NOTHING THIS

SCARLETT FINN

Also by Scarlett Finn

GO NOVELS
GO WITH IT
GO IT ALONE
GO ALL OUT
GO ALL IN
GO FULL CIRCLE

EXILE
HIDE & SEEK
KISS CHASE

WRECK & RUIN
RUIN ME
RUIN HIM

**THE BRANDED
SERIES**
BRANDED
SCARRED
MARKED

**FORBIDDEN
PREQUEL DUET**
ALL. ONLY.
ONLY YOURS

THE FORBIDDEN NOVELS
FORBIDDEN DESIRE
FORBIDDEN WANT
FORBIDDEN WISH
FORBIDDEN NEED
FORBIDDEN BOND

**BOMBSHELLS & BILLIONAIRES
(ROXIVERSE)**
NOTHING TO HIDE
NOTHING TO LOSE
NOTHING IN BETWEEN: ONE
NOTHING TO DECLARE
NOTHING TO US
NOTHING IN BETWEEN: TWO
NOTHING TO SAY
NOTHING TO GAIN
NOTHING IN BETWEEN: THREE
NOTHING TO YOU
NOTHING TO THIS PREQUEL: ONE WILD NIGHT
NOTHING TO THIS
NOTHING IN BETWEEN: FOUR
NOTHING TO DO
NOTHING TO NO ONE
NOTHING TO FEAR
NOTHING TO DENY
NOTHING TO BEAT
NOTHING TO THE WEDDING
NOTHING TO TELL
NOTHING TO IT
NOTHING TO SEE
NOTHING TO WIN
NOTHING TO OFFER
NOTHING TO PROVE

**LOVE AGAINST THE ODDS
STANDALONE COLLECTION**
SWEET SEAS
HEIR'S AFFAIR
RESCUED
MAESTRO'S MUSE
GETTING TRICKY
THIRTEEN
REMEMBER WHEN...
RELUCTANT SUSPICION
XY FACTOR

KINDRED SERIES
RAVEN
SWALLOW
CUCKOO
SWIFT
FALCON
FINCH

MISTAKE DUET
MISTAKE ME NOT
SLEIGHT MISTAKE

LOST & FOUND
LOST
FOUND

**THE EXPLICIT
SERIES**
EXPLICIT INSTRUCTION
EXPLICIT DETAIL
EXPLICIT MEMORY

TO DIE FOR...
TO DIE FOR TRUTH
TO DIE FOR HONOR
TO DIE FOR VIRTUE
TO DIE FOR DUTY
TO DIE FOR LOVE

**RISQUÉ & HARROW
INTERTWINED**
TAKE A RISK
FIGHTING FATE
RISK IT ALL
FIGHTING BACK
GAME OF RISK

ONE

SPOTLIGHT SOLUTIONS had employed her for seven years. Seven years. Damn, that sounded like a lot. More than a lifetime for some people. And it had gone by fast.

Rylee Hampton, Creative Consultant. Did that sound sufficient for seven years of graft? Working in the marketing department, as part of a large team, most of her time was spent sketching other people's ideas. Her job was her job, not the be-all and end-all, but there was such a thing as professional pride. She didn't want to be fired. Yet she could be facing exactly that, her and every other employee.

Being the end of the day, everyone was ready to go home, her included. They'd been ready until, less than an hour ago, an unexpected email hit the department's inbox, scuppering any chance of getting out on time. The message summoned an array of employees to the biggest conference space on the first floor. Usually reserved for product launches, corporate events, or visiting speakers, it rarely got aired out. If the three hundred or so other people in the room were an accurate indication, other departments had got the same message at the last minute as well.

What was the impromptu meeting about? God knew. Couldn't be anything good. Still, she wasn't worried. Nope. Why would she be? The corporation's competent infrastructure had undergone a couple of facelifts throughout her tour. So far, she'd survived the layoffs. Loyalty bought her consideration, didn't it?

Rumors persisted about the direction of the company, more so recently, but she'd switched off to them. Without a reliable link to anyone close to the top, it was impossible to figure out what was truth and what was fiction. Theories changed, becoming more embellished every week. The tide always rose. In time, it would fall again. Riding the Spotlight rapids was part of everyday life.

Others weren't so apathetic. Her marketing colleagues' mumbles and the rumble of surrounding conversation conveyed confusion and intrigue. The crowd was alive with questions and speculation. When was the last time she'd been in that room? The Christmas party? Maybe the mock expo. Damn, she wanted to go home, but there they were, waiting for the CEO to show up for an unknown reason.

There had to be some big announcement. Had to be. That would explain bringing so many people together and keeping the gathering hush-hush until the eleventh hour. The raucous conversation continued as groups predicted what might happen on the dais at the head of the room.

People loved to gossip, yes, but there was a thread of fear in the swirling excitement. In the current economic climate, everyone wanted to hold on to their jobs. Didn't everyone always want to hold on to their jobs? Big changes could mean big cuts. Redundancies, budgets, departments were already stretched thin.

Nichelle leaned in at her side to whisper, "Here comes Ted."

Their CEO. The sooner he got started, the closer she'd be to home.

Of her marketing colleagues, Nichelle was the closest thing she had to a friend. Though, in truth, her life outside of work was more important than her job. A social life, being "in" with her colleagues, was unimportant; she wasn't particularly close to any of them.

Polite and civil, she didn't have deep relationships at Spotlight. She kept her head down, did her job, and went home to the life that she loved.

From behind the dais, Ted ascended the stairs to the prominent spot at the central podium. Other members of the board shuffled onto the stage behind him.

Showtime.

"Everyone!" Ted called. "Please settle down!"

Always jovial with a smile on his face, Ted was a good boss, though not the smartest of businessmen. Word among employees implied he was understanding and generous. He didn't have the cutthroat spirit needed to close the deals that would ensure the corporation's, thus the employees', futures. Which was better? A superior who listened in the short term or one focused on the bigger picture?

She'd only met the man once, at a function in that very room. They'd spoken for a second. He wouldn't remember her, but she'd got a good sense from him, a good energy.

Ted tapped the microphone as the room quieted and the board seated themselves.

"Thank you, all, for coming today," Ted said, setting his hands on the podium. "I know this is spur-of-the-moment; you have jobs or homes you want to get to.

It's been a long day, so I'll make this brief. I'm sure many of you have heard the rumors about Spotlight Solutions and our financial troubles."

Redundancies.

Budget cuts.

The words rattled in her head.

So much for not being worried.

Tension gripped the room. It clenched her guts too. If this news related to downsizing, she could be in big trouble. Her four-bedroom apartment was already more than she should be able to afford.

"Oh God," Nichelle said and took her hand, eyes locked on the stage.

"Please nobody panic," Ted said and widened his grin. "We've been in secret negotiations for some time now and finally the day has come to say we have been rescued." The room relaxed somewhat, but still held its breath. "Spotlight Solutions has been purchased. I know it's unexpected, but the buyout secures everyone's jobs and our future projects." The room applauded. Ted held up his hands. "Please, save your applause for our savior, Mr. Jamison Dawes!"

Impact. Like a Mack truck.

What did he just say?

No. It couldn't be.

People kept applauding when a new person jogged up the stairs at the back of the stage. The man unknown to the room held up his hands to silence the crowd, presumably intending to introduce himself.

Oh, fuck. They needed no introduction.

Jamison Dawes wasn't unknown to her. Yep, they definitely knew each other. Intimately. Shit. Her mouth dried as it fell open. What the hell was he doing there? What did he think he was doing?

The applause died down.

JD went to the podium to shake Ted's hand. All

very posed and perfect, like politicians accepting the nomination for something. Steam should be coming out of her ears. Despite being such a prominent feature of her life, it had been a while since they'd laid eyes on each other. The last place she'd expected to see him was at her workplace.

Ted backed away to take a seat with the other board members. And she couldn't snap out of it.

Wearing a dashing smile, JD settled the room. Been a long time since she'd seen that smile. The damn smile that tipped the first domino; they'd been falling ever since. Crashing into each other, one after another, with an inevitability she'd almost come to rely on.

With that smile, he charmed every person in the place. Like lambs to the slaughter.

"Thank you," he declared. "Thank you, everyone."

Known as a shrewd businessman, personable and generous, Jamison Dawes—JD to her—was a good man, and extremely successful in his field. Good at lots of things, he was a philanthropist, a mentor, and making headlines gobbling up corporations around not only the country but the world.

Whatever he was saying, she heard none of it over the ringing in her ears. He could've recited *War and Peace* and there still wouldn't have been time to snap out of her daze.

A rushing of air overtook the ringing. A storm was coming. Seeing him up there, in front of her colleagues, *her* colleagues, talking, commanding attention, it was too much to take in.

Surreal was a better word. Too surreal to absorb.

The father of her children, that was his category in her life. A category that had nothing to do with her career. Their sparse direct contact happened through phone conversations and emails. Most communication was done by way of his mother, the conduit for his relationship with their twins. Marjorie Dawes satisfied formal visitation; JD showed up at his mom's to see the kids when he could.

Dumbfounded, she couldn't place him there, in her professional life, in her workplace. Spotlight had been hers, and only hers, and now he was there.

Why?

Why was he there?

Shit. Sitting only half a dozen rows from the front of the room had been a mistake, though not one she could've avoided without first knowing this was going to happen. JD finished his speech and stepped back to accept the adoring applause. Waving, he scanned the space. Damnit. Damnit. His gaze went right past her. Thank God. Relief. A reprieve. He'd missed her.

She'd breathed out too soon.

His attention stopped and returned to seek out… In a sea of faces, shouldn't she be invisible? What was she worrying about? He wouldn't—

Nope, he fixated right on her. Embarrassing that he seemed to try to place her, like he couldn't quite figure out her identity. The longer it took, the smaller she got.

It probably only took a few seconds; she shouldn't be offended. Given the unfamiliar environment, and that they hadn't seen each other for so long, it was no big deal. Right? Shouldn't she forgive him his second of hesitation? Definitely not her finest moment.

Eventually, he caught on and tilted his head like he was asking why she was there. So sorry for existing. Owner of the damn world, he didn't have to be so cocky. She was where she was supposed to be; he was the one encroaching on her turf. And what the hell could she do about it? Bupkis.

The father of her children bought the company

that employed her, and she'd been oblivious. This was going to take some adjustment… and she'd have to call her lawyer before speaking to anyone about it. Her lips were sealed. Officially.

Ted approached JD's other side and put an arm around him. The men shook hands again. Their current CEO said another few words. Ted thanked the room for their time and promised further information in due course, whatever that meant. Everyone was dismissed like her world hadn't just rocked on its axis.

Time to skate. When the first people stood, and the conversation level rose again, she leaped to her feet. No hanging around for her.

"I have to go," she said, shuffling past Nichelle.

The other marketing employees happily gossiped, speculating on the direction of the company now that this savvy hotshot had bought them.

Nichelle bent down to grab her own purse. "Wait, Rylee, I'll walk out with you. Wait for me."

At the end of the row, she didn't even care that her hasty pushing pissed others off. Nichelle tried to follow, further irritating their loitering colleagues. Winning friends wasn't on her priority list. If they wanted to be pissed off, they could be pissed off, let them crank up their blood pressures.

"It's okay, Nichelle. I really have to go. I'm already late," she said. "See you tomorrow."

Hurrying out before the masses corked the bottleneck at the doors, she needed to escape in case JD thought to corner her. As far as she was concerned, he could keep his distance forever.

Their rhythm worked for everyone, except him, apparently. Why did he screw with the status quo? The years hadn't dampened his arrogance that was for sure. It might have been attractive when they met, now, it was just annoying.

Damnit, she didn't like surprises.

TWO

DREAD OVER THE UNWELCOME surprise chased her home and through dinner. At her kitchen island, chopping carrots into sticks, her mind kept working. What would JD's next move be? Was this a game? What did he want?

The twins would like it if Daddy started working in town. How long would it last? His corporate MO: buy a company, spend some time shaping it, then move onto the next one, put an expiration date on her children's happiness. Always expanding his portfolio, JD often spliced companies into parts, keeping some and selling others. For him, it was all about growth... at least that's what his mother told her.

At some point, she'd have to talk to him. Damn. What would she say? Close though she was to Marjorie Dawes, his mother, she didn't want to put the woman in the middle. His sister, Brenna, on the other hand... she'd put herself right smack in the middle and would dare anyone to move her. After the kids, her friendship with Brenna was the most important in her life.

It had been anyway. How would that change with him in town?

He'd come in, mix things up, and then ride off into the sunset.

A storm front leaving carnage in its wake. And just like a storm, JD wouldn't notice or care about collateral damage.

Going through the motions, preparing for the following day, her other eye was on her twins seated at the long dinner table to the left of the kitchen island.

"But, Mommy, I eated lots of it," Kye complained.

"You eated less than me," Sky said.

Her four-year-old twins poked at each other's plates, comparing what remained of their dinner portions. Typical siblings, they each had a lot of love for the other and liked to show that by riling each other at every opportunity.

Switching to mommy mode, she cleared her mind. "Ate," she said. "The word you're both looking for is 'ate.' You'll keep on eating until you can both say you *ate* it all."

Someone knocked on the front door.

"Is that Grama?" Sky asked, bouncing up high on her knees, desperate to bolt from her chair.

She raised a hand to stall her children, signaling they shouldn't scurry to the door.

"No," she said, rinsing her hands and grabbing a towel. "You'll see Grama tomorrow. It's probably Auntie Brenna."

Both kids deflated with disappointment. Hilarious. Grama would take their side on the finishing their dinner debate, Brenna wouldn't. Their grandmother doted on her grandchildren. Their aunt enjoyed playing with people too much to give anyone an easy out.

Still smiling, she tossed the towel over her shoulder and went across the apartment to open the front door, expecting to see Brenna.

Instead, JD stood on her threshold. "You have an employee file," he said, which she guessed cleared up the question of how he'd got her address.

Astute, or arrogant, he answered the question before she'd asked it. Brenna and Marjorie had her address. If he'd gone through the employee files rather than asking his relatives, she'd bet that meant his family didn't know he was in town. At least she wasn't the only one blindsided.

Catching her breath, there wasn't much time to gather her wits. "At Spotlight Solutions? Yes, I have an employee file. Know why? Because I work there. And this is not there. This is home, not work. What are you doing here?"

He skipped over the last question. "You work there," he said, but it wasn't really a question. Good, he was supposed to be smart, and they'd clarified her position of employment already. "I had no idea."

Really? Sarcasm drawled through her brain. Spotlight Solutions was a prominent software firm. If he'd wanted something local, it would be the most attractive candidate for purchase. Not that she'd known it was for sale exactly. Given the company struggles, she'd bet he got it at a good price.

He couldn't have expected to buy Spotlight and keep it secret forever. It wasn't like he'd taken an anonymous position in the mailroom; he would take over as CEO. The person at the top of the pyramid was usually the most recognizable. Had she thought of him as smart?

Somehow, it fell to her to point out the obvious. "We met at a software expo," she said. "It never occurred to you that maybe I worked for a software company?"

JD looked almost baffled. "It never occurred to me to look."

"Of course not."

Speaking fast and matching his pace was a necessity. Talking before thinking things through was typical of them. Stubbornness, and their back-and-forth banter, had drawn them to each other in the first place. Old habits and all that.

They brought out a need in each other to get in the last word, to match each other quip for quip. Mature? No. It was what it was. Honestly, she hated how exciting baiting him could be and how easily she confused their repartee for having fun.

She was supposed to be mad at him, or at least demanding answers. Her heart rate kicking up was nothing more than an increase in adrenaline caused by him aggravating her. That was the reason. The only reason.

A little hand grabbed her knee and pulled at her until a tiny body squeezed around her leg.

"Mommy, I want to see," Sky said, blinking upward.

"You're not supposed to—"

Sky squealed. "Daddy!"

JD bent to scoop her up. "Hello, Sproutette."

Putting her arms around him, Sky glowed, then grabbed his face in both hands. "Did you be missing me?"

"Of course I missed you, sweetheart. You're my angel."

JD kissed the end of their daughter's nose. Though she rolled her eyes and folded her arms, it was kind of cute to see them together. These interactions weren't something she usually got to witness.

"Did you come to see my bedroom?" Sky asked but didn't wait for the inconvenience of an answer. "Mommy, Daddy wants to see my bedroom."

The kids were his ticket to getting inside. Not that she was keeping him outside exactly, but he'd tickled her suspicion by avoiding the question of why he'd shown up.

"No, he doesn't," she said and kept going before JD could correct her. "Daddy wants you to sit at the table with Kye to finish your dinner." Sky blinked at her father, giving her mother the chance to glare at him. "Because Daddy would never dare undermine Mommy's authority on something as important as feeding you."

His smirk stayed on their daughter, though it was for her, not the little one. "What are you having for dinner, Sproutette?"

"Pasta," Sky said, screwing up her face.

He gasped. "Oh, wow! Pasta? I love pasta!" he said with more enthusiasm than he would if talking to an adult.

The act worked like a dream with Sky.

The grumpy little one quickly reverted to her bubbling joy. "You want some of mines?"

Her kids might think they were smart, but watching out for their tricks was her full-time job.

Still, Sky had seen her father; it would be unfair to keep him from Kye. Sky also wouldn't give her parents peace, meaning she wouldn't get to the bottom of why JD showed up until they appeased their daughter.

Inevitable was inevitable.

"Uh, no," she said, entering the apartment, leaving the door open for JD to bring Sky inside. "If Daddy wants to eat with you, Mommy will fix him his own plate. You have to clear yours."

The scrape of her son's chair legs on the slate floor came before the front door even had a chance to close.

"Daddy!" Kye called out.

In a few weeks, their babies would turn five. Their little bodies needed the help of booster seats to reach the table, but both were professionals at climbing up and down either to get up or to get away.

Returning to her place on the other side of the kitchen island, she hung up the towel but faltered. The vision of JD standing at the foot of the dining table, holding both children, sent her mind back to the hospital on the day the kids were born. That was probably the last time she'd seen him holding them both together. Babies then, both considerably smaller, JD didn't make it look any more difficult now than it had all those years ago.

Shaking off the moment of sentiment, she cleared her throat. What had she been doing before he showed up to disrupt their lives?

"You had to come at dinnertime when I'm trying to get them both to eat, didn't you?"

Their inability to give each other a break was mutual. She didn't expect him to prostrate himself, and he didn't disappoint.

Haughty, JD was unapologetic. "That's why Daddy's here, to help you eat dinner," he said, moseying up the length of the table.

Putting each of the kids back in their chairs, he pushed them in at their places, then kept going to seat himself at the head of the table, in pride of place.

Typical that he should take the most eminent position in the room without invitation.

"Comfortable?" she asked, propping a hand on her hip.

JD tossed her a quick, impudent wink, then leaned

toward the kids who were poking at their food again. "Is it good, buddy?"

"It was," Kye grumbled.

Sighing, if JD wanted the responsibility of getting them to eat, she wouldn't take it away from him.

"Kye spent so much time irritating his sister that I think it's almost cold," she said, returning to her chopping. "But they have to finish it."

"Can Daddy have some?" Sky asked.

Trust her children to take advantage of every situation, just like their father. The twins were wily. Whatever her daughter's ultimate goal, she'd guess it had something to do with a particular movie.

"You know how busy Daddy is," she said. "He doesn't want to eat dinner here. He probably has other places to be."

"Not tonight." When she scowled at him, JD just bobbed his brows. "I'd love some pasta… thank you."

The food would still be warm. Going to the pot on the stove, she scooped a meager portion into a bowl and took it to him with a fork, dumping it onto the table.

"This is all quite domesticated, isn't it?" JD said, wearing a smile as he picked up the fork. "Civilized."

Oh, he was so proud of himself and loving every minute.

"It's novel for you," she said. "The rest of us call it life."

He popped a piece of pasta between his lips and surprised her by closing his eyes on a groan of bliss. "Oh my God, this is incredible," he said, forking up more to fill his mouth.

The pasta wasn't that good. She never worried about poisoning her kids, but her cooking skills weren't exactly of the highest order. The food she made was edible, though not as edible as their grandmother's, as she'd been told, many times, without subtlety. Four-year-olds were rarely subtle.

But he wasn't mocking her. It was a ploy. JD wasn't ignorant of the sway he had with their children and was using that influence for her benefit. Their twins idolized their father.

Utterly idolized him. There was no other word for it. He could do no wrong.

So although she sighed at his melodramatic reaction to the meal, inside, she was grateful. Their beautiful babies gazed at their father, eyes wide in wonder as he gobbled up the pasta like it was the most incredible thing he'd ever tasted.

She hid a smile.

"You two better hurry…" JD said, his mouth full, "or I'll be moving on to yours next."

So uncouth for a man known for his manners. It took all her energy not to laugh when both kids suddenly copied their father's exuberance for the pasta. He glanced over his shoulder and winked at her again.

Okay, so that got a small smile, but she shook her head too. "Wow, look at you three go. I must be in the wrong trade," she said. "I should open my own five-star restaurant."

"Maybe you should," JD said.

He'd done what was needed, the kids were eating. He slowed until they weren't looking anymore and tried to rise from his chair.

THREE

THEIR DAUGHTER was faster than him.

Sky leaped to her knees on her seat and grabbed JD's wrist before he could stand up. "Daddy!"

Lowering back into his seat, the caught JD surrendered to his fate. "Yes, Sproutette?" he asked, opening his mouth to pop the car Sky had attempted to deafen

Their daughter was arranging her remaining pasta into a row, not letting any pieces touch, and then eating them in order. "Are mermaids good?"

"Are mermaids good?" JD asked and glanced at her for direction; she gave a discreet nod. "Uh, yes, Sproutette. Mermaids are excellent. I love mermaids."

Kye blew a raspberry.

"Kye," Rylee warned. "We don't mock each other's interests. Your sister doesn't make fun of your mural, does she?"

Each of the children had chosen murals for their bedroom walls based on things they loved.

"Mermaids are for girls," Kye said.

JD's head tilted. What was he thinking about? His children's reactions to each other or the seashell bikinis?

It was left to her to play parent. "If Daddy likes

mermaids, that should be proof enough for you, son, that mermaids are not only for girls. Daddy's not a girl, is he?" Perfect opportunity to have a little fun. "I tell you what, sweetpea," she said. "If everyone clears their plates, Daddy will watch all *The Little Mermaid* with you, Sky. How does that sound?"

Her daughter gasped, glittering with excitement. "Really, Daddy? In my bedroom? You'll watch the mermaids?"

JD took his turn to glare at her, but she just plastered a grin on her face. She always wished he'd spend more quality time with the kids and wouldn't snub the opportunity to encourage him.

"He'll watch the mermaids," she said, blinking at him with innocence. "You did say you were free tonight, right? And you want to embrace your daughter's passions."

"Maybe I could take Kye to the park, toss the ball around and—"

"It's too late for that," she said. "Kye will watch the movie with you."

Though her son would bluster and gripe, it wasn't such a hardship for the little guy. He sang the songs and quoted the dialogue just as well, if not better, than Sky. Whenever she noticed him singing along, she'd never point it out or make him self-conscious, it was too sweet to interrupt.

Seeing their children happy and enjoying themselves was the greatest pleasure for any parent. As it should be for JD too. He'd stood up to presidents, met monarchs, and been locked in merciless negotiations with some of the most ruthless executives. He'd face any of those situations and come out on top. Yet thinking about watching animated movies with a pair of four-year-olds made him tug at his collar.

Rinsing her hands, she dried them again and went to stand next to where he was sitting, facing him.

Propping her ass against the table, she bent over to loosen his tie. "The Great Mr. Jamison Dawes," she murmured. Sliding the tie free of his collar to toss it over her shoulder, she unfastened the top two buttons of his shirt. "Afraid of bedtime?"

"Me? Afraid? No, I'm not afraid. I do this all the time."

Had he forgotten how well she knew her children and their routines? All their routines, even those that didn't happen under her roof.

"Your mom doesn't let them watch movies at bedtime. Usually, I don't either, but since you're here, I'll allow you to rebel with them." She leaned forward to whisper. "I won't tell your momma, I promise."

Sky climbed off her chair, drawing the parents' attention from each other. Their little one reached up to take her empty plate from the table and went past them into the kitchen to put it into the open dishwasher. Amazing.

"Can we have popcorn, Mommy?" she asked.

So much for their little bellies being full.

"Yes," she said, going to her daughter to crouch to her level and kiss her. "Sky, sweetpea, you're a good girl for putting your plate away. Are you trying to impress Daddy?"

"Daddy need to know the plate washer," Sky said, touching Rylee's hair. Her tresses always fascinated her daughter. "He didn't know."

"And Daddy will need to know where it is, so he can put his dirty bowl in the dishwasher, that's true. Good thinking, Sky," she said. Standing to smile at him, she ran a hand down their daughter's hair. "When was the last time Daddy did any kind of chore?"

JD didn't answer and probably didn't appreciate her smirk, though he didn't let it show. Funny how they kept locking eyes in a battle to maintain their poker faces in front of their children.

"Grama makes him," Kye said.

Ha! She snorted a laugh. "Your mom?" she asked. "Your momma makes you do chores? Oh, and I thought I couldn't love that woman more."

"I'm housebroken, Ry," JD said, rising to take his empty bowl to the dishwasher.

She twirled a strand of Sky's hair around her finger. "I wouldn't know."

"No, you wouldn't," he said, meeting her body with

his as she turned toward him. Their little one's soft hair drifted from her digit. Up close to JD was just an extension of the staring. Neither would break and back away. "I'm surprised, it's a turn on to hear you call me Daddy. Where are we on that fetish these days?"

If he thought flirting or talking sex would rattle her, he'd misjudged his audience. "That's what you are to my babies," she stated. "That's why I call you it."

"You gave birth to my children," he said. "That's why it's a turn on."

Much as she'd love to push this to its limit just to triumph, and she would triumph, she chose to be critical instead.

"Said babies are in the room, JD. One day you should read a book about responsible parenting. You get them on audio now, so you don't have to tax yourself. Do you talk like this when your mom's around?"

He smiled. Sky's little fingers moved into her hand and JD's at the same time. Their daughter swung each parent's arm.

"What's a turn on?" Sky asked.

Her lips curled in triumphant satisfaction. "Daddy will explain it to you, sweetpea. Why don't you get the movie set up and Daddy will bring the popcorn?"

Sky kissed each of their hands and then spun around to run to her room.

"I'll explain it?"

"Just be happy she didn't pick up on 'fetish.' By the time you go through with the popcorn, she'll have forgotten about it. She will have a list of a thousand things to tell you in her room. Be careful what you say around them."

"Usually I'm worried about what I say in front of my mom, so I don't have to worry about them."

She retrieved the popcorn and put it in the microwave to cook. "She'll love showing you her room," she said. "The mural isn't fully painted, but the outline is there."

"They both have murals? If the guy's slacking, I'll call him and—"

She laughed and went over to bag the carrot sticks in

individual portions. "I'm doing it myself," she said, taking the baggies across to the other side of the room.

"Momma, I don't want the carrots!" Kye whined when he saw her putting them in the fridge.

"I know, baby. Sky likes carrots. Mommy made apple snacks for you and you'll both share the grapes."

"I like the grapes."

"So does Sky," she said, going back toward the island. "You have to share. Besides, why are you whining about tomorrow's snack when you haven't even finished dinner? Sky's all done, and you're still at the table, little prince."

"Daddy sat with Sky," Kye whimpered.

She prodded JD in the ribs. "Go sit with your boy."

"We have to talk about work," he murmured.

Stepping back, she met his eye, landing a scowl of disapproval on him. "That's why you came here? Work? Not to see your children?"

His eyes narrowed. "You're judging me."

"Always," she said and prodded him again. Judging? Yes. Surprised? No. JD was the way he was. That was that. Getting upset or starting a fight wouldn't change anything. With most people, JD got away with a lot. Money did that. While she wouldn't necessarily start a war with him, she would never be one of those sycophants. If she was unhappy or questioning, she wouldn't hesitate to let him know. "Help Kye finish so he can watch the movie with you. Otherwise we'll be here all night."

"Will you be watching with us?"

Laughing, she moved the last of the daycare snacks to the fridge. "No, I have a ball-buster of a boss. I have work to do."

He propped himself on the counter beside her. "Want me to talk to him?"

She rearranged a few things in the fridge. "Ha! Yeah, right."

"Daddy!" Sky shouted from her room.

"We don't shout, Sky!" she called, closing the fridge to lean back and yell toward the mouth of the hallway beyond the end of the table. "Daddy is helping Kye with his food.

They'll come to your room when he's done."

"I'm done," Kye said, pouncing out of his chair. "Let's go, Daddy."

"Uh, if your sister can do her plate, you can too. Come on," she said and went to take the popcorn from the microwave to put it in a bowl.

Kye put his plate away. "I pick the next one."

Smiling at their son, she bent to kiss his head. "Of course, little prince." Straightening to take her amusement to JD, she handed him the popcorn. "Enjoy, Daddy. Between the two of them, they have almost every kid's movie ever released. You're in for a treat."

Kye took his daddy's hand to lead him toward Sky's room. JD looked back as though seeking escape, but he was only playing.

She'd known how her children felt about that man all their lives, while she'd spent most of that time judging him for his lack of involvement.

Her family had a routine. Her family and his. Why had JD suddenly decided he wanted to be a new cog in a machine that didn't need any spare parts? Their lives had been working just fine without him for years. Why was he choosing now to mix it up?

***

NOISE FROM THE MOVIE quickly faded into the background as she got lost in her sketches.

She needed to pee and—eleven p.m. With an inhaled shriek, she leaped from her desk to dart through the apartment into Sky's bedroom and came to an abrupt stop.

JD was asleep on Sky's bed with their drooling daughter sprawled on his chest. Kye was tucked under his father's arm, against his side, as dead to the world as the other two.

Her heart slowed as it swelled. They were adorable. There was love there; she could feel it thick in the air. She'd never seen this, had never seen her children share such an intimate moment with their father.

Maybe JD wasn't playing and had been telling the truth when he said bedtime was familiar. Though, from what she'd been told, he only showed up for half his scheduled visits, and his mother dealt with most of the parenting during that time. The children didn't mind because they had a great time with his family.

Could be this was their ritual in the times he did show up. Not knowing something about her kids' lives was disconcerting, but she'd always been happy with her and JD's limited contact. She never saw him, it never occurred to her to want to, yet there he was, sleeping in their daughter's bed with their babies in his arms.

Shirking the ridiculous sentimentality, she crept over to the TV and turned the movie off. When the light from the screen faded, the nightlight came on automatically.

Retreating without making a sound, she took JD's crumpled jacket from Sky's armchair and backed out of the room slowly, closing the door behind her. It didn't usually get closed, but she trusted JD to deal with the kids if they woke up afraid.

He'd come to talk work, and she'd roped him into being Dad for the night. If nothing else, he'd have learned his lesson about randomly showing up at her apartment. Kids had a way of hijacking anyone's agendas; her children were particularly good at it. There were times, like that night, she didn't mind giving them a helping hand. Maybe they didn't get all their wiles from their father.

FOUR

CHORES WAITED FOR NO ONE. With her schedule full at work, early morning was the best time to get things done. After her workout, she did a load of laundry. A second tumbled in the dryer while she updated her accounts spreadsheets.

Breakfast took no time at all to rustle up, though it lacked the required diners. The trio in Sky's bed stayed sleeping even after she turned up the radio and set the table.

The scent of bacon drifting down the hallway to the bedroom did its job and roused the first sign of life.

Kye appeared, bleary-eyed, yawning. "Momma," he mumbled.

Her gorgeous boy was always cuddly when he was sleepy. Going over to scoop him up, she tucked his face against her neck and returned to the kitchen to tidy up. Murmuring the words of a song she'd sung to them since they were babies, Sky's shrieking laughter interrupted the chorus.

Turning around, JD emerged from the end of the hallway holding Sky on his back with one arm while he tickled her.

Kye lifted his head and wriggled from her arms; Sky leaped from her father's. The pair raced each other to the table, trying to get first pick of the food she'd laid out.

JD scrubbed both hands back and forth through his hair. "You didn't wake me," he said, his voice gruff. "Is my jacket around?"

"Yes," she said and nodded toward the hooks by the front door.

He went over to dip his hands in each of the pockets. She carried juice in a pitcher to the table. Both kids drank from their cups and were disappointed to taste milk.

"I want juice," Kye said.

"The juice is for Daddy," she said and put a hand on the back of the same chair JD had sat in last night. "Join us for breakfast, Daddy."

Jacket in hand, he returned to them. "My phone isn't here."

"That's what happens in a house with four-year-olds," she said. "Things go walkabout."

Narrowing his eyes, he wasn't buying the innocent explanation. "Except the kids were with me."

She bent over the table to pick up his plate, filling it with bacon and pancakes. "Your children eat breakfast like it's the only meal they get in a day. If you don't eat fast, you don't eat."

"Daddy, do you like bacon?" Sky asked.

After putting JD's plate down at his place, she went around to help Sky cut her pancakes with the little one's plastic flatware.

"I hope so," Rylee said. "Or Kye will have a sore tummy from all the leftovers he'll have to eat." She glanced up at JD. "Kye's addicted to bacon. That's why we limit his exposure."

"I get bacon 'cause Daddy's here," Kye said, picking up a piece of bacon with his fingers.

"Yes, you do," she said and went around her daughter to get to her son. "Use your knife and fork, baby."

Whether he'd heard or was too preoccupied, JD didn't respond to the table conversation.

Something else bothered him. "My phone, Ry?"

Hmm, being out of contact with the world brought

out his prickly side. Interesting to know.

"No alarm went off," she said, continuing her mommy duties. She wasn't going to drop everything for him when the kids needed help. "If I'd heard it make a noise, I would have woken you."

"The hotel calls my room to wake me up, that's my alarm. I should've been up hours ago."

After cutting up Kye's food and putting his fork in his hand, she licked her fingers.

JD sat at the head of the table.

"Well, this isn't a hotel, JD."

"Grama wakes Daddy ups," Sky said. "Like momma wakeses me."

JD picked up Sky's little hand and bowed to kiss it. "Daddy's not staying with Grama."

That piqued her curiosity… and her concern.

"Why not?" she asked, pouring juice for JD. "She didn't say anything about a falling out."

Examining the spread for the first time, JD got interested. "It's nothing that dramatic. I just haven't gotten around to looking at apartments yet and she only has two bedrooms. Usually, I sleep in the den when I'm there with the kids. I keep saying I'll buy her a new place, but she doesn't like to move."

"I know that, and she likes her neighbors too. Your mom has a community around her that she loves," she said, trying to figure out the situation. Why would he want to look at apartments if he wasn't buying one for his mom? "Why would…? Wait, does that mean you're staying?"

Sky cheered. "Yay! Daddy, live with us!"

"Daddy, stay here!" Kye exclaimed, sitting up fast.

"Oh no, honey," she said. "I meant in the city, not in our apartment." Wouldn't that be a hilarious recipe for disaster? "Daddy doesn't want to stay here."

Except… interest lit his expression. "It's not a bad idea."

"JD," she objected, filled with dread.

But he didn't get it, or at least he played dumb. "What? You have an extra bedroom, and I can pay my way. It will just be for a few weeks 'til I find a permanent base… I can help with the kids."

As he smiled at their excited faces, she stood stunned. Was this really happening? In front of their kids and… She and JD had a one-night stand, not a relationship. They'd never lived together. As of yesterday, they didn't even have to look at each other at all. Now he was suggesting exposure therapy or something?

Not a good idea.

"Daddy can have my unicorn pillow," Sky said, moving her plate to push some of her bacon onto her father's.

Judging by the angle of his fork, JD intended to push it back. With a quiet cough, she drew his attention to her shaking head. Sky said she liked bacon because Kye loved it so much. Their daughter admired her brother more than she let on. But the little one wasn't actually that wild about it, she preferred the pancakes.

Her son was busy shoveling bacon into his mouth. "Daddy can share my room."

"Daddy can have his own room," she said.

Shit, did that sound like…?

"Great!" Had she just invited him to stay? "I'll have the hotel send over my things later," he said and picked up a piece of bacon. "You guys want to go to the movies today?"

"Yeah!"

"You want to spend the day with them?" she asked. "I'll have to call the daycare and—"

"Oh no, I can't take them myself. I can have an assistant…" Glaring, she spun to stalk to the kitchen. Breathe through the irritation, count to ten before reacting with outrage. Didn't matter, he'd got the message. "What?"

"They don't want to spend the day with a random assistant. They want to spend the day with their father."

"I have to work," he said. "Daddy has to bring home the bacon."

"I love bacon," Kye said. "Daddy like bacon?"

"He does," JD said.

"Mommy brings home bacon too," she said, packing their daycare snacks and drinks.

"Mommy doesn't have to. Daddy offered ten times as much child support as she accepted."

Oh, he was hitting all the wrong markers. "Mommy enjoys working," she said. They were heading into passive aggressive territory.

"And Daddy has to work on buying himself an apartment before he drives Mommy mad… Maybe you could use that extra money to speed up the sale."

"You want to come apartment hunting with me?"

"I do!" Sky exclaimed. "Can I have a bedroom?"

"Of course, Little Sproutette," he said. "You can have your own living room too. Your own pool, anything you want."

Sky pushed some pancake into her mouth, too much pancake. Didn't slow their lovely down though. "Can I have a unicorn?"

She laughed and finished packing the snacks. "See, this is why we don't spoil our babies," she said. "Grama wouldn't appreciate you segregating them. If you give them their own suites, you'll never see them, and they need supervision."

"We'll get somewhere open plan," he said. "Right, guys? And Grama will come stay when you're over."

God forbid he be alone with his babies. Despite the irritation, what she felt wasn't anger, it was closer to pity. He'd never fully embrace how incredible their children were as individuals if he didn't immerse himself in quality time with them. Although, she had to admit, last night was a good start.

Kye reached for more bacon.

She flipped around and held up a hand. "Ah, ah! Kye!"

JD intercepted the dish to pull it from Kye's reach. "I think you've had enough, buddy."

"It's time to wash up," she said, carrying the daycare bag over to hang it on the hook by the front door. "Mommy will clean up breakfast. Show Daddy where your bathroom is and he'll help you."

Sky took his hand to tug him from the table.

"Daddy doesn't know how to—"

"They'll show you," she said to what might have been mild panic. "Don't let them drown or get scalded. Just be an adult, JD." The trio disappeared down the hall. "Everyone, brush your teeth!"

Hoping they'd get along okay, the extra half hour she'd allowed should be enough, even if JD took his time with them. It would be a baptism of fire, but she wasn't Grama and wouldn't swoop in to save him. Unless she smelled smoke or saw blood, she was staying out of there. If he wanted to move in and be Daddy for a while, that was exactly what she'd expect of him.

***

FORTY MINUTES WENT by and still she waited for them to emerge. What were they doing in there? Something that wrought lots of movement and hilarity. The bathroom door had opened a while ago and she'd thought they were done and ready. Before she'd got there, little footsteps disappeared back into the room and the door closed again.

Checking her watch, worry rose. Time was getting tighter by the second.

Against her better judgment, and despite her aversion, she headed to the end of the hallway and opened the kids' bathroom door.

What the…? Water spilled every which way, including onto the floor near where Kye sat sticking foam letters to the tile. Sky was the one in the tub, swimming and sloshing around. JD, on his knees and shirtless, leaned against the side of the tub, his arms in the water up to his elbows.

His shirt was in a sopping heap in the corner. Even from her distance away, it was obvious his pants were wet. Not that she really needed to see to know, their daughter was adventurous in water.

Hmm, wow. She cleared the laugh from her throat with a cough. Restraining her amusement should get her a damn Oscar. Her babies were incredible.

Opening the closet just outside the bathroom, she grabbed some towels.

"Okay, fun's over," she said, crossing to Kye to pick him off the floor before going around JD to pull the plug.

Sky screamed and lunged up to throw herself at her daddy.

Setting Kye on his feet, she dried him off. "Quickest way to get Sky out of the tub is to pull the plug. She thinks she's going to be sucked down."

JD was behind her, so she only saw his shadow move when he stood up. "Daddy won't let anything happen to his mermaid."

Smiling, she wrapped her boy in a dry towel. "Go put on the clothes I laid on your bed, baby," she said, kissing Kye and turning him around. "Come here, Sky."

JD put Sky down to be dried off. Once her daughter's skin was drip free, Sky's hair got a towel dry.

Only one towel remained. She started to hand it off to JD, except one look at him shirtless had her pulling it back.

A smile crept onto her lips. "Wow, you're ripped," she said, surprised by the definition in his torso. Touching his pec, she drew a finger to his sternum and down. "Were you always this ripped?"

"I own a fitness company," he said. "I get all sorts of equipment for free… Working out clears my mind."

She stopped examining his torso to meet his eye, her finger motionless. "Defined, delicious, finessed."

One corner of his mouth rose. "Excuse me?"

Casting off the memory, her hand dropped. "Nothing."

Sky took her hand in both of hers. "Daddy helped to wash my hair."

"Yeah, and it's damn near impossible to wash a girl's hair in the tub. Who knew how tough it was to get shampoo out?"

She shouldn't be tickled that their daughter had taken advantage of the rookie but couldn't help it.

"When I said wash up, I meant hands and faces, and they have to brush their teeth."

"You meant…"

"They knew that," she said. "Your children are

master manipulators and your daughter wishes she was a mermaid. Put the pieces together. They played you. Much as I'd love to mock you for a while, I'm going to be late for work and now I have to dry my daughter's hair." Guiding Sky, she paused at the sink and was almost afraid to ask, "Why is my toothbrush in here?"

"Kye got it for Daddy."

Leading her daughter out, she called over her shoulder. "If you're moving in, bring your own toothbrush. Go help your boy get dressed."

***

DRYING SKY'S HAIR took longer than hoped, but the process was always prolonged when her daughter was excited.

Both of them were ready. She'd put the wet towels in the machine, and still there was no sign of the boys. In Kye's room, they found them on the bed playing a SpongeBob computer game… badly from the looks of it.

At least Kye was dressed; that was something. JD, on the other hand, had Kye's covers over his lap.

"Come on, we've got to go, baby," she said.

Kye looked up at his father who did a double take. "I think she's talking to you, buddy."

"Daddy has no clothes."

Damn, JD's wet clothes, right.

"I'd have called someone, except I don't have a phone."

"Hold on," she said, intending to leave the room. "Kids, give Daddy a kiss and say bye. I want you ready to walk out in two minutes."

Rushing to her bedroom closet, she snagged a couple of things and returned to Kye's room.

"Time to go, Mommy," Sky said, grabbing her brother to pull him along.

Rylee stepped aside to let the kids out into the hall to race to the front door.

"Here," she said, tossing the clothes to JD.

"What's this?" he asked, picking up the shirt.

"It'll do until you get back to your hotel."

"Why do you have guys' clothes? Who do they belong to?"

"My boyfriend," she said. "He won't mind." She turned away only to turn back. "Oh, and your charged phone is in the kitchen drawer under the coffee machine. There are spare keys for the apartment in there too. Have a good day."

Running behind would leave her frazzled for the rest of the day. Yet, she felt sort of lighter as she and the twins headed out into the world.

An unexpected new chapter? Yes. Where would it lead?

FIVE

SHE'D SWEAR she'd only just sat at her desk when her phone rang. Okay, maybe she'd been there an hour, but it had taken that long to orient herself and get her schedule in order. See, frazzled.

"Rylee Hampton," she answered.

"Ry, can you come upstairs?"

Whose voice was that? She didn't recognize the extension either.

"Who is this?"

There was a pause and then a mocking laugh. "The father of your children."

"Oh my God," she hissed, grabbing the phone closer to her mouth with both hands. "JD?"

"How many fathers of your kids are there? Did we get paternity on both of them?"

She scanned the open plan office around her, hoping no one was listening in. "Don't say that here. You better be alone."

"I am," he said with curiosity. "Will you come upstairs, please?"

"I…"

Hmm, dilemma. JD was her boss, but he wouldn't want to talk about anything professional. Still, maybe seeing him without the kids around would give her the chance to set a few things straight.

"Rylee," he said, drawing out her name.

Was he about to play the boss card or did he think he was being cute?

"I've never been to the top floor."

"Get in the elevator, press the button for the top. Walk straight ahead, through the bullpen and up the staircase that takes you to the mezzanine. From there, my office is right in front of you. You can't miss it."

"Will you be alone?"

Another pause. "In the office? Yes," he said. "Are you okay?"

"I'll be up in a minute."

Hanging up without waiting for another word, getting out while her supervisors were in their daily meeting was the best chance. Grabbing her purse, she dashed to the elevator, pleased the morning rush was over.

Why did JD call? She still wasn't totally clear on why he'd showed up at her place last night either. While the twins were around, they couldn't speak about certain topics. If JD was going to live in her home, she'd have to make that clear.

Thinking about him moving into her apartment put her into a trance for the rest of the elevator ride. Eyes focused straight ahead, lost in a swirl of what-ifs, she got through the bullpen. Only after running up the stairs and seeing three sleek, young blondes seated outside JD's office did she snap out of the daze. Why the parade of underwear models?

Walking straight into the double-doored office, she stopped inside, attracting the attentions of the four men present. So much for him being alone. The three on her side of the desk stared at the intruder. Ted, the CFO, and the COO. At least they were the former CFO and COO, she didn't know if they still held positions.

JD stood at his side of the desk. Apparently, if his held breath was any indication, she'd interrupted him mid-sentence.

He exhaled. "Gentlemen, would you give us the room," he said, without hesitating to dismiss them.

Shuffling aside, she let the men depart without taking her focus from JD.

The COO closed the door.

"Who is he?" JD asked.

"Uh…" She wasn't exactly following. "Ted Carmichael is the only name I know," she said. "The other two I know by position, not name… former position anyway. Are you restructuring?"

JD frowned. "What?" he asked, confused, then shook his head when he figured her out. "Them? No, the boyfriend. Who's your boyfriend? What's his name?"

"Baxter," she said, looking around the room with its pale gray carpet and heavy black furniture. "This room isn't very finessed, is it? It's too eighties. Though they are coming back… but not like this. It was Ted's, right? You'll have to redecorate."

"Are you serious?"

She admired the sparse-on-accessories bookcase to the right and the leather couches to her left. Both were too big to send the right message.

"Yes! Get a decorator in here fast. It seems like you're compensating for something you don't need to be compensating for." She rethought her words and smiled. "I probably just insulted Ted."

"What the hell are you talking about?"

His abrupt tone startled her. "The furniture," she said, confused by his scowl. "What are you talking about?"

"The boyfriend. Are you serious with him?"

"Oh, uh, I don't know." How was this his business? "Maybe."

In time. If they were together that long. The relationship was still in its infancy. They hadn't even discussed exclusivity. It seemed only fair that Baxter should live his life between their hook ups without her constraining him. The kids were her focus; she didn't need the complications men brought. JD didn't need to know any of that.

"Does he know you have kids?"

"Yes," she said, starting toward his desk opposite the door.

"Has he met them?" She shook her head and he exhaled. "Good."

"Good? What business is it of yours?"

"How long have you been seeing him?"

"A few months," she said and put her purse on the desk. "What's with the interrogation?"

"When do you see him?"

"JD, my life is not your business. Is this why you called me up here?"

"No, I called you up here to talk about work."

"Good, because that's why I came," she said and gestured to the chair behind him. "Let's sit and talk about work."

He sat, as did she, roles reversed. The office was his, yet she'd sort of taken the lead.

"I hear good things about you."

"Please tell me you're not asking about me," she said on a semi-groan. "No one knows the identity of my children's father and I intend to keep it that way."

His instant expression of offence was almost laughable.

"What?"

"Before the twins were born—you probably won't remember this—a squad of your lawyers descended upon me. You weren't present, ever, for the zillion meetings I attended. Suffice to say, I had to sign a contract. Yes, it was for child support and visitation, but it had other clauses too."

"Other clauses?"

"I was never to breathe a word of their paternity to anyone." She took a breath. "It worked for me. The kids have my name, I have my job. Your mother moved close, which was the concession I got for granting weekend visitation and child support... and paternity... without going through a court. Or going to the press probably. Marjorie has built her life here, been an excellent grandmother, and a friend to me. She manages to do both without ever encroaching on my life in any way that might compromise the situation."

"What are you saying?"

"You buying the company I work for, moving into

my life, it compromises me. My children go to daycare here. Our lives work. Until now I didn't have to worry about answering questions on who their father was or how much money he had… I don't know why you chose to do this, if you have some underlying motive or if it's just coincidence, but you have to abide by the rules."

Resting his forearms on the arms of his chair, he leaned back. "Which are?"

"First and foremost, you can't reveal to anyone that you're the father of my children."

"You said they go to daycare here." She nodded. "Inside Spotlight Solutions?"

"Yes."

"Our children are in this building and you're telling me I have to deny them?"

"I'm telling you it's in the contract," she said. "You don't have to deny it. No one will ask you; they'll have no reason to ask. Just avoid daycare in the lobby."

"Avoid it?"

"I will not ask our children to lie. Four-year-olds are terrible at it anyway. If they see you, they'll react. It's not just my life you've compromised, it's theirs too. Did you even think about them when you bought this place?"

"I didn't know you worked here," he said. "It just never came up."

They never talked and from what she knew, her name didn't arise in conversation with his mom or sister either.

"You expect me to believe this is all one big coincidence?"

Linking his fingers, he landed his forearms on the desk. "My mom moved to this city to be close to her grandchildren."

"I know."

"My sister followed a year later."

"I know that too."

"Until now, my goals have always been related to building up the business. It's taken up all my adult life. Amassing money is fun, building an empire is challenging, but you know the one thing I never had? Roots. When I took a step back, I realized I needed a base. I don't want to ping-pong around the planet anymore. I need somewhere to run things from… When I started thinking about where that might be, only one place came to mind."

Okay, that was… unexpected. A home; he was seeking a home.

"You meant what you said about settling down and buying an apartment?"

"I did," he said. "Where else would I do it? My family is here. My children are here."

"I'm not saying that you shouldn't have moved to the city," she said. "The kids will love seeing more of you. And I'll have one less thing to bitch about if you actually start showing up for them. I'm all for being wrong."

"But…?"

"But did you have to buy the company *I* work for?" she asked and took a deep breath. "It doesn't matter, it's done now. Until I have the chance to consult a lawyer, I'd appreciate it if you didn't say anything to anyone about… our link."

"Our children," he said. "Why do you have to consult a lawyer? I'm not here to take them away from you. You're an incredible mom."

Another surprise. A compliment? Was he trying to sweet talk her or did it just slip out?

"Thank you. But I meant the gag order," she said. "While it's okay for you to run around telling everyone who you are to my children, I could be sued for acknowledging it. I'll have to explore the language around the kids acknowledging you too. If you start telling people, and they start asking…"

"It puts you in a precarious position," he said, bobbing his head in understanding. "You know I would never sue you. At least, I hope you know."

The soaking guy elbow deep in her bathtub that morning wouldn't sue her. The slick businessman in front of her… she wasn't so sure about him.

"You're not like regular guys," she said. "You're not just… you."

"What does that mean?"

"You have a team," she said. "A team who felt it necessary to put this contingency in place. I don't know why they did or who they were protecting, but clearly, they thought they might need it, and if you truly didn't know about it, this proves they act without your explicit authority. Whether it's you or not, someone could use this against me. It's smart to protect myself."

He nodded. "I understand. I'll keep it to myself, if you do something for me."

Making a noise of surprise as she inhaled, shock and outrage were less potent than vindication. Now the compliment made sense.

"What something?"

"I need someone to work with me up here," he said. "Someone I can trust, someone I know."

"To work with you?" she asked. "What does that mean?"

"To take calls, sit in on meetings—"

"An assistant," she said. "You need an assistant." She jabbed her thumb backwards over her shoulder. "Is that why you're auditioning swimsuit pinups?" He smiled. "Seriously, JD, was the ad cup size and bimbo-IQ specific?"

"See why I need you?"

"I see why you think you need me," she said. "But I have a job."

"Working for me. You don't want me to pull rank, do you?"

Careful not to smile, she let her eyes wander as her tongue moved across her upper lip. "If you pull rank here, I'll pull rank at home."

"Deal," he said, startling her when he slapped the edge of the desk.

That was supposed to be a threat, not a condition. Before she could object, the door behind her opened. JD stood up; it seemed their private conversation was over.

"Need more time?" a male voice asked.

Twisting in her chair, a man about JD's age joined them. He was just as dashing too.

"No, we're good," JD said. "Rylee Hampton meet

Greg Birch. He's the closest thing I have to a grown-up friend."

Greg laughed as he came in. "Really? Guess I lost the pool."

"Guess you did," JD said. Was there any hint of recognition in Greg's expression? She couldn't decipher any. Either he didn't know who she was, or he had an incredible poker face. "She's my new executive assistant, effective immediately."

"Excellent," Greg said. "I prefer to get the formalities out of the way so we can get down to actual business. Want me to get rid of the others?"

"Sure," JD said. "Then bring the team in."

Greg left the room. Like she'd become invisible, JD sat down and picked up a pen to begin perusing some fat document that lay in front of him.

She sank back into her chair. "You should interview all the candidates before just picking a random person for the job. I don't have any experience with this."

"Sure you do. You did training and side jobs at college."

Taken aback, she gawped at him for a second, but he kept reading. "How do you know that?"

"You told me," he said, glancing up for a quick second.

Better that than he'd stalked or background checked her. Though she wasn't exactly sure he was right, she couldn't discount that it may have come up… on the night they met.

"How do you remember that?" she asked. His only response to the direct question was a shrug. Once it was clear he wasn't going to say anything else, she continued. "Do you have your own team or are the old one staying?"

"Ted and the others are staying for a transition period," he said and leaned back to open one of his desk drawers. "They're getting pretty impressive exit packages."

He produced a booklet and a stack of papers. After holding them up, he put them on the desk and pushed them across to her.

"What's this?" she asked, picking up the pile.

"You have a desk just outside my door," he said. "I'm orienting myself, smoothing over some wrinkles. Go on out and read as much of that as you can, understand it, then you can join the noon meeting. Is that okay?"

Leafing through the pages, she stood up. "Do I have to call you sir?"

"Yeah, or Master, or Overlord," he said, "whatever you like."

When she peeked over the top of the page, he was grinning. "What about jerkoff? Can I call you that?"

His amusement didn't go anywhere. "Sure, if you want everyone to know there's a different set of rules for you than for them."

Gritting her teeth, she acknowledged he'd won this one by holding up the stack of documents. "Better get to my reading, Overlord."

Steepling his forefingers over his mouth, he covered a smile and gave a single nod. Retreating from the office in reverse, she waited until the door was closed to roll her eyes.

As she turned, thoughts of JD shot out of her mind in lieu of sudden panic. A stampede of suits headed her way with Greg spearheading the pack. Stumbling aside, she caught her breath after fumbling her way to the desk chair. The herd went into the office, the door swung shut, and then there was peace.

She'd never wanted to be anyone's executive assistant. At least being in proximity to JD meant she'd be able to keep an eye on him and ensure he didn't blow their cover.

If he was planning to stay in town, they might have to revisit who knew about their children's parentage. Until she knew for sure, it had to stay a secret.

SIX

IT HADN'T TAKEN LONG to figure out she wouldn't be good at her new job. At that moment, she was supposed to be taking notes, and she was… when someone spoke to her directly. Keeping track of the technical stuff wasn't easy, which taught her something new and important: JD was way more intelligent than she'd given him credit for.

In addition to her, three others were present: JD, Greg, and a third guy, Jim, a little older than the formers. Respect, professionalism, the conversation was subdued but purposeful. Their familiar rapport betrayed they had history. Whatever that was or wasn't, the men seemed in no rush.

Listening to the boys' club wasn't the highlight of her week.

When the alarm on her dainty watch beeped, she almost whooped. "Ah," she said, turning it off and rising from her seat ready to make a beeline out of there.

"Uh, where are you going?" JD asked.

She pivoted to face him while gesturing at the door. "Lunch. It's five minutes to one."

"We go to lunch when I call lunch."

She smiled. "Not me. I go to lunch at twelve fifty-five every day and return at two p.m."

Though focused on the perplexed and affronted JD, it was impossible to miss the smirks of the other two men at the table darting between them.

"You take over an hour?"

She nodded. "If I need to," she said. "I do try to be back sooner; sometimes it's not possible."

His frown matched his impatience. "It will be possible now you work for me. You'll eat when I tell you to."

"And I would be completely fine with that, Overlord, except I have a date. It would be rude not to honor it."

"A date?" he said, flattening his hands on the table. "You're kidding." With a shake of her head, she widened her smile. "You're walking out on your job to get laid, and you expect us to accept that? Me to accept that?"

The assumption offended her more than it angered her. "Laid? No, Overlord, not laid."

Greg laughed, though he tried to mask it as a cough. That only inflamed JD's irritation; he started shuffling papers around the desk.

"Your boyfriend will have to go without his happy ending today. Unless you want to give up your position."

"If it's a deal breaker, I'm happy to return to my previous job downstairs." Please say yes. "They accepted the arrangement. I make up the extra time in the morning or at the end of the day."

"You have a responsibility to—"

"My children," she said, silencing him immediately. Her smile grew smug. "Yes, I have two beautiful children who go to daycare in this building. I eat lunch with them every day. Five days a week. They're expecting me… Would you like to see a picture? They really are adorable. They take after me more than their father, thank goodness."

After a fake laugh and no response from him, she continued her departure. Dealing with his objections put her behind schedule and she didn't want the kids getting antsy waiting for her.

Halfway across the executive bullpen, JD caught up to her. "You eat lunch with them every day?"

"Yes," she said, checking her phone for messages.

"I'll come with you."

Shaking her head, she pressed the elevator call button and tucked her phone away. "No way," she said. "There's no way to explain that. Besides, we're meeting someone."

"Wait, what? I thought—"

The elevator came and she stepped inside, prompting him to follow. "Go back to the office, JD," she said, but he didn't. "I told you, if the kids see you, they'll react to you."

"Good. I want them to react to me."

"We talked about this."

Others tried to join them.

JD put up a hand to halt them. "Get the next one."

They all backed out, leaving them alone. He stabbed at the door close button with a straight digit.

She selected the lobby. "Makes you feel clever to do that, huh?"

"Who are you meeting?" he asked. "Is it him? You said he hasn't met the twins."

"*He* hasn't and it's not him," she said, facing him to straighten his tie. "You shouldn't care who I'm meeting for lunch."

"I know."

What was that tone? Their eyes met and the air changed. Somehow, it got hotter and thicker, like it weighed more than before. Why were they standing so close? She hadn't even noticed until—did he have to be right there?

She shivered. "Did it just get weird in here?" Rolling her shoulders, the discomfort held on. "Why did it just get weird?"

His fingertip ascended to her temple and slid back into her hair, tucking an errant strand behind her ear.

"We were in an elevator just like this the first time I kissed you."

Obviously, their past was on his mind. That moment. The first touch of their lips. The combustion. The power of… them.

A strange sort of calm settled over her. The pull of his gaze, of having his complete attention, plucked at her barriers.

"We were."

"In the hotel and—"

"I was there, JD." Giving herself a mental slap, she pulled it together. "I don't need a play-by-play."

"You were pretty drunk."

Relaxing, her fingers curled around his tie. "So drunk that what you did to me was probably on the cusp of assault."

His lips curved until he laughed. "Just how I like my women."

Straightening her arms, she rested them on his shoulders. "It terrifies me that my son will look to you as an example of how to romance women."

His hands slid onto her hips and down to her ass. "He won't need any education on that. He's a Dawes, it's in his blood."

"To assault women? I hope not."

Leaning down, his lips warmed her ear. "You can try to claim assault the first time, but the second? The third…? You were definitely sober when I woke up to you riding me in the morning."

Though her hand splayed to pressure his chest, he didn't budge. The elevator doors opened, and she had to look, had to turn her attention to the lobby.

"Oh, Miss Hampton," the woman standing just outside the door drawled. Brenna. Exactly the woman she needed. "You're getting fresh in the elevator…" Her friend's smile faded when JD straightened up. "With my brother? Uh, what's going on here?"

Though confused, Brenna glittered with optimistic mischief.

"Hey, Nana," JD said.

When he started toward his sister, she stopped him with a shove.

"Brenna is my children's aunt," she said and leaned closer to whisper, "people at daycare know that."

Leaving the elevator, they let others in, keeping the cogs moving.

Brenna squinted at her, puzzled. "Yeah, and he should too. Do I have to introduce myself? I know it's been a while, but you remember I'm your little sister, right? You probably forgot. That would be why Mom and I didn't get a call about you being in town."

"In town?" she said. "He bought the damn building."

"Oh my God!" Brenna grabbed her hand to pull her closer. "And I stood you up last night? I'm a bitch. Damn, I missed the gossip."

"No, you missed Daddy enduring *The Little Mermaid*," she said on a laugh Brenna got in on.

JD didn't appreciate being the butt of the joke.

"He came over?" Brenna asked and linked their arms. "Does Baxter know? Oh, we have so much to talk about!"

"Did you make up with Lotta?"

Whispering, Brenna's embrace tightened on her arm. "Like I said, lots to talk about. Let's go get our dates."

JD caught her arm. "Ry…"

Brenna looked between them, then let her go. "Want me to go grab 'em?"

"Please," she said. Brenna faded from their side. "She'll be back with the kids in a minute. What is it, JD?"

"They let just anyone pick up our children?" he asked. "Security needs to be updated."

She picked lint from his sleeve. "Not just anyone. You wouldn't be allowed to pick them up," she said. "I have to list approved persons. Only me, Brenna, and your mom are on there."

Keeping one eye out, the twins could appear any second. He better spit out whatever was on his mind fast.

"Do you want to get dinner tonight?"

"Last night didn't scare you off," she stated.

"I'll take you all out. Anywhere you want. I'll fire up the jet, we can get out of state. No one will know us—"

"Dinner would be great, except I already have plans."

"Brenna can come, I don't see enough of my sister. And the kids think she's okay, right? They tolerate her?"

She laughed. "They adore their aunt, but my plans are not with Brenna," she said. He just kept looking at her, waiting for an explanation. The truth might not amuse him. "This is your weekend, JD. I drop the kids off at your mom's after work."

"After work, right," he said and took a step back. "I can't just pick them up from daycare?"

"You're not on the list," she said and laughed. "Bet you don't hear that much… I have to talk to my lawyer before we think about changing routines." Dejection settled over him. Damn, it didn't feel good to be the source. "Will you think about it before we make any decisions?"

"Think about what?"

"Do you want the world to know you sired your assistant's children?"

Pleasure replaced his negativity with a smile. "Sired? Damn, we should use that word more often. It's a turn on."

She smoothed his tie. "Did you explain that expression to your daughter? She'll be walking around the corner any second. You can take the chance now if you haven't."

"My daughter will never understand that expression. I'm having a tower built for her."

Grinning, she rested some of her weight on her palm. "Will there be a dragon on the stairs to kill any suitors who get too close?"

"Dragons? Try a security team, lethal laser nets and motion activated automatic weapons." Something about her smile in the silence that followed intrigued him enough to tilt his head in question. "What?"

"I've never seen you play protective daddy before."

The swagger that brought him closer was stopped by her backing up to press the button for the elevator.

Or, at least, it should've stopped him.

JD said what he wanted to say anyway, "It's a turn on, isn't it?"

"Shh," she said, unable to stop a whisper of a laugh seeping out. "Geez, JD." The elevator doors opened. "Go back to work before the babies see you."

"Be back by two," he said, taking his swagger into the elevator.

"Sure," she said. "And if the babies get upset, I'll make sure they know who to blame."

The doors began to close; JD winked just before they met. A moment later, her children came running around the corner with their aunt on their heels. The kids ran a circle around her and then headed for the door, giggling and joyously amped.

Brenna came to loop their arms together and they followed in the kids' path. "So…" her friend said. "What's going on with you and my brother?"

SEVEN

LUNCH WAS GOOD, the food anyway. Brenna had dozens of questions, most of which couldn't be answered while the kids shared their table. Though the topic wasn't completely embargoed. The little ones filled in a lot of details for their aunt, talking about having Daddy at the apartment.

The twins spoke about dinner, about him staying over, and about him moving in, which raised Brenna's brow.

Normally, Brenna didn't walk her all the way back to work or return the kids to daycare with her. On that day, she did.

"You're coming back to work with me?" she asked en route to the elevator.

Brenna linked their arms again. "Let's go get a coffee. Tell your boss there was a family emergency or something. It is Friday after all."

She pressed the elevator call button. "Because we all know there's more chance of having emergencies on a Friday."

Brenna shrugged. "Sure."

"I can't," she said, watching the numbers descend. "My only family is our children. If I tell JD there's a family emergency, he'll buy a hospital and maybe… a police department or something."

Brenna laughed. "Sounds like my brother."

"And that's another reason. My new boss is your brother. We're trying to hide our association. If he lets me cut out early, people will ask questions."

"He's like your top floor boss. I don't think top floor bosses know what goes on in marketing."

True. "They don't," she said, dreading the reveal of that day's development. "But your brother usurped me."

"Sounds kinky."

"I'm working as his executive assistant now. So, it's to his desk I go, not marketing."

The doors opened. As always, she kissed her friend. Instead of accepting the kiss, Brenna bundled her forward into the elevator and selected the top floor.

"What are you doing?"

"You know my brother hasn't really had a home all his adult life. You're lucky if he makes half of his visitations with the kids."

"We're slating him now?"

"No, not slating him, praising him. His slick move gives me an advantage too. I've never met any of his haughty top floor friends. That means I can parade around up there making his life miserable and, unless he wants to blow your cover, he can't tell me not to."

"He could tell me it's a security breach to have my friends around the office."

"Yeah, but he won't," Brenna said, squeezing her arm. "He loves us too much… and I'll tell Mom… oh, and his children. I'll tell his children. Don't forget them. He might think they idolize him, but they love Auntie Brenna more. If I tell them their father upset me, whoa!"

Brenna could always relax her. "Okay, you can come snoop around."

"And have a real conversation," Brenna said. "Tell me, if he's staying with you and this is his weekend with the kids, how does that work? Does Baxter know?"

"I'll take them to your mom's."

"Even though he's living with you?" Brenna's

incredulity opened her mouth except, yeah, she had nothing. "What does Baxter think about your ex living with you?"

Sliding a hand up the strap of her purse, she avoided eye contact. "I'm seeing him tonight."

"So he doesn't know?"

"Since when do you care about my boyfriend's opinions?" she said, twisting to smile like it was a tease. "Besides, I wouldn't exactly call JD an ex."

"Meaning he's a… current?" Brenna asked and gasped, tugging on her arm. "Did you have sex with him last night?" She gasped again. "Are you ovulating?"

The constant questioning and childlike enthusiasm were hilarious. "Geez, Bren, the guy knocked me up once. You think either of us would make the same mistake twice?"

"Uh, have you forgotten that your kids are delightful? I think you should have more… Would you have more?"

"Kids? Are you and Lotta still talking about it?"

"I don't know, kinda," Brenna said. "But don't change the subject." The elevator pinged and the doors opened. Out they went, through the bullpen and up the stairs. "Why not stay at Baxter's apartment this weekend? Leave Jamie alone with the kids at yours."

Troublemaker. Brenna would relish putting her brother in any stressful position.

"Your mom will swoop in and help him, you know that."

"Not if I tell her it's prep for a newborn."

"A newborn?"

"Sure, he'll have to prove he can handle two four-year-olds before we let him use your uterus again."

Another laugh. She guided Brenna to the desk, propping her on the end while she retrieved a chair. When she brought it back, she put it at the end of the desk and steered Brenna down into it.

"He doesn't want to use my uterus again," she said. "Let's talk about your uterus."

"No, let's talk about what you're going to do this weekend," Brenna said, watching her switch on her laptop and check what had materialized on her desk since she left. "Go to Baxter's, screw his brains out, break the news about Jamie gently, and leave my brother to drown in SpaghettiOs."

She returned to filling in the forms she hadn't finished before. "My children don't eat SpaghettiOs."

"All kids eat them," Brenna said, picking up a document from her in-tray. "You just aren't nice enough to give them to your children. Bet my brother has enough money to buy the whole factory. He could buy the twins *all* the SpaghettiOs in the world."

"Why are we talking about SpaghettiOs?"

"Because you don't want to talk about your uterus, or your boyfriend, and you haven't brought me coffee."

Pushing the papers aside, she rose. "I'll get coffee providing there's no more talk of my uterus or my boyfriend."

Leaving her friend at the desk perusing papers, she went downstairs to the coffee room—one of the first places she'd sought that morning. As long as there was coffee, she'd get through the day.

***

JD CAME OUT of an office at the end of the mezzanine, his mind full of a thousand thoughts. Most of them faded when he noticed his sister sitting alone at the end of Rylee's desk, looking through official work product.

"Are you lost, Nana?" he asked, plucking the papers from her hands to drop them into Rylee's in-tray.

Bouncing up from the chair, she shoved him toward the office. "No, Jame, go inside, I want to see your fancy office."

He went inside and straight to his desk. "What are you doing up here?"

His sister was still wandering around exploring when he sat down. "How come you never told Mom and me about this decision to move here?"

"I got the opportunity to buy this company and I took it. The decision to make this my base came later…"

"You still could've called us. We could've got you apartment listings and made sure you had a home straight away."

"I was fine in the hotel," he said. "I thought I'd be fine… Did Rylee say something?"

"No," Brenna said, sauntering toward the desk. "But those kids will break their hearts if you leave them." Inhaling, she came around and boosted herself to sit on the desk. "Are you going to seduce her?"

Didn't take her long to get to the point. Provoking a reaction or objection was exactly what she wanted.

He played dumb. "Who?"

Brenna gave his shoulder a shove. The juxtaposition jarred. Before that day, had anyone been so informal with him in the office? All it took was two women, two women unintimidated by him, probably unintimidated by anyone, and his balance was shaken.

"Rylee," she drawled.

"Why? You worried I might be your competition?"

Brenna leaned back, resting her weight on her hands. "Oh, I would eat that woman's pussy in a heartbeat," she said. His smile was knee-jerk. "She knows it too. It's no secret, even my girlfriend knows it. I've tried to take advantage of the mother of your children plenty of times. I've got her drunk, tried to feel her up—"

"Okay, Bren," he said, pulling himself into the desk.

Sighing, she swung her legs. "Yeah, I'm jealous actually. You've got the penis, so you get the babe. It's kind of unfair because I'm so much more compatible with her than you." Allowing her mischief to continue, he retrieved his contracts to keep reading. "You want to be a good brother and tell me about that?"

"Tell you about what, Nana?"

"Eating her pussy."

The words ceased to have meaning. Slowly, his eyes rose to his grinning sister. He didn't get a chance to speak before the office door opened and Rylee came in.

EIGHT

BRENNA WAS SITTING on JD's desk, facing him in his executive chair. He, on the other hand, was surrounded by paperwork, looking like his sister had just kicked him.

"What are you doing in here?" she asked her friend. "You were supposed to stay at my desk, *out*side this office, the CEO's office."

That was JD's role. The CEO. Not Brenna's brother or her ex. The CEO. In that building, they had to give him that reverence… or pretend to anyway. Picking her friend apart about it would be more than a little hypocritical given she hadn't got deference to him down yet either.

"Talking about eating your pussy."

If one of them had to do it, she'd put on her big girl panties and—wait, what did she just say? Shock froze her to the spot. Absorb, process, react. Uh… something.

She closed the office door to rush forward. "Brenna," she hissed.

"Was he good at it?" Brenna asked, all bold confidence.

"What?"

"Your night together, he ate your pussy… right?"

"What are you doing?" JD asked through gritted

teeth.

Oh, her friend was loving every morsel of this and didn't even have the decency to hide her pleasure.

"Let her answer the question, Jame," Brenna said. "Did he eat your pussy, Ry?"

"I… I really don't remember."

Brenna sucked an inhale through her teeth. "Oh, brother, that's not good. Either you were so bad, she's blocked it out, or you weren't much of a lover."

"He was a good lover," she said. Why was she so quick to jump to his defense? "Why are we talking about this? It was almost six years ago."

"You don't think it's weird that neither of you have ever talked to me or Mom about that night?"

"We know that night ended in the creation of two little people," JD said. "Isn't that all you need to know?"

Truth was, she did her best not to think about that night. She never let herself get bogged down by the details of what happened or how they'd ended up in that elevator together. At the bar, the sexual energy between them had been undeniable and only one way to vent it existed.

There were no words, no agreements…

As the bar got busier, the noise of others interrupted the intimacy of their little bubble, forcing them to lean in, sharing their flirtatious conversation, bringing them closer. At some point, JD mentioned his suite had a bar. She'd told him to lead the way… Sometimes she wondered what the hell made her agree to something so brazen.

In that hotel elevator, the need between them combusted. The bar in his suite was nothing more than an excuse. He'd cupped her face, drawn her to her tiptoes as he crouched to get lower and then… Their frenzied kiss left her dizzy. She remembered that. Too often she remembered that.

He'd rushed her against the elevator wall, his hands skimming her waist beneath her jacket. She'd arched into him and asked for more. The word "more" had actually come out of her mouth. Mortifying. Though that didn't stop her from sinking deeper into the memory.

JD hadn't hesitated. He'd given her what she wanted

in his plush, gorgeous suite. Not that she'd paid much attention to the furnishings. Flashes of being in his bed, under him, went through her mind, the feel of his body, his hands, his mouth.

"He did go down on me," she murmured.

"Oh, look at that smile." Brenna's tone slapped her back to the moment, but it was harder to shake the invigoration from her hormones still basking in those memories. "You must have been good at it."

"He did this thing with his tongue on my—"

JD cleared his throat. She stopped talking in sync with their eyes locking.

His brows rose. "Babe," he said.

The warning in that word gave her the chance to be stunned. Had she really just been talking about…?

"Sorry."

"Don't be sorry," Brenna said. "Tell us more. What did he do with his tongue?"

"I know I pay your rent every month, Nana, but you have a job, don't you?" JD asked. "You've got something else to do somewhere else. Ry and I have to talk business."

Sliding off the desk, Brenna slunk around it. "Business, sure," she said and made a show of kissing her cheek for several prolonged seconds. "Call me, gorgeous."

Used to Brenna's sense of humor, she just smiled and shook her head.

JD wasn't amused, even after his sister left. "Finish with the paperwork on your desk, then I want you to put together a branding package."

That cleared her thoughts fast. "What?"

"Give me two or three options; you have latitude on everything. I don't like wasting time on the creative stuff, it takes me too long. You're perfect for this."

"You want me to re-brand the company?"

"And rename it," he said.

"I don't even know what to… you want me to rebrand?"

"You're a creative consultant. Did you think I summoned you up here just to answer calls? Final schedule's your prerogative, you'll have to referee that. Most of the calls are directed to others; plenty of people in the bullpen can answer a phone. I need you for what you're good at. You have an important role here."

"You are constantly surprising me, JD. Do you want to tell me the plan? The corporate direction?"

"We're moving more into consulting while maintaining our current portfolio. I should be able to do most of it from here. There will be some travel involved—"

"I can't travel with you," she said. "Just so we're clear… We can't travel together." His brow twitched. Did she really have to explain why? "The twins."

Traveling for work was not something she'd considered before. That was one reason her job was so perfect, or it had been.

"They can travel with us."

"They've never been on a plane."

That startled him. "My children are almost five and they have never been on vacation?"

"They have, but I need written permission from you to take them out of the country. You and I never saw each other, so road trips were always easier… Sky likes being in the car and Kye just falls asleep."

"I'd have given you written permission," he said.

Apologies and contrition weren't required. He looked so sorry that she laughed.

"JD, you and I have never been close. There's always been an understanding between us, we never put words to it. Brenna enjoys playing people, don't let her get into your head. Don't let her mischief make you think you should feel something you don't or that you should've acted in a way that you didn't."

Confident she'd made her point, work was the next thing to—

"How do you know I don't?"

"You don't what?"

"You don't remember being with me? That's fine. You're right, it was almost six years ago. I'm fuzzy on the details myself." His eyes dropped to his fingertips as they straightened one of the papers on the desk. "But there's one thing I never forget."

Taking a few steps toward the desk, she wasn't sure what his reticence meant. "What are you talking about?"

"The next morning, after we made love, I asked for your number, told you I'd be in town, that I wanted to visit…" His gaze met hers. "You laughed, said with me on the west coast and you on the east, there was no future; that you were my rebound. You told me it was better to have a great memory than to hang on until it falls apart."

She couldn't remember it that clearly but had enough of a memory to know he wasn't far wrong. Those words sure sounded like hers.

"And what's wrong with that?"

"You took away my right to contribute to any decision about us. At the time, I'll admit, it pissed me off, but I let it go… then I got your email about the twins."

After her twelve-week scan, she'd begun her mission to find him. Getting a reliable number turned out to be impossible. An email was the best she could do.

"I told you and you sent lawyers. You didn't show up. Not until I was in the hospital with them."

"You didn't want to be with me. You made that clear. I was never given a chance to make a choice. You shut down any chance we had at a future that morning in the suite."

Had he taken her words so seriously? Hadn't he agreed? Now she wasn't so sure.

"I don't understand, are you…? Are you saying that you wanted to be with me?"

Breathing in, he picked up his pen. "I don't know, Ry. I was annoyed that morning at the hotel. You gave in before we had a shot. Maybe you knocked my pride, who knows? All I knew was I didn't want to build a family with you because of the kids. I figured if you'd wanted us to be with each other, we'd have found a way to come back together before you learned you were pregnant."

"You didn't want us to be together just because of the kids," she said, lowering herself into the chair at her side because her legs weren't up to holding her.

"I didn't," he said. "You were clear in what you wanted, and I honored that… And don't think it was all you, I was focused on building the business. We probably wouldn't have lasted in a long distance, whatever… I wouldn't have supported you with the kids like I should have… I haven't supported you with the kids like I should."

"You send a fortune every month."

"Money is irrelevant, Ry… I supported my mom's move close to you because it made my life easier. Through her, I had a link with the kids and someone to take responsibility for them when it should've been my responsibility and no one else's." Coming over suddenly stern, he held up the pen. "Don't get me wrong, I love my children more than anything. More than anything in the world. There's nothing I wouldn't do for them."

His vehemence made her smile, though she probably would have anyway. "I know."

"These changes, yeah, maybe they're sudden to everyone else, but I've been ready for them for a while. I want to be important to my family, as more than a source of income. Until now, sending money has been my way of telling myself I'm doing my duty. Parenthood is more than that."

"It is."

"You eat lunch with them every day?" She nodded. "Damn, I've got a lot of catching up to do."

"We can't tell them you own the building," she said. "Not yet."

"We're going to figure all this out. You're in charge. I don't plan to come in and take over your lives, but I won't neglect any of you anymore."

It warmed her to hear that. Her children missed out not having their father around every day. Not that she dwelled on it. They had love in their lives and were content. JD's move signified a new chapter for them.

"I'm going to call your mom and tell her to come over tonight," she said. "This is your weekend with the kids. If you're staying with us, there's no reason you can't have the apartment."

"What about you?"

"The three of you have to get to know each other," she said. He'd spent regular time with his children over the years but had never had to concern himself with being solely responsible for them. "Feed them three times a day, wash them if you can, and get them to bed at a reasonable time. Other than that, bathroom rules rule, watch them at all times, don't let them drown or burn… and climbing on furniture isn't advised either."

"Why are you making this so easy for me?"

Standing up, she smoothed her skirt. "Oh, it's not easy," she said. "Being a parent is the simplest, most difficult job you'll ever do… As long as I don't doubt your love for them, I'll never doubt your ability."

"Thank you, Ry."

Nodding once, she started for the door. Before she got there, she paused. There was something she shouldn't let slide. She may never get the chance to bring it up again.

"Your kiss," she whispered.

"What?"

Without turning all the way, she twisted to let her chin drift toward her shoulder. "The one thing I'll never forget is the way you kiss… No man's ever kissed me like that before or since… You… possessed me, valued me, it… I don't often think about that night, but when I do, or when I dream about it… It's your lips on me… that's the sensation that never goes away, never fades."

Fearing his expression, she didn't look at him, just took a slow breath and carried on out of the office to return to her work.

All those years ago, for that one night, they'd meant something to each other. They'd created life that meant more to them than anything else. In the years since, they hadn't been the best of friends, but they had a bond. They'd shared something no one else in their lives understood.

Jamison Dawes was the father of her children and a good man. They didn't have a future together as anything more than co-parents; at least they hadn't until he'd come back promising he'd changed his priorities. Maybe they could be friends, maybe it would never work out, but she'd give him a chance. Everyone deserved a chance.

Now she just had to convince Baxter that this was a good idea.

NINE

RYLEE FOLLOWED BAXTER into his apartment. Just. She stayed put by the door as he traversed the kitchen to enter the living room and turn on an end table lamp. Casting off his jacket, he sat on the couch to untie his boots. Once everything was neatly in the closet, he returned to the kitchen for wine and glasses

"You've been quiet tonight," she said, putting her purse on the kitchen counter. "Guess I monopolized conversation and didn't ask what's going on with you."

"You think that's why I'm quiet?" he asked. "Because you didn't ask about my day?"

Unbuttoning her coat, thinking she'd always liked Baxter's deep voice, that night, it worked against her.

"Then tell me why," she said.

He stopped pouring the wine and put the bottle on the counter. "You're living with your ex-boyfriend."

"He was never my boyfriend, Bax," she said, tossing her coat over the dining chair behind her. "You know it was a one-night stand."

"That's supposed to make it okay? All that means is you were so into each other you couldn't contain yourselves long enough to think about a rubber! And you expect me to just be okay with this guy living with you?"

She leaned on the breakfast bar, perpendicular to him. "Living with me and my kids. It's temporary, until he gets something else."

Peering at her, he wasn't reassured. "You believe that? What happens after the kids are in bed?"

"Do you really think we're going to sleep together again? Geez, Bax, it was almost six years ago. If we were going to make a go of a relationship, we'd have found the time to do it by now."

"You said you never saw him."

"I didn't."

"But you do now."

She threw up her hands. "This is crazy. I don't want to be with him."

He followed her into the living room. "What am I supposed to think? This guy shows up from nowhere, you tell me we can't go to your place because he's there, but you won't tell me anything about him. You never tell me anything about him."

"Because I can't," she said and dropped onto the couch. "I've explained that before, this isn't new information. Nothing has changed."

"What is he? Like a politician? A celebrity?"

She slipped off her shoes and picked up a foot to massage her toes. "Nothing like that."

"The guy has money, plenty of it," he said. "No way you'd be able to afford your place on your salary without serious child support or is it hush money? Is he married?"

She stopped massaging to glare. "Yeah, that's it, you found us out. He's married and I'm a whore," she snapped. "How the hell do you know how much money I make?"

"Am I wrong? There has to be a reason you don't talk about him. You should trust me. It doesn't feel like you trust me."

"Why are you obsessed with him? This is his weekend with the kids, just like it's been fifty times before. Why do you care about his identity now?"

"You won't tell me who he is, you won't let me meet

your children. There are more secrets in this relationship than truths."

Shooting to her feet, she didn't appreciate sitting under his looming form. "Thanks for clearing that up. If you didn't want me to stay here tonight, you could've just said that. If you want me to go, say it."

"Go? To him? Is that what you want?"

She growled in frustration as her head fell back. "Men and their goddamn egos!"

"That's your way of avoiding the truth," he said and turned his back on her.

"If I was so eager to have sex with him, why didn't I do it last night? Why didn't I just call you and cancel tonight?"

Extending his arm, he faced her again. "Maybe you're trying to make him jealous."

"Everyone really overestimates how much time I have to obsess about his thought processes," she muttered, heading toward her purse in the kitchen.

"Where are you going?" Baxter asked, chasing after her.

"You don't want me here, and I really don't have the time, or energy, to argue about this."

Clasping her shoulders, he brought her around to him. "I'm sorry. Seriously, I am. I'm jealous, you're right. Can you blame me? I don't want to lose you."

They didn't wax lyrical about feelings for each other. Did she have feelings for him? Did he for her? The night had taken them from casual to whatever this was without any detour. Things were changing left and right, and she didn't have time to figure out how she felt about it all.

"You're not going to lose me. He and I want nothing to do with each other beyond our children. Yes, he's moving to town and there will be a transition period, but it could work out for the best."

"How?"

"I'm going to see a lawyer on Monday. It might take some time to iron out the details but it's possible I'll be able to share everything once we do."

"And will you? Tell me everything?"

Would she? Could she? "Let's cross that bridge when we come to it," she said. He narrowed his eyes. "I don't want to make any promises when I have no idea what the lawyers will say. There may still be restrictions I have to adhere to. Please, Baxter, just trust me."

"Okay," he said and lowered, sliding his arms around her body to bring their mouths closer.

Before they made contact, her phone rang.

She froze and leaned back. "It could be the kids."

Though he wasn't thrilled, he exhaled and backed off, letting her fish her phone from the front pocket of her purse.

She read the screen. Looming over her shoulder, Baxter read it too: "Baby Daddy." With a huff, he stomped into the living room.

Though she didn't want him to be upset, she wouldn't take the risk of ignoring the call when something could be wrong with her babies.

"Hello?" she answered.

"Kye makes Daddy hate me."

Her daughter was in a grump. It had only been a few hours since she'd seen them, but she smiled at the warm love her daughter's voice inspired.

"Oh, sweetpea, he doesn't hate you."

"Daddy let's Kye pick all the movies!" Sky whined.

Closing one eye, with her back to Baxter, she blocked him out. Although he was on the other side of the room, she didn't doubt he was listening.

"Who are we telling on here?" she asked. "Kye or Daddy?"

"I want to watch Meemo."

"Nemo, sweetpea. You want to watch Nemo. What does Kye want to watch?" Waiting, she rested a hand on her coat on the dining chair. "Sweetpea?"

"Woody," Sky said.

"Kye wants to watch *Toy Story*."

"Daddy picked Kye. He loves Kye more."

It wouldn't help to smile, but her baby was so cute while breaking her petulant heart. "He does not. I promise. Daddy loves you both the same. You can watch Nemo after."

"Daddy says we can only watch one."

She glanced at the kitchen clock. "It is getting late. If you watch Woody tonight maybe Daddy will let you watch Nemo tomorrow."

"Auntie Brenna is visiting tomorrow."

"She's taking you out to buy your birthday clothes tomorrow afternoon, remember? Where's Daddy taking Kye?"

"Don't know," Sky grumped. "They're best friends. Come home, Momma. I need a friend."

Her heart broke a little. "Let me talk to Kye. I love you."

"Love you," she grumbled.

There was a scuffle on the phone and some mumbled words before her little guy's voice reached her ear. "Mommy?"

"Are you being good to your sister?"

He took a big breath, then stated his case. "She's whiny, Mommy. She's moaned all night. She is being mean. She should go to bed."

"You're not in charge, little prince. Daddy is in charge. And your sister isn't used to being around so many boys."

This was an odd shift for them. Daycare consisted of a mix of genders, but most staff were women. Being used to living with her, seeing their aunt and grandmother, they lived in a female dominated world.

Having his dad around more would probably benefit Kye, but the last thing she wanted was Sky pushed out.

"Boys are best," Kye said.

Breathing out a laugh, she pulled out the chair to seat herself at the dining table. "Oh, I love you, little guy. Put Daddy on the phone."

Her baby boy mumbled something that she decided was his declaration of love. Though it was equally possible he was moaning at her.

Another scuffle and then another voice on the phone. "Babe?"

"Are you playing favorites?" she asked, not thinking he was.

"What? No! Sky's—"

"She's feeling pushed out," she said.

"Kye and I were roughhousing and she got upset. She hasn't been herself since."

"She's not used to being around boys. Is your mom still there?"

"No, she made dinner and left." Really? That surprised her. Usually Marjorie grabbed any opportunity to be around the kids. "She's meeting us in the morning."

"I'm surprised."

"I was too. She said she had to leave, something Brenna told her about your uterus."

Despite her attempt to contain her laugh, it leaked out in a single blast. "I'm going to kill her."

"I'm not even going to ask."

"Don't," she said. "I don't suppose I could persuade you to rethink the movie?"

"Kye gets to pick tonight."

"Their aunt is over tomorrow night, she usually brings something ancient for them to watch," she said. "The babies—"

"We're going to the aquarium in the morning."

So much for honesty in this new beginning. "The aquarium is closed for refurbishment until the end of the month."

His snicker was smug. "I'm taking them to the aquarium."

"How are you—"

"My daughter made a request," he said. "If my children ask me for something, they get it."

"Show off," she said. "So Kye gets to pick the movie because Sky picked the activity? Remember she's going shopping in the afternoon."

"She and Brenna won't let me forget. Kye's going next week, right?"

"He is," she said. "I promised Sky we'd have a girlie afternoon; I'll do her hair and nails."

"You telling me I have to clear out next Saturday?"

"You could go shopping with your son."

He laughed. "Take him to my tailor?"

"He's a little young for that. My kids buy off the rack."

"I can change that," he said.

It was ironic that Brenna threatened he'd be a SpaghettiOs dad. Gifts were fine, to a point. She didn't want her children spoiled.

"You will not. Your mom takes care of all the spoiling they need." He laughed. "You should put the movie on or they'll be tired and grumpy all day tomorrow."

"Any last-minute advice before bedtime?"

She didn't have to think for long. "Don't sleep naked."

A sound from the living room matched the sound of surprise that came down the phone. She'd managed to shock both Baxter and JD simultaneously.

"Excuse me?" the latter asked.

"If they shout you in the night or get sick, you'll have to move fast… and you're pretty much guaranteed to wake up in the morning with at least one of them in your bed… so no late-night booty calls."

"Damn. I had a couple of Russian models on speed dial."

Opening her mouth, she kept her mock laugh loud. "I love to rain on your parade," she said. "Keep 'em safe."

Hanging up the phone, she looked down at the handset. She missed her babies and their voices already.

"I'm going to bed," Baxter said, pulling her from her reflection.

He was on his way to the bedroom when she left the table, his tone betrayed his grouchy mood. Hadn't they got over that fight?

Drawing in a breath, this wasn't going to be a quick fix. With two men to wrangle, she couldn't lose sight of her babies being a priority.

Life didn't like making things easy, but she didn't live in hardship. If she had to do a dance to keep things in balance, that's what she'd do.

TEN

"SO YOU DIDN'T have sex?" Brenna asked.

"No," she said, rearranging her salad.

It probably tasted great, she just couldn't get excited about it. Food was the furthest thing from her mind.

Usually, she looked forward to her time with Brenna. They ate lunch together several times a week. Without Brenna as an outlet, insanity was a real possibility.

"Did you want to have sex?" Brenna asked. "Did you… you know?"

Trying to figure out her friend, she frowned. "Did I what?"

Brenna shrugged. "I don't know, do whatever you do to get a penis interested."

Trust Brenna to make her laugh in a melancholy moment. "Get a penis interested? You're asking if I tried to initiate sex? No, I didn't."

"Why not?"

"Do you have sex with Lotta every time you share a bed?"

Shaking her head, Brenna caught some dressing as it dripped from a salad leaf. "That's different. Lotta and I live together. We share a bed every night. You and Baxter only see each other every two weeks."

"We see each other more than that." Sometimes. Rarely. "We go for dinner if the twins are with you or your mom."

"And you'll be able to see each other more now Jamie is in town… Do you want to go apartment hunting tomorrow?"

"You moving?"

"No. My brother can keep the kids, freeing us up. I say we go for a penthouse, a duplex maybe. How many kids do you want? You'll want at least four, right?"

"What's wrong with the two I have?" she asked, enjoying her salad a little more. "I'm not ready to trade them in yet."

"You might lose them to JD."

That stopped all thoughts in their tracks. "Why would you say that?" Panic was inevitable. "What's he said?"

"I meant their affection," Brenna said, reaching over to pat her hand. "He'd never take custody from you. You're an amazing mommy."

She relaxed. "He's had their affection since they first blinked up at him in the hospital. He'll always be their number one, I admitted that to myself years ago."

"And you have his, so I guess it balances out."

"What is your obsession with JD and me?"

Brenna put down her fork. "Oh, come on, he comes back into town without telling me or Mom and suddenly you're living together?"

"What do you think is going on? I'm with Baxter," she said. "JD knows it. We're figuring out how to co-parent, that's it."

"That's it, hmm?"

The jeering was beginning to grate.

Leaning back, appetite gone, she pushed the plate away. "You know, he's been back in town for two days and my life has been turned upside down. Why does everyone assume we're going to hook up?"

"Uh, maybe because the only other time the two of you have been alone, you made babies."

"And why am I the only one suddenly dealing with grief and harassment from every quarter?"

"Count yourself lucky that it's suddenly. Mom's been giving him grief and harassing him about you for five years."

That brought her up short. "She's what? Your mom barely mentions JD to me."

"Because she never wanted to point out his absence. Mom is always upset with him for not making more of an effort to be present... At least she says that, but she loves having sole responsibility for them. I think she always sort of wished you two got married." Brenna picked up her iced tea, took a long drink through the straw, then put down the tall glass. "Why didn't you get married?"

"We don't love each other, Bren. Why would we get married?"

"The babies."

"You have never talked so much about your brother in the five years we've been friends."

"I've never seen you two together for more than like ten seconds. I think I want to."

"You've seen me with Baxter."

Brenna kept eating; her expression didn't change much, but she didn't back down.

"Look..." Brenna said eventually. "I like Baxter, I do, and I think he's a good-ish guy, but..."

"But...?"

"I'm never going to like him more than my own brother, am I? And if it comes down to my niece and nephew having a stepfather who they *might* like versus a father who we know they do like..."

As Brenna went back to eating, her gaze drifted to the front window. She'd never entertained the idea of being with JD, not on a permanent basis. He'd shown no interest in becoming a family unit, a united family unit, and she'd been happy with her routine.

These ideas were being put into her head just because he'd chosen to become more present. She had a life. She had Baxter. JD's newest whim couldn't change that. Couldn't change her whole life... more than it had already.

Much as the seeds were being planted, she resolved herself not to even think about cultivating them. Not until it was clear JD was for real. How long would it take for him to prove himself?

All she kept coming back to was how complicated things were becoming, and she hated nothing more than complications.

****

ON SUNDAY NIGHT, she couldn't have been more ready for home. Despite attempts to be slow and unhurried, she missed not only her children, but her usual environment as well. Unlocking her apartment, she went inside with the sports bag she'd packed to take to Baxter's and opened her mouth, ready to call out to her babies.

The words dammed when a blonde woman appeared from behind the hallway wall. For a score of seconds, she stood stunned in silence.

"Oh my God," she exhaled. All the times she'd seen "hot, powerful men" stories related to JD in the media rushed through her mind's eye. He could get a model-type beauty like this, no doubt, but as her blood boiled, it wasn't his prowess or exposure that dominated her thoughts. "Get out."

"Miss Hampton."

Trying her damndest to hold on to her temper, the quiver in her voice gave a good indication of her struggle with restraint.

"Grab whatever shit you have here, leave, and don't ever come back."

"But Miss Hampton—"

"Get out!"

Startled by the outburst, the woman rushed past her, grabbed a purse and jacket from by the door and disappeared.

A fraction of a second later, JD came around the end of the hallway. "Ry—"

"Don't Ry, me," she said, dumping her bag and marching to him. "How dare you!"

Widening his stance, he folded his arms. "How dare

I… what?”

"Don’t play dumb with me, Jamison. I can’t believe you would do this. Either the children are at home and I’m going to rip the testicles from your body, or you palmed them off on your mother, which just proves to me what kind of father you are.”

The ease of his amusement vanished into the snap of his frown. “What kind of father I am? I’m a damn good father.”

"Because it suits you to say so? Because you think taking your dick out of the model’s pussy in time for Mommy coming home earns you some kind of reward?”

He got up close. “What the hell are you talking about? I have been nowhere near a….” Clarity slowed him, but he didn’t yield his position. “You’re talking about Anya.”

"I didn’t ask her name before I tossed her out on her ass. You know, you have some nerve,” she hissed. “I have been with a real, decent man, for months, and I haven’t even considered introducing him to our children, not once, because I wouldn’t do that to them. I wouldn’t introduce someone into their lives that will one day leave them. I don’t want my babies hurt; I don’t want them getting close to—”

"Neither do I. I don’t want you to introduce them to him.”

"So they’re at your mother’s?” she said and sighed, shaking her head as disappointment replaced anger. “I’m happy they’re safe, but really thought more of you, JD. I thought you could do this.”

He licked the glimmer of an ironic smile on his lips. “You know, I love this hole you’re digging for yourself. Keep going. Tell me more about what a terrible parent I am and how I’ve been screwing my mother’s housekeeper in front of our children, go on.” She blinked. “Yeah, that’s right, Anya is my mom’s housekeeper, not a nanny, not my whore. I’ve never touched her and the kids have known her for years.”

"I don’t…”

"I didn’t want the place to be a mess when you got back,” he explained. “Turns out I’m not super dad and there is a learning curve with this single parent thing, so I didn’t do it all. I didn't do the laundry or stack the dishwasher; I didn't make the beds or clean up the paints. I did feed them. I did keep them safe and entertain them. I did ignore work and spend every waking second in their company… and a few of the sleeping ones too because you were right, they did end up in my bed, both of them. And you know something? I couldn't wait to tell you how amazing it felt to wake up with them wrapped around me. I barely got a glimmer of it on Friday morning because they were up so fast and I was disorientated, but I've really got to enjoy them this weekend, Rylee, and it felt better than I could've imagined." He took a step backward. "Sad thing is, I was sort of proud of myself for getting through it and enjoying it… and I actually thought you might be proud of me too."

The kids ran around the end of the hallway as JD turned to walk away. "Mommy!" they hollered and threw themselves at her.

She crouched to hug them, unable to take her eyes from JD's path. Oh, boy, had she overreacted. Jumping to conclusions wasn't fair. She didn't like hurting him. In fact, she felt sick. The sensation was similar to what it was to disappoint her kids.

Right then, they were excited and chattering, so she forced herself to smile. Their excitement rubbed off. They'd had the time of their lives and fallen deeper in love with their father, if that was possible.

Yet she'd broken his heart. He should be proud. Looking after two hyper twins, who often decided to dislike each other, wasn't easy. She'd make it up to him… if she could figure out how.

ELEVEN

AFTER SETTLING THE KIDS with their coloring books in the kitchen, and trying to decide what to make for dinner, she ventured down the hallway and around to the guest room. JD's room.

The door was open. Although the bed was the same, the linens were fresh. An unfamiliar desk had appeared from somewhere and landed in the corner of the room.

At that desk was where she found JD.

Knocking on the open door, she waited on the threshold until he looked up. "I'm sorry," she said. "I shouldn't have… shouted."

"I love my children, Rylee. Why is it so difficult for you to understand that I love them?"

If he wanted to make her feel worse, he was going the right way about it. "I know you love them, JD. I do know that. I told you, if I didn't believe that, I wouldn't be making this so easy on you."

Pushing back in the chair, he folded his arms. "Are you making it easy on me?"

"I said I was sorry for shouting."

"For shouting?" he said. "I don't give a damn about you raising your voice. I give a shit that you think I'd prioritize sex over my twins. You're the one who's been on her back all weekend." Shocked and insulted, her mouth opened. Had he really just said that? "If you feel guilty, don't take it out on me."

"Guilty?" she demanded, storming forward. "How dare you! I haven't been out whoring myself, I spent the weekend with my boyfriend! Something I only do every two weeks because I spend the rest of the time caring for your children."

"*My* children," he said, thrusting up out the chair, sending it spinning as he stormed around the desk. "That's right, and I've been with them all weekend. When do you think I got the time to seduce a random woman?"

Her contrition dwindled. She didn't care when he came up close and sure wasn't going to back off.

"I imagine a man like you has them on speed dial," she said. "Is there like a central number billionaires use for slut takeout? Hookers for Hotshots Hotline?"

"Right, 'cause I need to pay for it."

"You pay for everything else," she said. "Isn't that what you've been doing with your family for years?"

"Oh, so that's why you're pissed? Because I've been working to take care of you and our children?"

"Don't give me that. You did this long before I got pregnant. You love your work, the company, the power."

Getting closer shouldn't have been possible, but, somehow, he leaned in to loom. If he was trying to intimidate her, he'd be disappointed.

"Not as much as I love my family!"

"And why the hell should we believe that? We've been here for five years, all of us! For five years your mother, your sister, me, your babies, we've all been right here, JD! And now we're the flavor of the month you want us to trust that we can rely on you?"

A frown darkened his expression. "You think you can't rely on me? You could have called me any minute of any day and I'd have been here for you or the kids."

He could infuriate her from afar, even in his absence, turned out he was better at doing it in person.

"The point is, we shouldn't have to call!" she argued. "You should've been here for us!" He didn't retort. Through the silence, their sharp breathing surrendered the adrenaline. "I… I'm sorry." She exhaled. "I don't know why I'm in such a bad mood tonight. I missed my babies. I missed being home. It's no excuse but…"

His hands rose to her shoulders, then slid down her back to pull her against him. "You should've come home." Closing her eyes, she relaxed. "Don't miss them. Be with them."

"This was your time."

"I'll have lots of time with them, as much as you allow. I'm a rookie, but learning is fun. Surprisingly." A few beats passed. "We're family, Ry; you and me and our twins. We do whatever it takes to support each other. I'm sorry if I've let the three of you down."

Compelled to comfort him too, she coiled her arms around his waist. "You haven't let us down. I shouldn't have said that."

"And I shouldn't have commented on how you spent your weekend. Your relationship is none of my business. You deserve time off to have fun."

Breathing in, her muscles grew heavier. "He's not happy," she said. "He wants to meet you."

"We can send the kids to my mom's if you want—"

"He doesn't know who you are," she said. "He knows nothing about you or us."

"You didn't tell him?"

The thread of curiosity in his voice could be construed as judgment. Being in his arms, warm and comfortable, she didn't want to push away or fight again. He smelled good, like male soap and expensive cologne… and her kids. Her precious babies.

"It's second nature for me to protect you, to keep us a secret."

"Protect me," he murmured.

"Protecting you protects the kids," she said. "Me and my babies live a normal life. I've always thought if anyone found out how much their father was worth…"

"You're worried about their safety?" he asked, instantly hitting concern. Calm and gentle but concern all the same. "Why have you never told me? Babe, we can get them security—"

"They'd ask why. They're safe now, while they're so young and under supervision at all times… We will need to talk about it again if our lawyers revisit the contract given you're in town."

"Have you made an appointment to see your lawyer? We should get everyone together this week."

"Are you okay with that?" she asked. "We don't have to change the status quo."

His hands opened on her lower back and splayed to press them closer. "I'm not going anywhere, Siren."

The word opened her eyes.

Staying loose, she leaned back to seek his gaze. "You haven't called me that since our night together. Is that what you call every woman you're intimate with?"

"Only you," he said. "No other woman's drawn me in the way you did that night, babe. You remember? I couldn't take my eyes off you."

Settling her head against him, she smiled when his embrace tightened. "I remember it was your hands you had a problem with."

"Soon as those elevator doors closed, I couldn't restrain myself anymore… Your finger touched mine and it was so damn soft, I… It broke me, babe. I snapped… and I never snap."

Her breathing slowed; had she ever been so calm? "I was sunk after that first kiss. I'd have given you anything for making me feel that way."

"You gave me two children, Ry. I've never shown you my true gratitude for that."

"We've never talked about the night we met."

"We've never talked." He pulled her closer. "You've never let me hold you like this."

With their lives being so disparate, they'd never had the opportunity.

"Feels good," she said.

He stooped to kiss the top of her head before squeezing her in his arms again.

It did feel good. JD was strong, his embrace secure. Since he'd arrived, she'd been off-kilter and overwhelmed, unsure how to make the pieces of her life fit together. But standing there in his arms, a weight lifted. Not that she didn't have the same responsibilities, but that she didn't have to shoulder them alone.

Pressure on her leg broke their embrace. JD must have felt it too because he stepped back at the same time.

There were the twins standing beside them.

"Hey, guys," JD said and crouched.

She liked that, how he so easily put himself at their eye level either by crouching or picking them up. Doing it made him accessible, showed that he was there for them. He didn't want distance between himself and their children, he wanted to be close to them.

Their bold baby girl looped her arms around her father's neck. "Cuddle me too, Daddy," Sky demanded.

JD hugged her with one arm and scooped the other around Kye to pull him close too. The way the father linked the siblings piqued her curiosity.

Being with JD wasn't something she'd ever considered. She'd always been an independent woman who didn't need a man to hold her up. This, what she was watching, was a physical manifestation of what this man was to their offspring. They adored him, she'd always known that, but in that moment, the fierceness of his love was frank, and she sensed how far he'd go to protect them.

The sheer intensity of it was odd given such an innocuous moment. Holding his children on this random Sunday night in the safety of his bedroom, he couldn't be more relaxed. Yet he seemed to be generating energy. The sensation was so strong, she got edgy.

"I'm going to start dinner," she said and touched her son's head as it was closest.

She only got a step away from the group when JD spoke. "Let me take you all out for dinner."

She looked back, his arm was still wrapped around a

child on each side. "I don't know if that's a good idea."

"Come on, it's a crime that we've gone all their lives without going out for a meal together."

"People will recognize—"

"We'll go out of town, somewhere with private dining…" He looked from Kye to Sky. "Mommy says you guys have never been on a plane. Do you want to go on Daddy's plane?"

Excited, both kids gasped, their little faces glowed.

"Daddy have a plane?" Kye asked.

"No," she said before JD could answer. "He's kidding, sweetpea. Aren't you, JD?"

Eyeing him, she needed his support. Until the lawyers had done their thing, she was still under a gag order. The kids wouldn't be able to keep secrets, asking them would be unfair.

JD gave each kid a squeeze. "Go find your best clothes, guys. Daddy will get you there so fast you'll feel like you're flying."

Excitedly chattering at each other, the kids ran out of the room.

As JD stood, she moved in close again to whisper, "You can't ask them to lie."

"And don't ask me to lie to them," he whispered back. "I do have a plane and I won't lie to them and say I don't."

"But if you start showing them this whole glamorous side of your life, they'll talk at daycare."

"I've taken them to nice restaurants and in the back of limos, all sorts."

"Yeah, saying they went to eat food with Daddy or rode in the back of his big car is not the same as saying he took them on his private jet and had their own personal hostess feed them truffles."

"Then I'll give Nadia the night off," he said. As soon as she opened her mouth in shock, he smiled. "I'm kidding, babe."

Pressing a hand to his chest, she tried to push away, but he put his hand over hers to keep her there.

"It's not a joke, JD. I could get into serious legal

trouble if the kids tell people who you are."

His smile widened. "Babe, you don't really think I'd let anyone hurt you in any way, do you?"

With curled fingers, he rested the pad of his thumb on her cheekbone. She didn't like looking into his eyes and believing him.

"All I'm asking for is time to talk to my lawyer," she murmured, moving her face against his hand. It would be harder for him to argue if she came across as yielding, rather than defensive. "Overlord."

"I'd prefer if you'd call me 'Daddy' at home. Reminds me of what we made together… I knocked you up. I'm the only guy in the world who's done that."

His swagger almost made her laugh. "Let me guess, that's a turn on."

He slid his hands onto her hips. "Is that why Bren was talking about your uterus?"

She laughed. "God, don't ask me about that, please."

"Okay," he said, easing in to kiss her hairline before turning her around. "Go put on a pretty dress. Kye and I will spoil our girls in private dining tonight."

She headed out but called over her shoulder. "Go help him get dressed or he'll end up in half jammies, half Hulk costume. I'll get Sky."

"You got it, babe," he said just before she disappeared into the hall to get ready for the evening.

She and JD had proved they could go from zero to a hundred fast when it came to losing their tempers with each other.

Maybe it came from his business experience or her parenting skills, or maybe a bit of both, but they'd been mature in calming down and apologizing, compromising.

They were finding their way in this new reality. She could tell, reining JD in a little every once in a while was going to take practice… and patience.

TWELVE

"OH, I'M SORRY, I'm sorry," she said, rushing into JD's office only to find him working alone at his desk. She stopped short and sealed her stunned lips for a second. "I thought I was late. Where are the others?"

"Everyone is running late today," JD said without looking up from whatever he was scribbling on. "Got everything you need?"

"I think so," she said, heading over to the tripod already set up with her cards. The top one was inverted. "You didn't peek, did you?"

"Babe, if I had time to peek, I would have," he said. She put her laptop on the multimedia unit to attach it to a lead. He froze in his writing to frown. "Did I sign a check to Glitter Unicorn earlier? Did I read that right?"

"Rainbow Unicorn," she said, turning her smile to her computer as it booted up. "It's for your daughter's birthday. Brenna's handling the plans."

"Who knew a real live unicorn could be bought for five thousand dollars? I'm not cleaning up after it. The thing probably craps bigger than Sky."

She laughed along until his words sank in then spun around. "Five *thousand* dollars? She told me five hundred.

What the hell?"

"Maybe it was five hundred," he muttered.

Oh, yeah, like there was no difference between the two numbers. Rolling her eyes, she went back to setting up her presentation.

JD was a details man. After living with him for two weeks, she'd learned that much. Slipping up on a number like that was unlikely. Obviously, he thought he was funny, or wanted to give her a heart attack.

Another thing she'd learned? He was a workaholic. It was a wonder he'd ever managed to find any time for the kids given how hard he toiled.

Each night he made the effort to be home in time for dinner, which was nice. Inevitably, soon after it, he'd slip off to the desk in his room. The only people capable of forcing the man away from there were his children. If the twins got the idea he should participate in their game or movie night, they'd drag him from his desk and, for the last two weeks, he'd complied.

Most nights she entertained them and dealt with bath and bedtime, but they always insisted he come kiss them goodnight in their beds and he did without complaint.

After the babies were asleep, he'd go back to the office or to his desk in his bedroom and that's where he'd stay. Without fail, on her way to bed at night, light still glowed beneath his bedroom door. The guy kept going when she was dead on her feet.

If the kids got up in the dark, ninety percent of the time, they ended up in her bed. Every once in a while, one or both of them would sneak in with JD. He never complained.

One thing was for sure, mornings were easier with him around. Sure, there were some days he was on the phone, but he'd still help with cleaning up while he talked. He'd gotten better at seeing through the kids' manipulation too.

Yes, they were in a routine. Sometimes they'd fight about something BS, it was never serious. Despite the addition to their apartment, her space didn't feel smaller. No one was encroaching on her territory. Probably because JD only made his presence known if the kids were around.

Sometimes she chastised herself for liking the picture too much. One day soon, he'd be moving out of the apartment and wouldn't be around to help. The kids' hearts would break when Daddy moved out. If he meant what he said about building his base there in the city, he wouldn't be going too far. Hopefully, he'd still see them more.

"How did you get on downstairs?" JD asked, pulling her from her thoughts.

"Oh, uh. Fine, yeah. But note to you, if you want to send me to brief and scold my old boss, you might want to warn the guy that I'll be the one coming to the meeting."

Her presentation was ready to go, so she turned to face him again.

He still scribbled away. "I'm sure you did fine."

"I did. That's not the problem. I wrangle two four-year-olds on a daily basis, I can handle one forty-year-old. But I am starting to feel less like an executive assistant and more like a marketing director." She slid a file from the front of her laptop case. "I reviewed the marketing plan you sent me."

He stopped writing to make eye contact. Finally. "And?"

"You have more money than sense," she said, taking it to the desk to open the file. "I did a cost-benefit of the new plan versus the old one. While there are plenty of good opportunities to be had, I don't think throwing money at the problem will have the desired effect."

"So you suggest…" he asked, picking up the file to peruse her work.

"Slow and steady," she said, snagging a pen from his desk. "We shouldn't make sweeping changes up front. Think of it as a soft opening. Leak some details of the new strategy, ease the transition from old to new. You'll find that puts a lot of staff at ease as well as shoring up the current customer base. If you go in too hard and heavy with this relaunch, people will spook and bolt or assume it's out with the old… We don't want our current clients to feel undervalued. Once we have them used to the idea and they're familiar with the new brand, then we have a private launch. For existing clients and staff only, previewing the changes before the big relaunch to attract new customers. It makes everyone in our existing network feel like part of the team. If they think of us positively, they'll recommend us to others. I don't have to tell you that positive word of mouth is still every corporation's best friend."

As his gaze ascended to hers over the top of the file, the edge of his mouth sloped up. "You're sexy as hell."

Smirking, she pointed the pen at him. "That's sexual harassment. I reviewed the handbook when I caught you checking out my ass the other day."

"The other day…" he said, mimicking her, "you unbuttoned my shirt."

"That was at home, it doesn't count, and you were lopsided."

"Sky did my buttons."

Her smile became a grin. "There's something sweet about a father who'd leave his shirt buttons lopsided all day so as not to offend his daughter."

"Have you seen our daughter when she's offended?" he asked and blew out a sarcastic breath. "She's a force to be reckoned with… she takes after her mommy."

"And Mommy couldn't be prouder. My daughter won't take shit from anybody, especially a man."

"And our son? We'll let him be pushed around?"

"If you think our son is easily manipulated, you haven't been paying attention. That boy is smart as a tack." She went around the desk to slide a hip on it. "He does that thing you do."

JD leaned back in his chair, rocking side to side, innocent amusement written on his face. "What do I do?"

"You know. That stay quiet, intimidate everyone by not letting them know what you're thinking thing."

"Intimidate?" he asked, leaning toward her, propping an elbow on the desk. "Do I intimidate you, Siren?"

"Me?" she asked, raising her brows. "No, not me. But you do drive me nuts when you don't tell me what you're thinking."

"Sometimes I do that for your own good."

She laughed. "What does that mean?"

The office door opened, drawing both of their

JD stood up. "We'll have to finish this later," he said to Greg and Jim. "I have to take care of a family matter."

The men stood. "Jamie," Jim said. "If something is going on that impacts the company—"

"Let's leave them to it," Greg said, putting a hand on Jim's back and exchanging a suspicious nod with JD.

Just how much did Greg know?

THIRTEEN

STILL PEERING AT JD, she missed Greg and Jim departing the room, leaving their lawyers and a third man just inside the door.

"The twins," JD said. Not talking to the lawyers, he was looking at her. "That's where you came up with the name." She nodded once. There was a beat of nothing, then he grinned. "I love it." She barely had time to feel relief before JD switched focus to the lawyers. "Okay, show us what you've got. This is the final draft, right?"

He gestured them over to the boardroom table at the opposite end of the room, behind the new couches she'd had the decorator bring in. Sometimes it seemed like JD did nothing himself. If something needed done or she raised an issue, he'd taken to giving her full authority to resolve it. Probably because he didn't care enough about it to do it himself.

One thing he wasn't so loose and easy about was the situation with the lawyers and the contracts.

"Yes," Mr. Andrews said. "We'll go over it all. Providing everyone is happy, we can sign today and make it official. Hence why we brought our notary friend."

"Can't wait," JD said, coming up behind her to guide

her into a chair like he was eager to get on with things. He pushed her in before taking his own place at the head of the table. "Show us what you've got."

Since her first meeting with her lawyer on the Monday morning after JD moved in, JD had insisted on dealing with his lawyer himself. Leaving the negotiation to his team the first time around had been a mistake, according to him, one he vowed to never make again.

Mr. Andrews, JD's lawyer, was the one to take them through and explain each clause of the contract. The document seemed smaller than the one she'd signed originally, but its significance was so much greater.

"This contract does everything you instructed us to do," Andrews said, his particular focus on his client. "I don't think I have to tell you it greatly reduces your protection. The shield that was built before the subjects were born has served you well for a long time. I can't see why—"

"Those subjects are my children," JD said. "The original contract should never have existed, though I appreciate that was a failing on our side. That contract should have been shredded as soon as my children started talking. Are we expected to deny them throughout their educational career? I will attend events, plays, parent-teacher meetings. How would we explain that if no one knows they're mine?"

JD plucked the pen she'd been clutching from her hand.

Before he could sign, her hand landed on his, prompting him to look at her. "Please be sure about this, JD… It's a big change for all of us and one we won't be able to undo."

"It should never have been done in the first place," he said, freeing his hand from under hers to sign his name in the designated places.

When he was done, he put the pen in her hand. As she tried to lower it to the line she was supposed to sign, it shook. Until now, she and her children had been afforded relative obscurity. After this, nothing would be the same. Her children would never be anonymous again.

She couldn't.

She couldn't sign.

Inhaling, she twisted to find JD's gaze. "I want to interview bodyguards," she said, a thread of panic in her voice. "It will be expensive, but I'll find a way to contribute."

JD cupped her face, smoothing his thumb across her cheek. "I'll take care of it."

"They're going to kindergarten after the summer. They could be exposed to… We won't be there."

He offered a comforting smile. "You don't have to explain. I'll take care of it."

"We can postpone signing the contract," Andrews said. "I'll add a financial provision for security that caps your exposure."

JD's hand dropped to the table with a thud. "Did you just use the phrase 'caps my exposure' in relation to the safety of my children? You see everything around us? Remember every property you've ever visited around the world that's owned by me? I'd sell it all if it made my children smile. I'd conquer the damn planet if it meant keeping them safe."

Her hand slithered over the top of his to soothe him with a squeeze. "Shh," she whispered. "Don't get angry, Overlord. He meant nothing by it."

JD's hand turned to link their fingers. While she used her other hand to rub his forearm, he gazed into her. The longer they held that contact, the more he seemed to calm. He'd comforted her without dismissing her worry. Whatever their children needed, she didn't doubt he'd provide.

"I apologize," Andrews said. "Given this unexpected development, a postponement may be wise. There is no clause to include additional children. We didn't believe it was necessary, though your sister implied—"

"His sister thinks she's funny," she said, leaning closer to JD, tilting her head, asking without words if he felt better.

He answered by picking up her hand to kiss her knuckles.

Once they were both breathing normally again, JD switched his attention to the lawyers. "If there are future children, Rylee and I will sign our names together on a completely different contract. I don't want to postpone, and Rylee trusts me to take care of all the financial needs of our children, especially security." He touched her face again. "Don't you, Siren?"

"I do."

JD was beyond generous. She couldn't imagine him ever withholding anything from their children or from her.

"This document is about disclosure," JD said. "It lifts all barriers and allows us to freely acknowledge each other without fear of repercussions. Everyone must understand that my family is to be embraced and aided, not to be punished or denied."

"Yes, sir, but Miss Hampton is not technically your family."

"She's the mother of my children." He didn't skip or hesitate a second. "Short of my children themselves, I consider her the closest family I have," he said. "It's ridiculous to tell the children they can be honest about their parentage and then demand their mother call them liars or remain mute. Furthermore, I object to her being treated like she has done something wrong. The very existence of the contract in the first place is such an affront that we should all be grateful to her for giving us the time of day."

"Baby," she murmured, inching closer. "You're getting yourself upset again."

"Damn right I am."

"Can you gentlemen give us a minute, please?" she asked.

The lawyers gathered their things.

"No," JD said, his brow creased in a frown. "Sign the contract, Ry, and then these gentlemen can go. We don't want them hanging around more than they have to." Picking up her hand to kiss her knuckles again, he wrapped each of her fingers around the pen. "Please."

If she was just going to sign the contract after calling them back in, it made sense to sign it and let the lawyers go on their way.

Inspired by his determination, she clutched the pen tighter and put her autograph everywhere they needed it before pushing the contracts toward the lawyers. In a daze as the notary did his thing, she stayed numb during the conversation JD had with the trio of men before getting up to show them out.

She hadn't so much as left her chair. JD came back over and swiveled it around to crouch in front of her, something he did with the kids when he was being tender or understanding.

"Talk to me, Siren," he murmured, gathering her hands. "What's wrong?"

"It's gone," she said. "There are no more rules."

She couldn't match the glee that became a grin on his face. "That's right. I can finally claim my family without obstacles."

Without her putting up obstacles was what he was really saying.

Her mind raced; there wasn't time to nitpick. "We have to tell the kids."

Standing up, he guided her to her feet. "Let's go get them now."

She glanced at the clock above the powder room door. "They're gone already." His instant look of concern motivated her reassuring hand to land on his chest. "Brenna picked them up. This is your weekend. She's bringing them back to the apartment later… We didn't know what time you'd be out of the office, so she said she'd stay with them… I'm supposed to have dinner with Baxter."

"Are you looking forward to that? You can tell him the truth, no more secrets."

Shaking her head, she inched nearer. "Not before we've told the kids," she said. "They should know first."

He squeezed her shoulders. "They know I'm their father, it's not a big reveal for them."

"No, but they don't know about your means or that you own the building they spend their days in." Feeling a sliver of anxiety, she touched the edge of his tie. "Have you decided if you're going to hang around?"

"Hang around? You mean have I changed my mind about living here full time?" he asked and scooped a hand around her face to bring it up. "I'm going nowhere, babe." They looked at each other for almost a minute, saying nothing. "Why don't you delay your date until tomorrow night? You and I can make a plan while Bren has the twins." Smiling, he brushed his thumb across her cheek. "We can be seen in public now. Where's your favorite restaurant?"

Tipping her head further back, she curled her fingers around his lapels. "A seafood place by the water," she said. "But if you take me there, your daughter will never forgive us."

He leaned down. "We'll tell her we had steak. Do you like seafood?"

She nodded. "It's my favorite. But Sky tells me sea creatures are mermaids' friends and so she makes me feel guilty if I suggest eating it."

"When was the last time you ate there?"

"A long time ago, it's expensive," she said. His brows rose. "I don't mind gouging my children's father as long as I'm making him a co-conspirator in my crime."

He shrugged. "I'm pretty sure we're going to screw them up anyway. Isn't that what all parents do?"

"Yep, and there's always the added bonus that if she runs away, she becomes Grama's problem."

JD was laughing when the office door opened and Greg came in. Though she tried to be discreet in removing her hands from his lapels and stepping away, there wasn't much space behind with the chair blocking her.

"We're going to dinner," JD said, running a hand down her arm as he headed for his desk.

"It's barely five," Greg said.

"Brenna has the kids." JD shut down his laptop and gathered some papers. "She'll drop them off at the apartment later. We have to get some things straight first."

Shock reverberated through her. "What?" she asked, amazed to read the lack of surprise in Greg. "JD?"

He was all at ease. "You told me not to make it difficult for you," JD said, picking up his things. "But Greg knows exactly who you are and all about the kids." Still standing dumb when JD came over to thread his fingers between hers, it was too confounding for words. "Come on, babe, we'll go home and change. Does this place have a dress code?"

"I…" Her laptop bag was over his opposite shoulder and his own computer and files under his arm. "We won't get a reservation tonight."

"Oh, we will. Let me worry about that," JD said, pulling her toward the door. "Let's go home."

FOURTEEN

"THAT WAS BEYOND amazing," she said, folding her arms on the edge of the restaurant table.

JD topped off her wineglass. "The guilt makes it better," he said. "Now we share a secret."

"We'll have to find some way to betray Kye." She put her menu on the edge of the table. "We don't want to play favorites."

The server came to pick up the menus. "Did you decide on dessert?"

"Yes," she said, straightening her back. "Can we have a cheesecake and a chocolate mousse to go, please?"

"To… to go, ma'am?"

"Is that a problem?"

The server glanced around like he was being pranked. "I'll speak to my manager."

"You do that," JD said with booming authority. "While you're asking questions, I'll be making calls to ensure this restaurant is out of business in under a month. This woman gets whatever she wants. It's my job to keep her happy. Don't keep her waiting."

"I apologize. He's not himself. I've had to let him down gently," she said and reached over the table to take JD's hand from his wineglass. "He spoils me every chance I give him. But I have to keep telling him over and over again, this is sex, that's it. That's all I want from him. Raw, animalistic, sweaty sex. I won't leave my husband for him. My children would never forgive me for hurting their father."

Both men stared at her. She picked up her wine and gulped some down while still holding JD's hand.

"Pack up that dessert for us," JD said. "Clearly you can see you're interrupting me stealing a woman away from another man."

The server stumbled in his retreat from the table.

A moment later, she laughed and let go of JD's hand. "He's having a memorable night."

"I'm confused. Am I the father of the kids you're hurting, or do they belong to your imaginary husband?"

"Don't think it matters," she said on a shrug.

He raised his brows. "Do you think sweaty is a requirement of good sex?"

"Yes," she said and drank more wine. "If you're not sweating, you're not exerting enough energy."

"That's right," he said. "I forgot you like it hard."

Sinking back in her seat, she drew a fingertip down the side of her glass. "I'd make slow love with my husband. It's my extramarital lover's job to overwhelm me with his passion."

His smile widened before it disappeared behind his glass. "I'll remember that."

She glanced at her watch. "Brenna will have the kids home already and we haven't even talked about anything."

"Is that why you wanted your dessert to go?"

Shaking her head, she touched her wine-damp lip. "Kye's on a cheesecake kick at the moment. He'll adore you if you bring him back some… and Sky enjoys licking the mousse from a spoon… she's always loved the bubbles."

"The kids and I are going to the zoo tomorrow," he said. "We're going to my mom's for lunch after. Will you join us?"

"I don't want to intrude." She shook her head. "Your time with the kids is precious."

"You let me intrude on you guys last weekend," he said. "They like it when they have both of us at their beck and call."

They sure did. Their kids loved having the attention of both their parents and their extended family as often as possible. "That is true."

"Was Barry okay with postponing your meal?"

"Baxter," she said. "He was okay with it. He wanted to know why, I told him I'd explain at dinner tomorrow. I'm sure he'll understand I want to talk to the kids first."

"Are you worried about telling him?"

"No," she said, twisting the stem of her glass between her fingertips. "Should I be?"

"Some men find me intimidating."

The swagger in his tone betrayed his tease. Though, no doubt, there was some truth in that. The glint in his eye provoked her dormant competitiveness and her own desire to play.

While being grown-ups around the kids and in the busy hierarchy practiced with rules and deference at the office, they had little time to think. The opportunities to relax as themselves, as they could in social situations like this, were few and far between.

"I've seen both your dicks," she said, picking up her wine and breathing out slowly.

Narrowing one eye, JD tried to figure that out. "Meaning…"

"I already know which of you is the better lover."

"How many nights have you spent with him versus the one shot I got to make an impression?"

"Oh, you made an impression, Mr. Dawes. My figure has never been the same since I spent that one night with you."

"I don't remember you being in better shape back then," he said. "Your body's still worth a second look."

"Oh thanks, that's so romantic of you, JD." She touched her upper chest and pretended to swoon. "I'm lightheaded."

"That's the roofie I slipped into your wine," he said

and extended his arm to expose his watch from beneath his cuff. "I should get you in the car before you pass out."

Smirking, she held her glass closer to her chest. "Explaining that to your son would be interesting," she said. "You also seem to have forgotten that I'm a single parent of twins and you're living in my apartment. Most nights I'm so tired you could probably slip into my bed and have your way with me, and I wouldn't have the energy to object."

His eyes stopped smiling as they became more intense, compelling her to lower her glass. "Energy or inclination?"

That had to be rhetorical. Did he expect an answer...? She wasn't sure she'd have an honest one for him. They sat there, just looking at each other, losing track of time. The moment was broken when the server came back with two boxes, presumably containing their desserts.

JD sat up to say something about the restaurant logo on the boxes being unacceptable, setting the server on edge again. The boy thought he'd done well, but her date wasn't doing much to encourage him.

Her date. That description made her think twice. It wasn't a romantic date. They were parents, friends, and colleagues. Complications in each other's lives. Still, it was in their children's best interest that they get along. There was nothing sexual about their association.

Sexual. There was another word that stuck in her mind.

Now there was nothing sexual about their association. But there had been... once. Their link began with sex. When they'd first laid eyes on each other, sex had been in the forefront of their minds. Did attraction like that just evaporate?

They were older, far more mature, and far more capable of keeping their impulses in check.

"Babe?"

Stolen from her daze, she read JD's concern, which suggested he'd tried to get her attention more than once.

"Sorry," she said. The server and boxes were gone. "The kids not getting their dessert?"

"They're not getting it in boxes that provide Sky with evidence we ate Flounder."

Neither had eaten that specific fish, but his point was valid. "You can tell her during your father of the bride speech at her wedding."

"Don't forget about the tower," he said, pouring the remainder of the wine into her glass. "No man is getting near my baby girl."

"She might not be your baby by then," she said. "Who knows how many more kids you'll have."

"Think I'll care less about Sky if I have other girls after her?"

She shrugged. "You haven't talked about your intimate life," she said. "Do you have a serious girlfriend?"

"If I did, you'd have met her in the last two weeks. We live together, Ry."

"You haven't met Baxter."

"I know he exists."

"Should we come up with rules?" she asked. "The kids are older now; it's harder to hide things from them. If you're going to be in town, I guess you'll want to be dating."

"I'd say the most important rule is that as long as the four of us are under the same roof, the apartment belongs to the kids. We shouldn't have any… intimate time there."

Perfect first rule. Ensuring the kids had a safe haven was most important.

"Agreed," she said.

The server came back with two blank boxes.

JD handed over a credit card without saying a word. "Babe, you seem distracted."

The last thing she wanted to do was share her muddled thoughts. "I'm tired."

"Want next week off?"

Her boss had the authority to grant that wish. Damn, complications. Her boss. Father to her children. Her roommate. Former lover. Tormentor. Friend?

Brenna was her best friend and didn't exactly offer an impartial ear, understandably. Did JD have someone to lean on? Greg was his friend, but she had no clue whether their colleague knew about their history or that they'd shared a night together. Either way, she'd have to look Greg in the eye at work. Maybe it was best to be in the dark. Gossip didn't interest her.

"I want to go home and hug my babies," she said. "Will you take me home, JD?"

He nodded once and stood up to come around and help her from her chair. The server rushed back and, from the corner of her eye, she noted JD handing over a significant cash tip.

JD put his card away and then laced his fingers between hers. "Let's go hug our babies," he said, picking up the desserts in his other hand.

It was nice to have support, to have someone take care of things. Life was going to get more complicated as people absorbed the truth of her children's parentage. As long as their babies were okay, and had the support of both parents, they'd work everything else out. JD would do his part; she had full confidence in that.

He was a good father. Though that wasn't exactly something she could be proud of herself given it was luck of the draw. Serendipitous. Still, she had done a good job of picking a counterpart. Primitive biology at work, she presumed. He loved their children, and she couldn't ask for anything more than that.

FIFTEEN

THE HIGH OF HER DAY with JD and the kids carried her through to meeting Baxter for dinner.

It didn't last long beyond that.

They'd met at a gastropub, nothing fancy, just a great place to eat. She loved their cocktails and the friendly staff; she'd been there a bunch of times.

In fact, they'd eaten there so regularly that she'd decided on her dinner order before arriving. While giving their drinks requests, they ordered food too.

"So…" Baxter said, his attention moving from the darkened window next to their faux-leather booth to the bright lights hanging above each table. "Do you want to tell me now why you canceled on me last night?"

Still smiling, optimistic about the conversation, revealing the truth should be freeing.

"I didn't cancel, I postponed."

"Usually when it's his weekend, I have you the whole time."

"I know," she said. "And this is sort of his fault." Though Baxter frowned, she flashed a smile. "Well, not his fault, but… we had a meeting with our lawyers yesterday afternoon and signed new contracts."

"New contracts? You mean…"

"Yes," she said, flattening her hands on the table, pushing her arms straight and shoulders back. "The gag is officially gone; I can say anything I like. Everything. Anything is allowed."

"Rylee…"

His stunned expression enhanced her glee. Had he believed it would ever happen? Had she?

"We had to talk to the kids last night, hence the postponement. It was only right to talk to them first."

"But…" he said, squinting. "They knew who he was, right? They knew he was their father… didn't they?"

She nodded. "Yeah, there were other things they weren't aware of though. We had to loop them in."

"And… it went well?"

Thinking about their evening poured warmth into every cell in her body. They'd had a lot of fun with the kids, as to how much they took in…? It was difficult to tell when kids got giddy.

"I don't know that the kids got what we were trying to explain to them. But they're four, you know, they'll get it eventually… when I loosen the reins."

"The reins?"

"Sometimes I haven't let JD do certain things with them. I won't have to worry about that so much anymore."

"JD?" he asked, his brows rising. "That's him. That's their father?"

Another smile and a nod. "Jamison Dawes," she said and frowned in wonder. "I don't know where I got JD from. Everyone else calls him Jamie."

From his puzzled expression, she guessed he was figuring it out. "Jamison Dawes," he said. "Why do I know that name? How do I…" he trailed off. "Jamison Dawes… the billionaire?" He panted out his disbelief, but wasn't done, another memory hit him. "Wait, didn't he just buy your company?"

She held up an innocent hand. "I didn't know he was going to do that… and I already tore into him for it. Though, in his defense, he didn't know I worked there."

"He didn't know where the mother of his children worked?"

Lifting a shoulder, their drinks appeared right on time. "He has enough on his mind. He's busy and doesn't waste mental energy figuring out where I spend my days."

"Apparently he fucking does, didn't you say you'd started working in the new CEO's office?"

"Yes, but…" When he put the question in such an impatient way, it didn't sound great. "He needed someone familiar. He asked me to do the rebrand. I'm not sure I'll stay in his office after that's done."

"Rylee…" he scoffed out her name but didn't follow it with anything.

In anticipation of his point, she stayed silent while the server put their drinks on the table.

At least she did until the server was gone and the pregnant silence continued. "What?"

"You… you fucked this guy," he said, ignoring his drink, while she raised hers to her lips. "You fucked him."

"Five years ago… almost six."

"You fucked him, had his children, and you're living with him. Now I find out you're spending all day alone in some top-floor office with him?"

Breathing in, she let her eyes drift to the side. "And…?"

"And? And he's a fucking billionaire!"

His raised voice drew the attention of diners and staff. Great, just what she needed, a show.

She offered the strangers a nervous smile before leaning over the table toward Baxter. "I don't see your point, Bax," she hissed. "Though I am getting to grips with your attitude. What is wrong with you?"

He pushed against the edge of the table, reinforcing the tension in his shoulders. "Why aren't you with this guy again?"

"Why would I be with him? Because he's my boss or because he's squatting in my house?" she asked. "If people made romantic choices based on those roles, we'd have a lot of CEOs in polygamous marriages and no such thing as roommates.”

"You have kids together."

"I'm confused," she said, sensing an increase in his anger. "Do you want me to be with him? Are you telling me to be with him?"

"I'm telling you I don't understand why you're not… Has he made a move on you?"

"JD? Since when?" she asked, her upper lip curled. "Not since the night we were together. He would never compromise me like that."

Baxter didn't look to be buying it. "Why not?"

"Because he respects me," she said. "Because I'm the mother of his children and our relationship is about the kids, not about sex. Sex complicates everything, there's no way we're compatible beyond that. If we tried to make ourselves be something we're not, we'd only end up hating each other."

"So you are attracted to him?"

"What?" she snapped. "Where did you get that?"

"You just said there's no way you're compatible beyond sex, that means you think you're sexually compatible."

Putting down her glass, she ran a hand through her hair. "Jesus, Baxter," she exhaled his name, but he wasn't appeased. "Was the sex good? Is that your question?"

"I want to know if you think about it now. Do you think about having sex with him?"

"No!" she said. The quiver in the back of her throat made her feel like a liar. "Look, sometimes JD and I have an… energy." His mouth opened. "But it's not something we'd ever act on. Honestly, ninety percent of the time we're more interested in competing. We're selfish together. We'd be too busy racing to our own orgasm to worry about pleasing each other." His eyes widened. "Shit, Bax, I… what I mean is that we're not interested in any kind of relationship. We're not. We don't care about each other that way. I care about what he means to my children, that's it. Honestly, if you met him, you'd see, he's just not husband material."

"Why not? What's wrong with him? Seems to me he'd be a perfect husband; he's got the cash for it."

"Cash?" she asked. "Funny, 'cause that's what JD

used to think the world was all about too. You'd be sick if I told you how much he tried to pay me in child support before the twins were born."

"Is that supposed to make me feel better?"

"I have no idea why you don't feel just fine," she said. "So what if the father of my children has a few bucks? I don't know why that changes anything."

He leaned in. "It's more than that," he said, lowering his volume. "You work with him. You live with him. Shit, Ry, why are you living with him? The guy has enough money to rent a whole damn hotel if he wants."

"The kids asked him to stay," she said. "I told you that. It means something to them to have their father around every day. They've loved having him at the dinner table and cooking breakfast for them."

Disbelief and some kind of resentment bubbled out of him. "He cooks?"

"He's a better cook than me," she said, slanting back when the server brought their food.

The man could clearly sense tension at the table, or maybe he'd heard the shouting.

"What else does Mr. Fantastic do?"

So much for looking forward to eating; her appetite had disappeared.

Baxter was heavy-handed in arranging his plate and adding more ketchup to his burger.

"What is wrong with you, Baxter? Since we got together you've wanted to know about the twins' father. Now I'm being honest with you and you're being… unreasonable."

He stopped dealing with his food to glare at her. "You call this unreasonable? All this time you've had a brilliant billionaire in your back pocket, and you never thought to even so much as hint that—"

"Do you know something? I never thought about JD's bank balance, never thought about it. I really didn't. I used to think about how many weekends he failed to show up when he was supposed to have the kids. About the hours they spent with their grandmother wondering if Daddy was going to grace them with his appearance. I'm sure this is a shock to you, but I never considered JD brilliant either. I didn't think about his business or wonder if he was any good at it. I thought about my children and if he'd disappoint them again."

"Seems that's all changed, huh? Now you've moved him in."

"Yeah, and maybe that's why," she said. "Even if I hated the guy, I still have to recognize that he is the father of my offspring, Baxter. That's something you'll have to get used to if you want to continue this relationship." In the silence that followed, she tried to read him, but he gave little away. "If you don't, that's your choice."

SIXTEEN

"I WANT TO MEET HIM."

Her head shook before she even thought to speak. "No. No way."

"I have to meet him," Baxter said. "Did you think you could keep us apart forever?"

"In time, maybe, once you've had the chance to get used to the idea."

"Did he have the chance to get used to me?" he asked, sounding snide. "You told him my name, right? Does he know you have a boyfriend?"

"Yes, he knows," she said, doing her best not to sneer. "And I told him your first name. I really don't think he gives a shit about who I'm seeing."

"Have you met his girlfriend?"

"He doesn't have one," she said, forcing herself to pick up a fry.

Baxter raised his hips to retrieve his phone from his pocket. "Let's find out."

Her wrist loosened, dropping the fry. "What are you doing? You don't have his number," she said, hoping he hadn't invaded her phone at some point to copy the "Baby Daddy" number from her contacts.

He turned the phone around to show an online

search bar bearing JD's name. "World of instant information. Don't tell me you never Googled him."

"Never," she said. "Well, yeah, I did, back when I found out I was pregnant, but that was about as useful as an umbrella in a forest fire. Sometimes I see stuff by accident, but I never—"

"Gabriella Wellesley," he said and flashed the screen at her briefly, just long enough for her to glimpse an image of JD with a svelte blonde. "Billionaire heiress and model."

"He's not seeing her."

He lifted the phone closer to his face and swiped some more. "They look pretty close to me… Oh yeah, check out that one."

Showing her again, he extended his arm to give her a better look at JD on the beach with the same blonde. In a tiny bikini, little was left to the imagination. The girl had an amazing figure. Amazing enough to make her blanch at the sight of JD standing, holding the woman, his hands resting on her pert, almost-naked butt.

Baxter swung the phone away and kept swiping. "Wow, this guy doesn't seem to have a type. There's a redhead, a brunette. One from here, one from there… is he just working his way through the continents?"

"You should know better than to believe everything you read on the internet," she said. "He's not seeing anyone."

"Looks to me like he is… wonder which one he'll introduce to your kids now that the gag is gone."

"He wouldn't introduce any of them to the kids," she said. "And he isn't seeing anyone."

"Think you know better than the internet?"

"Yes," she said. "Because I heard it from the horse's mouth. He isn't seeing anyone."

Adjusting the angle of the phone, Baxter's ogling apparently became reading. "Hmm, maybe you're right. This article here says he and Gabriella broke off their engagement a month ago. Funny, that's like right before he showed up here… Guess the kids are the flavor of the month."

"Don't," she said, losing her battle with the sneer. "Don't do that. Don't imply he's only here because his relationship broke down."

"An engagement, that's a big deal," he said. "Did she ever meet the kids?"

"What?"

"This woman, the billionaire heiress, did she meet the children?"

"No."

"Because you asked him that too?" Baxter put his phone on the table. "You don't really know what he did with the kids on his weekends. Maybe she stayed with him at his mother's."

Maybe. She couldn't refute that. She'd never probed into who the kids met at his mother's, as her encounter with Anya had proven. If JD was planning to marry this Gabriella woman, and he'd told the kids about it, she couldn't imagine neither of them would mention it to her.

"I'll ask him about it."

"Why?" Baxter asked. "Does it matter? If he's going to marry her, the kids will have to get to know her. If they've broken up, it doesn't matter now, does it?"

"It matters if JD is introducing random women to my children."

In asking, she'd tread carefully, having used her only free pass when it came to accusing JD of prioritizing sex over their offspring.

"A fiancée is hardly random."

"She is if they're over now," she said. "He can propose to whoever he wants, but he better be damn sure the relationship is going to last if he wants the woman to be a part of my children's lives."

"You're getting defensive."

"You're upsetting me," she said, shoving at the plate, unable to consider eating. "I don't want to think about something like that."

"About Jamison with another woman?"

"About my children getting attached to someone and being hurt when they're snatched from their lives," she said, and grabbed her purse from the bench beside her while shuffling to the edge.

"Where are you going?" Baxter asked, tensing, leaping to the end of the booth.

"Home."

"To him?"

The exit in her sights, she didn't wait when he pulled out his wallet to throw money on the table. Yanking on the long metal bar granted her blessed freedom into the nip of the evening air.

She was striding down the block when Baxter caught up at her side.

"Go away, Baxter," she said. "Go home."

"No," he said and tried to grab her arm, but she pulled it away. "You can't even stand to stomach it, can you? Thinking of him with another woman makes you sick and you expect me to believe you feel nothing for him?"

"This has nothing to do with him," she said.

"Are you kidding? You couldn't wait to get out of that restaurant and rush home to confront him about this other woman!"

"Stop it," she spat and tried to walk faster. No way she'd ever outrun anyone with legs so much longer than hers. "Goddamnit, I thought you'd be happy I could finally tell the truth."

"Yeah, and I might have been if this didn't open its own can of worms. Shit, Rylee, can you tell me you wouldn't feel the same if the situation was reversed?"

"Would the mother of your children threaten me? No! I know the children are the priority. They need two loving parents. If those parents can get along, that helps them. It helps the kids, Baxter, that's it… Maybe if you had children, you'd understand."

This time he got hold of her arm and spun her around to face him. "And maybe one day we will, but you better remember that I'm your man. I'm your future. You can't prioritize him over me."

"What? That's not what I'm doing."

"You're with him every minute and with me for a few hours every other weekend. This relationship won't last unless you make room for me in your life," he said. "More room."

"Bax, I… I don't know if we're ready for that."

"It's been months." But not a lifetime. Commitment had never come up. Until that point, everything was casual. He had his life, she had hers, and they got together whenever their schedules matched. "We're ready."

Were they? Much as she knew her next words would aggravate the situation, she had to be honest. "Me and the kids, Baxter," she said. "I don't know if me and the kids are ready for it."

Letting her go, he stepped back. "Didn't take long for him to come between us, did it?"

"This isn't JD's fault," she said. "You're making assumptions. This is a big development in my life. No one's known who the father of my children is and now the world will. I don't know how this will change things for the kids, but they have to be my priority."

"And it never occurred to you that I could help you? That I could be a support to the three of you? Why is it your default to keep me on the outside?"

Until then, she'd had no other choice. Being unable to reveal the truth meant there had always been a secret between them. Now that need for secrecy was gone… Had she been using it as an excuse to keep herself from getting too close?

"I need you to… to be patient," she said. "Please, we'll figure this out, just… give me time."

He backed away. "I'm not a patient guy."

Turning around, he strode off, and she watched him go. Confused, tired, and upset, figuring out what she wanted from her relationship with Baxter was no easier than guessing how her life might change now the world knew the identity of her children's father.

SEVENTEEN

AFTER BAXTER DISAPPEARED around the corner, she forced herself to hail a cab. The apartment was only a few blocks away, but walking felt like too much. She didn't want to think; she just wanted to be with her family. Her kids always helped her feel better about everything, especially when the Earth was tilting on its axis.

Using her key to go into the apartment, she dropped her purse and scanned the mess in the kitchen. No sign of the kids, but she could hear something further inside. Heading down the hallway toward the sound, she ended up pushing JD's slightly ajar bedroom door further open.

The trio were on JD's bed watching a movie on the TV that shared a wall with the doorway she was standing in. All their attention swung around to her. Kye was lying across the foot of the bed, his head propped on his hand. JD sat in the middle of the bed, in front of his pillows, hairbrush in hand, doing something with Sky's hair. Their daughter was content between her father's legs, stretching a hairband.

"Momma," Sky called. "Daddy's making my hair wavy."

"I called Brenna," JD said, frowning at whatever he was doing to Sky's hair. "I don't think I followed the instructions right."

Just like that, they accepted her. No one asked questions or needed explanations. No one accused her of anything or made demands.

Dragging her feet, she slipped off her shoes and climbed onto the bed. Forcing her boy onto his back, she held his cheeks in her hands and pressed a kiss to his forehead. That wasn't all. Her gorgeous, precious boy got a kiss on each of his eyes before she kissed his lips.

Kye laughed when she moved on and did the same thing to her daughter. When she was done kissing Sky, she crawled up the bed some more and gave her daughter's back a little push.

"Slide down a bit," she said, taking the hairbrush from JD's hand and climbing over his leg to sit between them to take over with Sky's hair.

"Mommy saves the day," JD said and kissed the back of her head before slouching against his pillows.

After removing the ties and pins to put them aside, she took JD's wrist to pull him into a sitting position again.

"Watch," she said to him. "Every good daddy should know how to braid his daughter's hair."

"In case of braiding emergencies," he said, smoothing a hand down Sky's hair as she brushed it. "Her hair's as soft as yours."

"I wish," she said, putting the brush aside to run her fingers through the length of Sky's tresses.

Within their daughter's locks, JD's fingers tangled in hers; his torso pressed against her back. Sky and Kye laughed at the movie on the screen ahead.

JD's breath warmed the shell of her ear. "Everything okay?" She nodded and gave his fingers a squeeze before extricating hers to separate out the hair for braids. "Did he hurt you?"

Physically or emotionally? She hadn't intended to be back home that night. The fact she was in the apartment at all told him something had happened. Tipping her chin toward her shoulder, she kept her volume low and continued braiding, so as not to draw their daughter's attention.

"I'm not your responsibility," she murmured. "I'm Mommy, you're Daddy, that's it."

"Mommy," Kye called out.

"Yes, sweetpea?"

"You should put your jammies on."

"Yeah!" Sky exclaimed. "Can Mommy sleep in our bed tonight, Daddy?"

JD's bed was communal property? That was funny. Just like Sky to claim ownership. Kye scrambled up the bed, bypassing his sister and mother to wrap his arms around JD from behind. She didn't have to look to know it. Her boy's hands caught in her hair as he threw his arms around JD to clamber up onto him.

"Watch the girls, buddy," JD said, picking her hair from Kye's hands.

"Can she, Daddy?" Sky demanded. "Can Mommy cuddle with us?"

"Thumb wrestles, Daddy," Kye said.

Pushing Sky further down the bed to between JD's feet gave her space to shimmy down the bed and the boys more room to play.

"Daddy!"

Kye's exuberance tempted her to smile and peek over her shoulder. In demand, JD scooped their son around to sit on his torso and lay down, pushing his groin hard against her ass. Not that he'd notice, being too busy locking his hand around their giggling son's.

"Daddy!" Sky screeched.

"Daddy's playing with me!" Kye said. "You can't talk to him!"

"Hey, don't fight," JD said. "You know the rules, you shout, and I send you to your own bedrooms."

Sky whined. "But Daddy, you didn't tell Mommy she could—"

"Mommy won't fit in bed with us."

"We can squish," Kye said, then squealed and bounced on JD, moving them all with the motion. Kye pushed his back against his mother's for extra traction. "Sky!"

She'd just put a tie in the end of Sky's hair when Kye

called to her.

"Oh, boy," JD said when Sky jumped up.

Their daughter ran around to sit on her father's chest, blocking his view and pushing on his thumb with both hands, holding it down so Kye could pin it.

Spinning on her butt, putting her back to the TV, she crossed her legs and watched her children overtake their father. Two tiny people, who spent large portions of their life whining at each other, could take down the great Jamison Dawes when they worked together.

Kye screamed. "I win!"

"My turn!" Sky called.

Both kids bounced on JD with such exuberance, she worried they might hurt him.

"Guys, be careful with Daddy," she said, snagging her son to pull him back into her lap.

"Have to help Sky," Kye said, wriggling away from her grip to help his sister triumph over their father.

The kids' laughter reached new exuberance when JD roared and grabbed them both, tossing them onto their backs in a tickle trap, drawing them back if they tried to escape.

"Mommy!" Sky called through her laughing. "Mommy! Save us!"

"Mommy!"

"She can't save you now," JD roared like a comic book villain.

She laughed. "Oh yeah?"

Seemed he'd forgotten his vulnerability in only wearing boxer-briefs and a tee-shirt. With her nails, she caught the hair on the back of his thigh and gave it a tug.

"Ow," he said, slapping a hand to the injury and twisting to scowl at her. "That hurt."

"Try getting a wax," she said, bobbing her brows.

"Mommy," Sky screeched, struggling to get up.

Kye climbed up onto his daddy's back.

JD caught Sky. The little one laughed and screamed simultaneously. Dragging his daughter back under him, he tickled her some more while Kye tried to sit up and balance on his father's back like he was playing horsey.

When using the same weapon, plucking the hair on his leg, she didn't expect JD to rear up. One of his arms coiled around to balance Kye on his back for as long as it took him to twist and bring the other arm around her waist to swing her around in front of him.

He took her so completely off guard that she fell fast and had to brace so as not to land on Sky. Shit, he swiped her body beneath his, and she curled on her side, sheltering her daughter who was rapt in hysterical laughter.

"Mommy, save me!" Sky screeched.

JD came down over them again on all fours; she guessed Kye was still on his back. With her legs now between his, she pushed Sky under her body, using her weight to keep JD away from the little one. Widening her legs between his, she wouldn't let JD close his knees, and helped Sky wriggle downwards, creating an escape tunnel between her own thighs.

"Sky!" Kye screamed when Sky appeared from between their parents' legs.

She flopped around just as Sky vaulted off the end of the bed.

"Cookies!" Sky called and ran for the door.

Like it was a call to arms, Kye threw himself away from his father and leaped off the bed to run after his sister.

"Guys!" she called and put a hand on JD's braced arm, expecting it to move out of her way.

"Let them," he said.

Still out of breath and underneath him, her eyes met his. Although he remained on his hands and knees, heat rose between them. Was that the humidity of their breath or... something else?

"It's late for cookies."

With a fingertip, he stroked her tousled hair from her forehead, drawing it down her temple. "If they win, they get a cookie before bed."

She smiled. "Daddy relaxes Mommy's rules."

"Does he?" he asked, his fingertip continuing to her jaw.

Her rules for the kids... Was he on the same page?

"I meant—"

"I know what you meant… You can sleep with us tonight if you want. Like Kye said, we can squish. I just didn't want to put you in an awkward position."

Making a show of glancing around, she used her gaze to make a point of their current position with her on her back under him. "Didn't you?"

"This isn't meant to make you uncomfortable; I'm trying to look in your eyes."

And that explained exactly nothing.

She smoothed a wrinkle on the seam of his tee-shirt. "Because?"

"Because then I'll be able to tell if I have to ruin the bastard for hurting you."

EIGHTEEN

THE FEROCITY in JD's gaze erased her discomfort.

"I told him who you were," she admitted in a whisper.

"And? He didn't take it well."

She shook her head. "And he put things in my mind I don't like."

"What things?" he asked, brushing his curled fingers across her cheek.

"Did the kids ever meet Gabriella?"

Surprise and confusion joined his frown. "Gabby? No," he said. "How did you—"

"He Googled you," she said, trying to sound as non-accusatory as possible. Biting her lip, she slipped her fingers under the sleeve of his tee-shirt, fidgeting to distract herself. "I didn't know you were engaged. I'm sorry it didn't work out."

Moving away, he sat up between her knees. "It was a complicated situation," he said, touching her shin, reminding her she was still wearing her dress and it was riding kind of high, not that anyone noticed. "Her father thought the alliance made good business sense, and it did, but I was never sure about the engagement. Gabby said we should try it on for size, we did, I didn't get any more comfortable. So I broke it off."

She pushed up onto her elbows. "You broke it off?"

He bobbed his head. "Yep, about three months ago."

"Three?"

"The media only got wind of it a few weeks ago," he said and frowned at her. "I figured you'd have known all this."

"I don't follow the business news," she said and then laughed. "I barely follow any news, I have two kids, you know."

He smiled. "Gabby was never…"

"Never what?"

"Stepmother material," he said. "She didn't want kids. In fact, that was one of the issues between us."

"She didn't like our children?" she asked. "God, what a bitch. You should've dumped her the minute you found that out. What's her address? I'll take her down a notch or two."

He laughed and shifted to lie down at an angle, resting his torso on her thigh as his legs twined around her other one.

"I know she'd have fallen in love with the twins if she met them," he said, propping his temple on his fist with his elbow on the mattress beneath it. "But she wasn't interested in having more, I wanted the option."

Her lips moved when his free hand slid onto her stomach. That distant glaze over his expression suggested he was acting without thinking. He seemed a million miles away, watching his hand stroke the fabric of her dress, low down on her abdomen.

"I hope you don't expect to get them from there," she said.

She wasn't offended and didn't make any move to stop his caress. It seemed to comfort him, though she didn't know why.

"It's amazing, Ry," he said, relaxing his hand on her just above her pubis. "This body created the two most important things in my life… and I never appreciated it."

"My body?"

"What you did for me," he said. "What you went through… I wasn't there for any of the pregnancy. I missed it all. I regret that… And I don't regret a lot in my life."

"Even telling me your suite had a bar?"

He snapped back to reality to fix on her. "Especially that," he said. "Damn, Rylee, the kids are the best thing I ever did in my life… the best thing I've ever been a part of… though I admit I didn't do much."

"I didn't get morning sickness," she said. "I craved tortilla chips and would eat them by the ton… I was utterly exhausted for the first three months and the last three."

"If I'd been around, if I'd known that, I would've been able to help."

"How?" she asked, pushing the pillow deeper under her head to make seeing him easier. "You couldn't have gone to work for me."

"I could've taken care of you. You never have to work another day," he said then rolled slightly to aim his voice toward the door. "Sprouts, back to bed, come on!" He rolled back to find her smiling. "What?"

"You're a good dad, JD."

The kids came running back in. Cookies aloft in Kye's hand.

"Uh, no cookie crumbs in bed," JD said as the kids climbed onto his bed again.

"For Mommy," Kye said, crawling up the bed to thrust the packet at her.

"Oh, my prince," she said, taking the cookie pack while snagging her boy to tuck him under her arm.

Kye settled against her. Sky was still hyper and jumped on the bed a couple of times. When JD put an arm out to make sure she didn't fall, Sky grabbed it for balance and climbed up to sit on her father.

"Daddy, can I have more cookies?" Sky asked, bouncing on him.

"No," he said. "I think you two should go brush your teeth again. It's time to settle down."

Though they whimpered and moaned, they went with their father when he picked them up to carry them into the bathroom. She sat up and retrieved the remote control from the nightstand to return the movie to the point it had been at before the hilarity.

She was sitting cross-legged in the middle of the bed

when JD carried the kids back in.

"Momma, sleep with us," Kye said, reaching for her.

"Momma needs to get up," JD said, passing Kye to her.

He kept hold of Sky as she got off the bed. She rocked her boy while JD pulled the blankets back and laid Sky down. Kye would be asleep soon, he was exhausted, and she didn't object when JD took their son to put him in the bed with his sister.

"Daddy!" Sky called.

He bent over the bed to stroke Sky's hair and kissed her forehead, then Kye's. "Daddy will come through in a while. You two finish watching the movie." Stepping back, he put an arm around her. "Mommy and Daddy are going to talk grown-up things for a while."

Sky was already watching the film. Though Kye seemed a little more discerning in the way he examined his parents, he was too tired to care and finished on a yawn.

JD guided her out of the bedroom, dimming the light and pulling over the door before leading her down the hallway.

"Grown-up things?" she asked.

"You need a glass of wine, and I want to hear more about your pregnancy."

"Okay, but we have to clean up in the kitchen first."

"The kids and I planned to stay home in the morning and do the chores. We'll do that and you can lie in. We'll take care of it."

"Please don't call Anya again," she said. "I can't handle beauty that intense before coffee and a shower in the morning."

"No Anya," he said, leaving her at the head of the kitchen island, her back to the dining table, to pour a glass of wine.

She appreciated that he elected to drink lemonade and stay sober, being the designated parent.

"Just a quick drink," she said, when he put the glass in her hand.

His smirk came with a wink. With her crowded in

front of him, he went around the table and up the four stairs into the living room that took up the large corner area of the apartment. The curved couch in the middle faced the entertainment unit. Two windowed walls showcased the evening city.

Sitting down, she drank, then put her glass on the coffee table to curl her legs up onto the couch.

Wrapping an arm around them, she set her focus on JD. "Do you miss Gabby?"

Startled by the question, he paused mid-movement before settling on the couch. "Not really… We were together years ago, when we were young. It didn't work out. I missed her when we broke up back then. That's when I grieved the relationship. We came across each other again by accident about a year ago. I think it was nostalgia that hooked us up… I guess what they say about never going back is true, because this time around was never quite as… intense as I remember it. She was different, I was different. It just wasn't the same."

"Everything's different when we're young," she said. "And every experience we have changes us."

"Then I guess you better start at the beginning."

The way he settled deeper into the couch put a smile on her lips. "What are you talking about?"

"Your experiences. I want to know."

"About the pregnancy?"

"About everything," he said. "I'm listening, Ry. I want to know everything."

Though dubious at first, they quickly slipped into easy conversation. The night they'd met, they'd talked. Conversation had flowed; humor and innuendo blended into the discussion all the way through.

She needed a night like that again. One where she could just be a woman and have an adult conversation. JD was there to deliver and for that, she was grateful. Not only was he a great father to her children, but he was becoming her friend. She needed one of those now more than ever.

NINETEEN

THE KIDS PERSUADED her to go to the batting cage with them in the afternoon. Well, JD invited her to join them when the conversation came up over lunch. She'd told the twins that was their quality time with their daddy. JD chose that moment to explain to the kids how Mommy was scared she wouldn't be able to do it. Ha! A challenge. Didn't take much to be goaded into it.

In the end, she wasn't sorry she'd joined them. After an afternoon out with the kids, they'd gone for burgers, then come home to get ready for the week ahead. Both exhausted kids struggled through bathtime and went to bed without a fight.

She got ready for bed, then returned to the hallway to peek around each of the kids' bedroom doors. Both were already in slumber. Music drifted from elsewhere, so she drew Sky's door over without actually closing it and went toward the sound.

In the living room, JD scrolled through the tracks in her digital library. "You're quite the rock chick, Siren," he said, leaving the stereo to go sit on the couch.

A glass of wine was on the table beside the rest of the bottle.

"I have to get up early for work tomorrow," she said, sinking onto the couch and curling her legs underneath her. "I don't want to be late."

Sitting with her, JD handed over the wine and picked up his lemonade. Were they up for a repeat of last night?

"I promise not to dock your pay."

"Do that and I'll raise your rent," she said, sipping the unknown wine, nice, light, sweet. "This is amazing."

"Two thousand dollars a bottle, it better be."

She almost choked on her next mouthful and barely managed to catch a drip of wine on the edge of the glass without spilling it. "Two thousand... what?"

He laughed. "I'm kidding, babe, relax."

"Idiot," she said, shoving his shoulder. "I could've choked to death."

"Would it have been worth it if it had been two thousand dollars?"

"Maybe," she said, holding her glass closer.

"It's peanuts to us, babe, either way. If you'd let me, I'd show you."

"My life is just fine as it is, thanks. My kids are happy."

Which was the main aim of her existence.

She wouldn't pass up another conversation with him. Before their discussion the previous night, laughing was a distant dream. Funny how people got stuck in their routines and forgot what they were missing. Awake until the wee hours, they'd explored all kinds of topics together. Trust between them was growing. She trusted him with the kids, but this was different, interesting, and unrelated to their offspring.

"Are we going to talk to the daycare tomorrow?"

To put him on the list?

A knock at the front door interrupted the chance of an answer.

Finishing her mouthful, she put down her glass and stood up. "Bren has this book she wants me to read." She descended the stairs to the kitchen. "I thought she'd give it to me at lunch tomorrow. Guess she decided to bring it over."

"What book?" he called after her, remaining on the

couch.

Opening her arms, she lifted them above her head in an exaggerated shrug. Brenna was a law unto herself. Maybe JD's sister wanted to see what they were doing since a text exchange earlier revealed she wasn't staying with Baxter.

Brenna would be desperate to know what happened, though she hadn't expected her friend to just show up.

Throwing her head forward, she laughed to herself when messing up her hair. Just before reaching the door, she slid down the strap of her nightdress and chewed her lips a little. If Brenna wanted to believe she'd interrupted something, she'd get a show, and, later, a ribbing for falling for the prank.

Deepening her breathing, she took a big gulp of air and pulled open the door with a panting breath. Except the moment she saw who was on the other side, all of her deflated.

"Baxter?"

From checking out the hallway, he turned, and did the same to her. Shit.

"Is he here?"

Getting with it, she stepped forward, holding the door close to her back. "You know better than to just show up here."

"Things didn't end right between us last night. I want us to deal with this as adults… I want to meet him."

"You can't meet him," she whispered.

Heart racing, adrenaline drove her to panic. JD was in the apartment. If he thought his sister was there and not going away, he'd come to the door to either invite her in or scare her off.

"Why? Why not?" he asked, his eyes trailing down over her again. "Is he looking for his boxer shorts?"

"Don't do that," she said, scowling at him. "Do you think I'm more likely to let you in if you start that crap again? You're not coming in because the kids are here. You know you're not allowed inside when the kids are home."

"You have to let me meet them sometime too," he said. "What the hell is going on? We were fine before he showed up."

Baxter must've come with good intentions; it hadn't taken him long to become unreasonable. Though, she had to admit, answering the door in a rumpled state didn't help matters. What an idiot. Her, she was the idiot.

Taking a deep breath, it was on her to deescalate the situation. "Bax, the family is going through a lot of changes. We're trying to find our feet."

"All I'm asking is to be part of that family, Ry. I want to be involved. I don't want to be pushed out."

What should she say? What could she say to make him feel better? They'd been on completely different pages if he thought they were serious enough to—how could he think they were serious? They only talked or texted to arrange dates and barely knew each other. Had she misled him or was he making up their connection in his own mind?

"Babe, what's taking so—"

When the door was yanked open, she stumbled backwards and came up against JD just learning his sister wasn't their guest. To steady herself, she used his form, and, great, yeah, that was when her hand landed on skin.

Twisting, she gasped at the sight of him shirtless. "Shit."

He'd probably seen her progress to the door, and figured he wanted to get in on the joke of teasing Brenna. Backfired on both of them. Now the joke was on them.

"What happened to your shirt?" Baxter said, cold and blank, with more menace hanging in the air around him than she'd ever seen.

Giving in to the inevitable, she closed her eyes and took a breath before speaking. "Jamison Dawes meet—"

"Baxter Ames," JD said and put one hand on her hip before extending his arm around her to offer his hand. "Right?"

"Yes," Baxter said, somewhat disarmed by JD's indifference as they shook hands.

"It's a pleasure."

Once he'd let go, JD snagged one of his jackets from the hooks just inside the door to drape it over her.

"You're covering her up?" Baxter asked, regaining

some of his bristle. "What for? I've seen her in less."

Baxter had a point. Seemed like an odd gesture given she was in a short cotton nightdress with straps of only an inch or two, she wasn't near naked. She'd shown more skin on dates. Still, it gave her back just a sliver of dignity.

"Who hasn't," JD said. While she recognized his sense of humor, Baxter wouldn't. She jabbed an elbow back into JD's stomach causing him to half laugh, half recoil. "Right, uh, we won't invite you in. Our kids are four, there is always a chance of them popping up any time. We don't have strangers in their home at night."

"Strangers?" Baxter said, scowling at her.

"Yes, strangers," JD said.

Baxter still fixated on her. "I want to meet them."

Though she opened her mouth, JD spoke first. "That's not going to happen tonight," he said. "Sure won't happen without a ring on her finger either." He shunted her forward, using force that was probably payback for her elbowing. "Take Ry." He prodded her once in the back. "Finish your conversation here. I'll put your wine in the fridge. Shout if you need me."

With that, the door landed against her back and stopped without latching.

"Shout?" Baxter hissed. "And you're drinking wine with him? Is he trying to get you drunk?"

"We have work tomorrow," she said. "We were having a drink before going to bed… our own beds. He's drinking lemonade. It's not like we're getting drunk together."

"So he's limbering you up?"

"No, it's been a stressful weekend; he's being a friend. Geez, Baxter, is this the way it's going to be from now on? You've met him. What more do you want?"

"To meet the kids."

"They're asleep," she said. "Even if they weren't, it's too late for them to think about new people… and JD has a point."

"What point?"

She folded her arms. "Weren't we talking about it being wrong to introduce random people into their lives? It can't be one rule for their dad and a different one for me."

Please say JD wasn't eavesdropping.

"You're saying you won't introduce me until we're engaged?"

That was a terrifying leap. "They don't take to new people and there are going to be a lot of changes in their lives now JD's identity is public."

"I can't believe this. One word from him and you shut me down… again!"

Stepping toward him, she lowered her voice. "Screaming in the hallway won't endear you to anyone. If you wake the kids, you'll scare them, piss me off, and make an enemy of JD. None of those things will work out for you."

He sneered. "Are you threatening me?"

"Threatening? No," she said. "But I am saying I'm too tired for this. If you want to meet JD properly and have a conversation, I'll set it up, but honestly…"

"Honestly, what?"

"We should… take a step back."

"A step back? You're breaking up with me? Here on the doorstep?"

"You came here uninvited," she said. "What we had worked great. We had great fun. But this is the first real hurdle we've faced and it's putting us in perspective. Our lives are too different. I can't have fights like this all the time. I can't have my kids used as pawns, and I do not want you getting into a pissing contest with JD."

Up until then, she'd never had to deal with any boyfriend competing with JD. Would this kind of reaction and conversation be part of every relationship she ever had from then on?

"I can't believe this… I can't believe you—"

Moving back, she opened the door some more, ready to retreat inside. "Go home, Baxter."

"No, I—"

"No." He tried to move forward, but she planted a hand on his chest. "You can't come in here. Go home."

"Rylee—"

"Goodnight, Baxter."

Going into the apartment, she closed the door and locked it before he could think about doing something stupid like rushing in after her.

She hadn't intended to break up with him. In truth, in the long run, freeing him from her orbit was a kindness, whether he believed it or not.

Bed was close by and it called for her to rest. Maybe the world would be lighter and make more sense in the morning… Judging by past experience, that was a helluva wish.

TWENTY

"BROKE UP WITH HIM?" Brenna asked from her place on the couch. "Give me details. You broke up with him? Like it's over?"

Sitting on the floor at the coffee table in JD's office, she divided the various food items they'd picked up from the market

"I don't know," she said, nudging her friend's knee with her elbow, glaring up to silence her.

Brenna rolled her eyes in apology as the office door opened. JD came striding in with Greg behind him.

Noticing them, the men stopped.

JD crooked a brow.

She smiled and licked her fingertip. "Conference room two is free."

"So is my office," he said and headed for his desk. "Or it's supposed to be. What are you doing in here? I thought you ate with the kids every day."

On reaching his desk, he pulled out the chair and two little roaring people leaped out from underneath. Doing his fatherly duty, and probably because he was a little taken aback, he put a hand to his chest and gasped, pretending they'd really terrified him.

Sky laughed.

Kye jumped up and down. "Did we scare you, Daddy? Were you scared?"

"Terrified, Sprout," JD said, picking up his boy while Sky climbed into his seat. "How are you doing today?"

"This is a big office," Sky said, pushing against the desk to spin the chair.

"Sweetpea, stop spinning, you'll get dizzy," she said, shifting onto her knees to reposition the paper plates on the opposite side of the table. "Come over here and eat, please. Daddy has to work."

JD caught the back of the chair to stop it from spinning and put Kye down. Their son ran across the room, seeking his plate.

Sky climbed up to stand on the chair to reach for her father. Picking her up, JD pressed a kiss to her cheek. When he tried to put her down, she locked her arms tighter around his neck.

"Daddy, who is that man?" Sky asked.

Damn, talk about tenacious. Their daughter's feisty spirit would get her into trouble one of these days, especially if she aimed it outside of the family. But her confident little girl would stand her ground and get herself out of any messes she got herself into; Sky's wits were impeccable.

"That's Daddy's friend Greg," JD said.

"Is my daddy your boss?" Sky asked.

Brenna laughed out loud; she tried to be more discreet about enjoying Greg's obvious discomfort. Reaching over the table, she straightened Kye's plate and gave him a napkin.

"Uh, yes," Greg said. "Your dad is everyone's boss, honey."

"He's not the boss of Mommy."

Brenna laughed even louder and slapped a hand onto her shoulder. "That's right," Brenna exclaimed. "We know who wears the pants in their household."

Greg didn't know where to look or what to say, poor guy.

She pushed up, bracing her hands on the coffee table

to sit on the couch.

"Sky, that's enough. Come over and eat with your brother, please."

She pressed a long, sloppy kiss to her father's cheek as he put her on her feet. JD was too polite to wipe the slobber from his face, though there was probably a part of him that liked bearing his daughter's mark.

Sky came over to get her lunch plate. She ignored her daughter's grumbling about the salad and gave her a napkin. Leaving the kids with their aunt, she carried a plate and a napkin to JD's desk. She put the sandwich down and moved in close to wipe away Sky's kiss with the napkin.

"I liked that there," he said, resting a steadying hand on her waist.

Smirking, she was careful not to rub too hard. "It's inappropriate for the CEO to wear young women's kisses in the middle of the day."

"Really?" he asked and slid his other hand onto her waist. "When is it appropriate for him to wear them?"

"At home," she said. "At night."

"She goes to bed kinda early."

"Then, I guess you're out of luck," she said, tossing the napkin to the desk.

With a tighter grip, he pulled her closer. "Isn't there some rule of substitutes in your apartment?"

One side of her mouth rose as her head tilted the other way. "Are you flirting with me, Mr. Dawes?"

"Greg," Brenna declared. "Would you like a sandwich? Come and sit with me here on the couch. It seems polite for us to entertain ourselves with our backs to those two while they strut around each other."

"We are not strutting," she said, pushing away from JD, who pinched her, stealing her focus once more as she moved away from him.

It could've been her imagination, but it suddenly occurred to her that her hips moved with a little extra swagger. Did they? Why would she be doing that?

"Really? 'Cause I'm pretty sure the windows just steamed up," Brenna said. "And why did we choose to come up here to eat?"

Greg sat beside Brenna on the couch, as he'd been directed to, so she went to the opposite couch and sat behind her daughter, monitoring both kids as they ate.

"Because Daddy has asked to eat lunch with the sprouts," she said, opening Sky's sandwich to put the lettuce back inside as the little one tried to push the salad off to the edge of the plate.

"Momma!" she whined.

Leaning back, she cleared her throat, and fixated on the other side of the room, over Brenna and Greg's heads.

"Daddy likes his sandwich," she said, projecting her voice, forcing JD's attention from the papers on his desk.

"Huh?" JD asked. She eyed Sky, who was probably blinking at her father in wonder. "Oh, yeah." Grabbing up the plate she'd put on his desk, he took a huge bite from his sandwich and made noises of delight, getting a laugh from her and the kids. "It's amazing. Love it."

Sky grabbed her sandwich and tried to take a bite as big as her father. Rubbing her back, she didn't want their little one to choke.

"Take your time, sweetpea."

JD came over and dropped onto the couch beside her, taking another bite. "Don't eat too fast, I want the rest of yours," he said around his food, making a show of leaning over Kye to examine his plate. "Leave that tomato, I want that."

Wearing a grin, Kye grabbed the tomato and stuffed it into his mouth. JD made a sound of horror and Sky grabbed for her cherry tomato to eat it too. Caught up in the moment, she grabbed the cherry tomato from JD's plate and sucked it between her lips. For a second, he just looked at her, stunned. The kids whooped and leaped up to climb onto the couch with their parents.

"Go, Mommy," Sky said, stealing the other tomato from JD's plate to put it in her mother's mouth.

With half a pack of the fruit still in the store's bag, they weren't short of them. Still, the kids seemed determined to remove all from their father's reach.

"Don't choke Mommy before she's signed the life insurance papers, guys," JD said, patting her on the back.

She swallowed. "If Daddy dies, I get to run his empire until the babies come of age, right?" she asked and turned sultry eyes on Greg. "Want to get together later?"

"Yeah, funny," JD said, sliding his hand into hers on the seat of the couch. "You pair get down and finish your food. Daddy has a meeting in an hour. My bank manager isn't much of a picnic guy."

"That isn't what he told Rylee last week," Brenna said, wiping her lower lip with a fingertip and bobbing her brows.

"He wasn't serious about that," she said, helping the kids settle at their food again. "And please remember my children are in the room?"

"Tom hit on you?" JD asked.

"Not really. He was being polite."

Sky was arranging her plate when she asked, "Auntie Brenna?"

"Yeah, babes?"

"Can I be a lesbinum too?"

In less than a second, glee spread on Brenna's face. She wasn't sure she wanted to look at JD, Greg was gobsmacked.

"You sure can, babes," Brenna said. "I'll show you all the best places to pick up chicks."

"I don't like boys," Sky said, with all the innocence of a four-year-old. She was still arranging her food, opening her sandwich to line up the contents, as she always did before taking a bite.

"I don't like boys either," Brenna said. "I think it's growing up with a brother that does it. Living with them sucks."

"Yeah, Kye's stinky," Sky said and shoved her brother, who was oblivious to the discussion.

"I did not turn you into a lesbian," JD said. "And stop recruiting my daughter."

"Oh, come on," Rylee said. "It wouldn't be that bad if Sky was gay. At least you wouldn't have to build a tower for her."

"Are you kidding? I'd build it even higher," JD said. "Women are relentless."

Brenna settled back on the couch, holding the plate against her chest as she picked up crumbs with a fingertip.

"We are that, brother… But I have a feeling it would be your little princess doing the chasing. She knows what she wants."

"She doesn't know what a lesbian is," JD said. True, though Sky didn't know what heterosexual meant either, or, hopefully, anything about sex at all. "She's repeating a word she heard… probably from you."

"Probably," Brenna said. "There's no need to be quite so affronted about it. I remember you and me bonding over ogling plenty of hot women in our younger days, placing bets to see who'd get the furthest."

"When we were kids, Bren."

"There's nothing I wouldn't do with a woman that you probably haven't done too, which reminds me…" Leaning forward, over her crossed legs, Brenna discarded her plate to focus her complete attention. "You never told me what this tongue thing was that you like, Ry."

"Tongue thing?" Greg asked, finally returning to the moment.

Brenna glanced back at him. "Yeah, apparently Jame does this thing with his tongue on Rylee's pussy that just drives her wild."

"Okay," JD said. "I guess I have to say it too: my children are in the room."

"They don't care," Brenna said, looking from one of them to the other and then reaching into the bag beside the couch to pull out two pots of pudding. "Who likes chocolate?"

The kids bounced and grabbed for it.

She snagged the pots from Brenna to set them on the table. "After their sandwiches."

Sky and Kye glanced back.

"Daddy's not eating," Kye said.

Setting her eyes on him, she and the kids waited until

he took another bite of his sandwich. After that, the twins returned to their lunches.

"Will you tell me now?" Brenna asked when the kids were occupied.

"I didn't think you were sleeping together yet," Greg said, putting his empty plate on the table. "When did that start up again?"

"They're not sleeping together now," Brenna said, pausing to make eye contact. "Are you?"

"No," she drawled like she was talking to one of the kids.

Brenna turned to Greg. "This was something they did on the one night they spent together."

"And they're still talking about it now?"

Brenna shrugged and pointed at him. "Exactly."

"It was that good?"

"Good enough to impregnate her," Brenna said, gesturing at each twin in turn. "Twice!"

"I don't think I impregnated her with my tongue," JD said.

This conversation was getting away from them.

"Can we not say 'impregnate' around the children, please?"

"It's biology," Brenna said. "They should know about the birds and the bees."

"Not at four."

"They're almost five," Brenna said.

"I like bees," Sky said, licking her finger, then wiping it on her daddy's slacks.

"Bees are for babies," Kye said.

She held up both hands. "Okay, everyone, let's finish our food in peace, please!"

Too tired, she didn't attempt to build another sandwich for herself. Her mind raced. She couldn't even think clearly enough to put food together. Happy to stay slumped on the couch, exhaustion ran through her veins.

JD swung his plate around, offering her the other half of his sandwich. "Boss has to eat something."

Straightening, she took the plate. "We're not at

home."

"We're with family." He winked. "You're the boss."

TWENTY-ONE

JD SEEMED DISTRACTED during his afternoon meeting with Tom, his personal accountant. She'd noticed when he called her in to sign some papers. From the loose smile on Tom's face, she guessed he'd known who she was all along too.

The papers were something to do with trusts for the kids, and a bunch of other things she didn't recognize. The men talked to each other over the top of her as she put her signature in the indicated places. That was trust. Hopefully, she hadn't just signed up to another deal they'd have to undo in five years.

Tom left, giving way to a meeting that involved Greg. All business this time, so she steered clear. Well, she did until the clock on her desk shocked her. The meeting was running way over its allotted time.

Marching into the office, she didn't even pretend to knock. Those who didn't know of her relationship with JD could whisper all they liked. She didn't have to concern herself with being sued anymore; that was the only thing, previously, that held her back from being too familiar with the CEO.

"Time to move on, gentlemen," she said, striding over to the desk wearing a broad faux smile.

Going around to JD's side, she rested a hand on his shoulder to lean across and gather up the documents from in front of him.

"Who's this?" Eli Savoy asked.

"My assistant," JD said, a smile in his voice. "She's bold."

"I see that," Eli said. The older man was wearing a suit that probably cost more than her apartment. "I love bold women."

"Don't we all," Greg said.

Holding the files to her chest, she cocked her hip toward JD while addressing their guest. "We have a schedule to keep, sir. I mean no disrespect."

"Disrespect is not when I feel when I look at you, Miss…"

"Hampton," she said. Her cellphone rang. Shifting the files, she retrieved it from her pocket. The daycare number? A surge of panic hit her. "Excuse me." She answered the phone, fighting to subdue her worry. "Is everything okay?"

"Yes, Rylee, don't panic, but…"

Dumping the files back on the desk, she turned away. "But…?" she said. "Oh my God, Marie. What happened?"

"The kids are fine. There's nothing to worry about," Marie said. "But, uh, Kye is… he's giving us some trouble."

Edging closer, her hand sought JD's shoulder, but she couldn't look at him. "Trouble?" she asked. "What kind of trouble?"

"This is…" The more awkward the daycare nanny got, the more she worried. "He says he owns the building; that Sky is everyone's boss and… we have to do what we're told."

Her panic faded to an irritation that she landed on JD. "You're kidding me."

"No, I… I think you should come down here."

"Absolutely," she said. "And I'll bring his father with me."

Hanging up the phone, she shoved JD's shoulder.

"Kye?" he asked.

Spinning around, she widened her false smile again. "I apologize, gentlemen. Mr. Savoy, Greg will have to see you out. Mr. Dawes and I have a family issue to deal with."

"Family?" Savoy asked.

Sidestepping, she gave JD space to get up. "Our son's gotten too big for his boots."

JD swept his jacket from the back of his chair to put it on. "I'll call you with those numbers later in the week," he said and took her hand. Savoy seemed too surprised to respond. "Excuse us."

Eager to get downstairs, she tugged JD along, through the bullpen and into the elevator. Alone in there, the doors closed, and she straightened his tie.

"I can't believe this," she muttered. "My beautiful baby, my sweet little angel… Just a few weeks living with you, and he's become an arrogant jerk."

Adjusting his tie, she busied herself smoothing his lapels. "I'm not clear on what he did."

Planting both hands on his chest, she wasn't shy about glaring. "He told the daycare Sky was the boss and everyone had to do what she said." His grin wasn't shy, but she wasn't amused and held up a chastising finger. "No, this is not funny, JD. Our children are not going to be spoiled brats."

He tried to relax his face but didn't do a great job of it. "Right, no, of course. It's not funny." His smile twitched again and he bent a little lower. "I love that he gave his sister the top chair. How do you think they decided? Drew straws? Rock, paper, scissors? Maybe she leveraged bacon in the negotiation."

"I think you should stop enjoying this," she said. "You should consider this your first official daddy assignment. If you think I'm explaining this one to the daycare people who take excellent care of our children every day and have been nothing but kind—"

"We'll give them a raise."

"Money is not the answer to everything."

Resting his hands on her shoulders, he skimmed them down her upper arms. "Trust me, babe, when it comes to underpaid, underappreciated employees, they never say no to a raise."

She breathed out. "I suppose since we're there, we should add your name to the approved list… If this is as mortifying as I imagine it will be, I may never show my face there ever again and you'll be picking them up every day."

"Our children are spectacular, aren't they?" he asked, taking her hands in his, holding them to his chest.

"I told you not to enjoy this."

"It's tough," he said, raising her hands to kiss each one. "I like playing Daddy."

"Yeah, well, you can play Daddy with your kids' teachers," she said. His hold loosened to let his arms snake around her, pulling her against him. "Parenting shouldn't turn you on, JD."

Lowering to nuzzle her hair, he hummed. She smiled, thank God he couldn't see her face. She should put up a bigger fight to him holding her. He wasn't just giving her a hug of comfort, she could feel his mouth in her hair, moving closer to her ear.

"Being part of your team," he murmured. "That turns me on."

"I'm the mother of your children," she said, pressuring his chest with her bent arms trapped between them. "Where's your show of respect?" His hands glided lower until he cupped her ass to give her a squeeze. "Dawes!"

"Oh, that's hot."

She squawked when he squeezed again, but the exclamation was masked in a laugh.

The elevator doors opened. She slithered a hand between his and her ass to link their fingers and guided him from the elevator, through the gaping people in the lobby waiting to use it.

"Excuse us," she said and dragged him toward the daycare.

Entering the large doors to the childcare reception, the windows behind previewed the daycare kids. None of the dozen or so kids there were hers. Oh, God, was this bad?

Reception was unmanned. Marie, supervising the kids on the other side of the glass, noticed them. The patient woman gestured them through and went to the door at the end of reception where the kids were usually waved through.

"This place isn't secure," JD said, glancing around.

The setup had always impressed her. People had to go through a coded door from the reception to the kids. Hence why Marie was currently on her way to meet them on the other side of the window.

"Be polite," she whispered, then changed her mind. "In fact, no, be an arrogant asshole, then they'll know where Kye got it from."

"Thanks," he muttered.

She patted his ass. "Have you got your wallet?"

"No, it's upstairs. Why? Do I need it? Think they'll ask for ID."

Hilarious. "We might have to pay for their silence," she said from the corner of her mouth just before Marie opened the door. She pasted on contrition. "Marie, I am so sorry about this."

Grabbing JD's hand, she stepped back to put him front and center.

"Mr. Dawes," Marie stuttered and looked from father to mother.

"Yes, uh…" Introductions. Her job. Formal ones anyway. No one in that building was ignorant of his identity these days. "Jamison Dawes meet Marie."

"I don't understand what…"

The daycare provider was at something of a loss. This was it, the moment that would change everything.

Sighing, she surrendered to it. "He's my children's father."

Marie's mouth opened slowly in sync with the widening of her eyes. Shock. Yep, she recognized it, wouldn't get used to it though.

"Oh, I…"

"Yeah," she said. "That's how I feel about it most days too."

"I understand there's been a problem," JD said. "Are the children okay?"

"Yes," Marie said, trying her damndest to cast off her surprise while crossing to go into the cubbies room where the kids hung their jackets and changed their shoes each day.

Sky and Kye were seated at the side of the room with a teacher who passed to join Marie.

"Excuse me," she said, making quick eye contact with JD, signaling him to stay with the teachers while she went to hunker down in front of the kids. "You two are in serious trouble."

"Daddy owns everything," Sky said, swinging her legs.

"Daddy does not own everything," she replied. Kye kneeled on his seat. She picked him up and put him back on his butt beside his sister, continuing with the disapproving eye.

"We told the truth, Mommy," Kye said.

She breathed out. "Yes, son, Daddy owns the building. This building. Not every building. The people here have taken excellent care of you for a long time." She gathered up both of their hands. "Treat them with respect. They're your friends. You should always be nice to your friends. And they look after you. They keep you safe when Mommy and Daddy have to work."

"But Daddy is the boss," Sky said. "He loves us."

"He does," she said. "And he would do anything for you. But Daddy is a good boss, who takes care of the people under him."

Someone touched her head; she tipped up her chin.

JD stood behind her. "There's more to being a good boss than giving orders," he said in quite a stern voice, stern to be used with the kids anyway. "Get your things, we're going home... There are some things we all need to talk about."

Rising to stand, she stayed by JD when their kids crept away to get their coats. They knew they'd upset their parents, but she wasn't sure they understood exactly what they'd done wrong.

JD was right. They needed a family meeting.

TWENTY-TWO

SHE'D JUST FINISHED tidying up the kitchen when JD came down the hallway to join her.

"He's okay," JD said. "His nightlight went out."

After their meeting, the kids had been given chores while dinner was prepared and then were put to bed early. The slumbering children were JD's signal to go to the desk in his room. There he'd stayed until Kye called out for him. Within seconds, he'd answered the call.

Inspired by JD's commitment to the company, she too had been working after the kids went to bed. Unlike him, her concentration hadn't been up to the task. That's when she ended up in the kitchen. Cleaning helped her numb out and clear her mind.

Instead of returning to his desk, JD came to join her.

Well, maybe not her. He went to the fridge for a bottle of juice.

"We'll find our groove," she said, folding a towel while he gulped down the drink and sat on a stool at the end of the island. "Our kids aren't jerks. This was just a teething problem… right?"

Lowering the bottle, he wiped his mouth with the back of his hand. "Right."

She tossed the towel to the island and sagged forward, catching her weight on her elbows against the counter.

"I hate that I believe you even though I know you're full of shit," she groaned and straightened her arms until her face made contact with the cold stone.

"Babe, we're not going to let them be jerks," he said, stroking the back of her head. "We've got this. We're good. Trust me."

Rolling herself sideways, she peeked up at him, still half strewn on the island. "I do trust you. I do."

Trailing a finger across her cheek, he tucked her loose hair away from her face. "I know you do, Siren."

Something played on her mind.

Licking her lips, she propped her temple on her arm. "Can I talk to you about something, JD?"

Though he kept stroking, scrutinizing his finger on her skin, he tipped his head in concern. "Anything, babe."

"I was just… this might seem insane, but I… I was thinking—" Her cellphone rang, startling them both. Fearing it could wake the children, she darted to her purse and snatched it out to read the screen. "It's Baxter."

JD left the stool, bottle in hand. "I'll give you privacy… and I'll get the kids if they wake up."

"Thank you," she said, answering the call, holding the phone to her shoulder for a few extra seconds to give JD the chance to disappear down the hallway. When he was gone, she raised it to her ear. "Baxter?"

"Don't hang up."

Stretching an arm out, she swung herself into a dining chair. "I read your name on the screen. If I'd wanted to avoid your call, I could have." Silence. "Why did you call, Bax?"

"You were right. I was an idiot," he said on a sigh. "I want another chance."

"Baxter, you're a great guy, but—"

"Don't give me the great guy speech," he said. "We had something good. Didn't we? We always had fun together, right?"

"Yes, but—"

"I heard what you said, and I've been thinking about

it. I want to get together."

"Baxter, there's no reason to—"

"The reason is I want to be with you," he said, either passion or desperation in his tone, maybe both. "I want you, Rylee. And I don't want to lose our relationship because of one bump. You said it yourself, this is our first real trial. That has to stand for something; it has to mean something. You talked about compatibility, we're compatible. We made it to four months with no big fights or dramas. We want to be together; we were meant to be together."

Going through such a stretch without incident might make them seem compatible. It hadn't been enough. She admitted to herself that a part of her craved friction in a relationship. Not major conflict or unhappiness, but a teasing playfulness that would get her blood moving.

Arguing, putting up a defense, showed there was something to care about, to fight for. Being able to put words to those principles, voicing them, was a sign of security. A strong relationship, a secure relationship, of any kind, meant being able to say what you wanted to say without fear the other person would be harsh in their judgment or turn their back on you.

She and Baxter had been good together. Fun was exactly what it was. Once in a while, seeing Baxter gave her a chance to switch off from reality. Worrying about the kids or work wasn't necessary when they were safe with their grandmother. As for Baxter, in that off time, there was no need to get wound up or be on the defensive.

And the first time her real life spilled into her relationship with Baxter, the whole thing collapsed like a house of cards. Baxter was not her future.

"We should get married."

Lost in her thoughts, figuring out the foundation of her relationship with Baxter, it took a second for his voice to break through.

Although she heard the words, they didn't quite make sense. "We should… what?"

If he thought a snap decision that would affect her children's lives forever was the way to fix the situation, he needed to get a clue.

"You said JD couldn't introduce a woman to your children without putting a ring on the woman's finger first. I've been thinking about that and—"

"You thought we should get engaged just so you could meet my kids?"

"He couldn't object that way, could he? He'd have to consent if—"

"Baxter," she said. Incredulous to the point of dumbfounded, she was confident in her next request. "Don't call me again."

Hanging up the phone, she stared at it for a minute, unsure whether she should laugh or throw the thing against the nearest wall.

Okay, so she didn't have the inclination to replace the phone. Better to put it back in the pocket of her purse and take the bag with her down the hallway. Turning off lights as she went, bed was the best idea. Maybe everything would be fixed by tomorrow.

Just as she was about to enter her bedroom, the narrow band of light under JD's door caught her eye.

He was still awake.

He'd probably get a kick out of Baxter's insane, unromantic plan. She almost went to tell him about the conversation. Before she'd taken so much as a single step, she faltered.

Why the reluctance? Going to speak to JD at night never caused hesitation in the past. Something was different. What was different?

She was single.

Insane that such a minor detail should make such a huge difference. She'd never considered looking beyond Baxter for anything physical while they were involved. Though she and Baxter never had an explicit conversation about being exclusive.

Brenna once asked if they were. All she could say was if she wasn't fulfilling Baxter's needs, she wouldn't judge him for looking elsewhere. Her kids were her life; she'd made that clear to Baxter more than once. He'd never complained about only seeing her two or three times a month. That infrequency meant, as a single guy, he had a lot of free time. What he did with that time was up to him. It would've been selfish to ask him to sit around waiting for her.

Entering her bedroom, she closed the door and got ready for bed.

She and Baxter were on such different tracks about the relationship. How had that happened? They both had fun, they'd admitted that, but it had never gone beyond that. Not for her. She didn't need emotional validation from a man and had been happy to have her recreational ones taken care of by him.

Until JD showed up in their lives full time, Baxter had never pushed her about meeting the twins. Had she led him on? Been blind to his true feelings? The truth was, she wasn't interested in marriage with him. Baxter had potential. She was sure he'd want to get married and have kids, but she couldn't be that woman. Did she even want more kids? Probably not. The twins gave her so much. She needed nothing else, anyone else, to satisfy her maternal needs.

She couldn't be what Baxter deserved, and she'd thought he'd known it too.

How had their wires gotten so crossed?

Sliding beneath her covers, she reached for the light switch by the bed. She didn't quite get there before someone knocked on the bedroom door.

The kids wouldn't knock.

Sinking back onto her elbows, she checked the covers were over her chest because her nightgown was kind of sheer.

"Yeah?" she called.

The door opened a few inches.

JD slid into the gap. "Crying yourself to sleep?"

She smiled. "Wouldn't want to miss an opportunity to take advantage of me if I was vulnerable, would you?"

"Exactly," he said. "They'd revoke my guy card." They shared a smile. "Seriously, babe, you okay?"

"He wasn't my great love, JD. It's sad, sure, but I have kids, and a job, and a home to keep me occupied."

"And an intrusive ex barging in to take over your

life."

"That too."

"Okay, I just wanted to check in."

"JD," she said as he began to slip out. He waited for her to say something else. "Are you my ex?"

Shifting a little, he straightened, bringing himself a few inches deeper into the room, resting on the doorframe with the door still in front of him.

"What else would I be?"

Shrugging, she sat up, folding her legs beneath the covers. Her hands rested in the basket they formed.

"I don't know. Brenna called you that too and I... I don't know, it doesn't sound right."

His chin rose, facilitating his peering. "What would you rather I be?"

"I don't know, I... to me 'ex' says relationship and, well..."

"We never had one of those," he said. "You're right about that."

"It's weird and I don't know why... maybe it's because of the kids. I don't like throwing the term around like we were something that we weren't... I hate the idea they might think we gave up on each other."

Sliding his hands into his pockets, he slouched a little. "When we didn't have a chance to see how it would work."

"Right," she said, pushing back against the pillows. "One day they're going to ask us what happened... What are we going to say? That it was just sex? That we couldn't keep our hands off each other? I know when they're adults they might understand, but... Is it okay to tell them they weren't enough for us to give it a try, to see if we'd be able to tolerate each other?"

Baxter's proposal, such as it was, had been so insulting she couldn't even think about it. He'd only tossed it out there to progress their relationship to a place that would manipulate JD's declaration about the kids.

She and JD had never even tried to make progress beyond that first night.

Pregnancy wasn't a reason to invent love, or feign

that it was there, and love, as far as she was concerned, was the only reason for any couple to get married. But how did they know what was between them? How could they ever have known?

Except, she wouldn't be thinking this way if JD hadn't shown up like he had.

Nauseous, her mind was too full. Her life, which had made perfect sense for so long, was suddenly complicated and confusing.

Because of the kids, especially with them being older, they couldn't play at having a relationship. It would be serious from the first second; they were parents for goodness' sake. Surely, no relationship could stand up to that kind of pressure. They shouldn't even consider it.

Intellectually, that was the smart choice. Yet, she was left with the vision of her babies' expectation shining on her as they waited to hear the story of how she met their father. The only version of the truth was that they were hot for each other. That was it. Sex. That was all that existed between them. All that had ever existed between them.

"Things are good with us, Ry. They're going to see that we more than just tolerate each other. We're friends," he said and pushed away from the doorway to start toward the bed.

She held up a hand, stalling him. "Don't," she said. "Don't come over here."

He smirked. "Why not?"

Man, he enjoyed her conflict.

She squirmed. "Because I'm in a weird mood. My head's screwed up. I make bad choices when I don't feel grounded."

"Yeah? Do you do that often? What kind of things do you do?"

"The last time I woke up pregnant."

Sarcasm didn't dissuade him; he swaggered another step. "That won't happen again," he said. She raised a brow. "Sky was lining up the tampons in the bathroom."

Their daughter's habit of organizing things won again.

"Oh, yeah, I'm on my period, that's the only reason you're not going to get me pregnant again."

"What other reason could there be?" he asked. "Your eggs love my swimmers."

Grabbing one of the scatter pillows she'd pushed aside, she threw it across the room at him, but he ducked out of the way, laughing.

"I can't help that your sperm were overeager," she said. "You weren't satisfied with fertilizing me once, you had to do it twice in the same night."

"I'm twice the man."

"Yeah, yeah, stud," she said and tossed another throw pillow at him.

It got him in the gut. "There's no room for a guy in that bed with those pillows."

There weren't that many. They were a comfort, a substitute for her babies, who'd kick them out of the way when they came to cuddle.

"There's room for my babies," she said. "From here on out, Kye's the only male I need in my life."

"He'll be happy to hear that," he said, sauntering away. "You know where I am if you need me, babe."

"JD," she said. He turned as he got to the door. "I'm glad you're here."

He winked. "We're family. This is where I'm supposed to be."

Before closing the door, he slipped a hand through to turn off the light, leaving her in mellow darkness. He was right. This was where they were all supposed to be, the children safe in their beds with Mommy and Daddy ready to fend off the monsters and put their meals on the table. They were family and as long as they were all safe, she couldn't ask for anything more.

TWENTY-THREE

STANDING IN JD'S OFFICE, six easels angled before her, three higher, three lower, they displayed six color schemes for the new branding package JD picked.

Admiring them, she tried to discern, objectively, which she liked and why.

The task got considerably more difficult when JD left his desk and came over to stand behind her.

All she could think about was his height and the solid column of his supportive body. The thump of his heart against her shoulder blades, the angle of his chin on her crown, betrayed just how close he was to her. Not that she needed evidence. His warmth warned her he was there. Her instinctive reaction whenever he approached was so acute, it went into overdrive at just the suggestion of him these days.

"The blue and white is, uh… typical," she said, breathy, losing her concentration when his hand crept onto her hip. "But the… the red, it's… powerful…"

"You smell amazing," he said.

"I smell like whatever Kye was spraying all over the place this morning."

He hummed his approval. "My cologne. No wonder you've been driving me crazy all day. You're wearing my scent."

"Can you concentrate, please? I need you to pick something."

Concentrate. They were supposed to be concentrating, but he massaged the front of her hip, urging her ass against him. The other hand snaked around to undo the button on her jacket. Splaying his fingers on her abdomen, the thin cotton of her blouse was no defense for the heat of his entitled hand rising higher, pressing her body against his.

Two weeks had gone by since she'd broken up with Baxter. Now last thing on a Friday, they'd made it through two full working weeks and had nothing to think about except their family weekend ahead.

Entitled hands weren't alien these days, not that she could complain. Her own hands had grown more and more brazen by the day.

Familiarity bred between them. Living together, working together, parenting together, the strands of their lives were weaving and twining, tightening and growing stronger with each progression. They got through each trial and over each bump, together as a family.

"What do you want, JD?"

With a firm grip, he rocked her against him. "That's a loaded question, Siren," he said into her hair. "God, I could hold you all day."

"I meant color scheme," she said, sliding her hands over the top of his. To take his hands off her body? Maybe that had been the idea, it didn't work out. Pushing against him, his fingers parted to accept the counterpart of hers. She urged the hand on her belly higher until he was almost cupping the underside of her breast. At the same time, his other hand slithered from her hip across to a more central position, tantalizingly close to the growing thrum of her pussy.

Kissing the top of her head, he buried his mouth in her hair. "I had a dream about you last night."

"JD, the color scheme," she said and laughed.

Frequently, it was getting hard to keep him on topic while his mood favored this more salacious direction.

"Whatever you want, babe. Anything you pick is fine

with me."

"It's your company."

"It's our children's company. Everything we build here is for them."

Groaning, she unlocked her knees, forcing JD to take some of her weight. "Oh, why do you have to say things like that?"

"It's a turn on?" he murmured, a smile curling his lips. "I like making you weak at the knees."

That wasn't the only weak spot. So far she'd refrained from being explicit about that. How long would their restraint last before it snapped? Though anyone looking at them now certainly wouldn't pick "restraint" to describe their position.

Greg came in. While he did pause, he didn't look overly surprised by their entwined stance.

"You still here?" Greg asked her. "It's after six."

"Oh shit," she said, pushing out of JD's arms. "I said I'd get the kids at six."

"I have a few things for you to sign," Greg said to JD, holding up a folder.

Dashing for the door, she called over her shoulder. "They're cooking for you tonight. Your mom's coming over. Please don't be more than an hour."

"I'm right behind you, babe, I swear," he said just before she ran out.

***

HE RETURNED to the desk and sat down.

"What?" JD asked his number two still standing by the door holding up the folder. "You expect me to sign them in midair?"

"Are you going to marry her?"

"Am I going to…? What?"

"We're not blind, you know, none of us. You two are hooking up."

"We live together."

Greg came to the desk, opening the folder to sort out whatever was inside. "Is that a yes? Marry her and get her pregnant. It's what you both want. I've never seen two people more content to just be a family. Your two sprouts are up here every single day. You're blocking out time just to entertain the three of them."

"The business isn't suffering."

"No, it's booming. Who knew you being so happy would make you so productive?" Greg sat down and pushed the folder toward him. "Rylee was okay when you told her about the California trip?"

He raised his eyes to his friend for a brief second, then went back to reading. "I'm not sure I really have to—"

"You have to go. You cannot snub our suppliers. This is important and will dictate our rates for years. They don't give a damn about your kids or your fiancée, they just want some face time."

"She's not my fiancée."

Another visitor interrupted. Unlikely as it may be, he found himself hoping that Rylee had come back and brought the kids with her. He'd see them at home and have them all weekend, that didn't mean he wasn't eager to see them as soon as possible.

Except it wasn't Rylee or the kids, it was Brenna.

"What are you doing here?" he asked.

She flashed Greg a fake smile. "Would you excuse us… please?"

Brenna meant business, she wasn't there to mess around.

Greg drew his eyes away with a silent signal of good luck. He'd need it. The second his friend departed, Brenna slapped a hand to the center of his desk to bend over it, getting into his face with her frown.

"She needs you to take control. She's more vulnerable than she lets on. She's swearing off men, swearing to focus only on the kids. It's not healthy. It's time to get off the bench, brother. Step up to the plate. Take a swing."

"Okay, enough with the sports metaphors," he said, closing his eyes for a moment. "What are you talking about?"

Standing straight, she balled a fist on her hip. "Wow, if you're really asking that, you are in more trouble than I thought. Rylee, idiot brother, you're in love with her."

He laid a hand on the desk, fighting to remain calm. "Okay," he started. "I know Mom's been grooming you for this role all your life, but you don't have to bust my balls when she's still around to do it. I'm seeing Mom tonight, I'm sure she'll find plenty of opportunities to snark at me when Rylee is distracted."

She blew out a breath. "Do you know I had to pick my jaw off the floor when Rylee told me you two aren't sharing a bed yet? I mean, seriously, what are you waiting for?"

Yanking the folder toward him, he started to sign. He didn't know what exactly, but it served as a distraction.

"You know, she just got out of a relationship, and she has two children to—"

"Your children, idiot. She's never introduced the kids to any man she's been involved with. You are perfect. She already knows they can tolerate you."

He sneered, but she matched it. "Doesn't change the fact that she just broke up with—"

"She didn't love Baxter, he was casual. The fact that he tried to make it more than that freaked her out. She didn't want to be married to him. She wants to be married to you."

He stopped. "She said that?"

Brenna's shoulders dropped as she lamented his question. "Of course she didn't say that. Rylee would never say that. But I know her. I know it's what she wants."

"Like you know I love her? You want to get your facts straight, Nana."

Holding up a hand, she counted off each of her fingers. "You live together. You work together. You have two children together. You spend every waking moment together. You spend more time with her than you do with the kids!"

"I won't be living in her apartment forever."

"Have you even looked for another place?" He slapped the folder shut and stood up. "Has she asked you to leave?"

Rounding the desk, he marched across the room with Brenna in his wake. "Leave it alone, Bren."

"Both of you are doing this crazy dance around each

other."

"It's sexual," he said, grabbing his jacket from the closet. "It's an attraction, that's all."

She scoffed. "Yeah, right, okay. So fuck her and get it over with."

"She's the mother of my children, Brenna. I have more respect for her than that."

"First it's sex and now it's respect, how many more steps until you admit… You. Love. Her."

He held up a finger. "Stop it. Enough. I mean it, Bren, don't say any of this crap to Rylee, she's been through enough. Our business is our business. Not yours. I don't get all up in your relationship, do I?"

He started for the door and she followed. "Because I'm in a loving relationship. I can admit my feelings to the woman I love. You do the same and I'll back off."

Ignoring her, he left the office. Greg was at Rylee's desk writing something.

"Good. I was coming to find you. The folder is on my desk. Everything is signed. I'm going home. If you need anything else, Rylee and I will be at the apartment or on our cells all weekend."

Greg stood. "No worries. Have a good weekend."

"You too," he said and walked away.

"Think about what I said," Greg called after him.

He just waved over his shoulder, unwilling to stop and debate his love life anymore. He got to the elevator call button, and, pressing it, was startled when Brenna pounced up beside him.

"What are you doing?" he asked.

She was watching the numbers above the door, doing a good job of looking pleased with herself. "Oh, didn't I say? My niece called and asked me to dinner." The elevator came and she stepped inside, flashing a proud grin. "I don't tell you enough just how much I love your children, Jame."

Suddenly his feet were heavier; he had to force himself to join his sister. He loved his kids too, oh so much, but sometimes he wanted to wring their necks. God hope Brenna hadn't included the twins in her and their mother's conspiracy regarding his relationship with Rylee. He'd have to set some rules about that.

For now, he had a night of torment ahead. Man, his daughter knew how to set him up good.

TWENTY-FOUR

"HOW YOU DOING, SIREN?"

JD approached her in the kitchen just moments after she'd finished cleaning up.

"You've done well tonight," she said. "I'm proud of you."

"Me? They're my family."

"I see more of them than you do. And they like me more than they like you."

Sliding his arms around her, he pulled her against him. "True," he said, rubbing his chin side to side on the top of her head.

Sinking against him, she breathed out and slid her hands into the back pockets of his jeans.

Her drowsy eyes landed on the front door at the other side of the space.

"They're playing board games?"

"In the living room," he said. "I'm putting my money on Sky."

"Kye will wipe the floor with them. But he'll be so charming that your mom and Brenna won't notice they've had their asses handed to them."

He exhaled a murmur of a laugh and held her tighter,

slowly beginning to move like they were dancing to an inaudible tune.

"You know…" she teased. "We have a clear shot at freedom right now."

"We do?"

"The front door is right there. I bet we could be out of here for a half hour before they even noticed we were gone."

"Plenty of time to get to the jet. Where would you like to go?"

"Venice," she said. "Oh, or Monaco."

"Monaco?"

"Sure. The kids couldn't be mad about that because they'd hate it there."

Still slow dancing, holding each other, every muscle relaxed while the smile in his tone grew.

"You don't think we'd miss them?"

"We'd come back," she stated like it was obvious. "Soon as I wipe you out in Monaco." Breathing in, she sighed out her plan. "We come back, sell this place and use the money to buy ourselves a trailer in Michigan or Texas… You need to buy a wife beater and start drinking beer from the can."

He laughed. "I do?"

"Sure. You can sit on a lawn chair wearing a ball cap making enemies of the neighbors by sleeping with their wives while they're at work or out hunting."

"Thought you wiped me out."

"Your fortune, yes, but women sleep with you 'cause you're hot, not because of your money… at least at first."

"What will happen to the kids?"

"They'll grow up resenting us, which they're going to do anyway. Kye will speak with a twang, wear pants that are too big and borrow your jalopy to go park with girls on weekends."

"And Sky?"

"Will start wearing crop tops and hoop earrings, shouting about how grown up she is and how we'll never understand."

"I think she'll do that anyway."

"Maybe."

"And us?"

"We'll gradually descend into alcoholism and resentment. Going out to bars at the weekend, I'll flirt with other men to piss you off. I'll throw myself at them until they take advantage, then you'll pin them down in parking lot brawls. I'll drag you away before the cops show up and we'll scream at each other back at the trailer, but I'll mop up the blood and clean your wounds, while telling you how stupid you are for getting into fights."

"And I'll agree with you, but say I lose my head when I see other men touching you."

She smiled. "Exactly." Another sigh. "Then, with too much alcohol and regret in our systems, and the realization that our kids ran off and abandoned us long before, we'll start the cycle all over again. You'll knock me up right there against the aluminum siding."

Running his hands up and down her back, he released a sound of satisfaction. "That's some future we've got ahead of ourselves."

She opened her eyes that had closed somewhere along the way and glanced across the room again. "And it all starts with walking out that door."

JD kissed the top of her head. "I'll race you to it."

"Would you do it?" she asked. "If it was really going to play out that way?"

"Babe, it would never play out that way."

"Because you'd never let me fritter away your fortune?"

"No, because I'd never let my daughter wear crop tops. Are you crazy? Those things attract boys."

They were still laughing when Brenna's voice interrupted them. "What's so funny?"

"Damn it," JD said. "We missed our chance."

"Your chance for what?" Brenna asked. "What are you talking about?"

They were still dancing. The oddest thing about it was that it didn't feel odd.

Brenna didn't even comment or look at them like it

was weird in the slightest.

"I want to take the kids to Disney this summer," she said. "Will you take the family to Disney, JD? The kids would go nuts. I want to take them while it's still magical to them."

"I'll hire 'em the whole park."

Giving him a quick squeeze, she backed out of his arms. "We don't need the whole park; people are part of the experience."

"Can I come?" Brenna asked, sitting on a stool.

"Sure, and Lotta, and your mom," she said, going to join her friend. "We'll have everyone."

"She's determined to fritter away my fortune." JD leaned over her to get some nibbles from the bowl laid out earlier. "Because I haven't bought her a trailer in Texas."

She pushed her elbow into him and, tipping her chin to her shoulder, addressed him without seeing him.

"If we bring your family, we'll have trusted babysitters on site."

"Ah, good plan, Siren."

There was something saucy about the way Brenna's lips twisted. "And why would you need babysitters?"

"So I can throw myself at other men," she stated matter of fact, scooping up some nuts.

Brenna's smile gave way to confusion.

"It's the only way I'll notice her."

With her brow pulled down, Brenna looked from one of them to the other and back. "And society calls me queer? Straight are the strange ones."

Spinning around, Brenna hopped off her stool and went to join her mom and the kids in the living room again.

"You should invite Greg," she said, propping herself against the counter, facing JD.

"Invite him where?"

"To Disney."

"All he'll want to do is talk work," he said, coming closer to lean forward and set a hand on the counter on either side of her.

"We'll get him out the habit. He doesn't have anyone around here. I feel bad for him. He needs a support network."

He narrowed one eye. "Is that code for a girl?"

"No, but, oh," she said and pushed her shoulders back. "I know a girl in my old department who is nice. We could nudge them together."

"Matchmaking? Is that really what we're doing now?"

She popped one of her almonds between his lips. "He's your friend, JD. He should be part of the family too. He better come to the kids' birthday party in the park next weekend."

"I'll remind him."

From his smirk, she wasn't sure he'd ever invited him, or if he had that Greg had been receptive.

"Want me to call Nichelle?" she asked. "Your mom will come over and watch the kids. You could pay for dinner somewhere fancy, help Greg impress her."

"Will that impress you?" he asked, angling closer.

She laid a hand on his shoulder. "All you've got to do to impress me is take out the trash… and do your share of bedtimes."

"You're an easy woman to please. I'll set it up," he said. "Monday?" She nodded. "Greg and I have never been on a double date before; this should be interesting."

"Don't be talking work all night," she said, feeding him the last nut and taking his hand. "Remember the goal is to get him laid."

"That's his goal," JD said, looping his arms around her to move her body in front of his. "We set the scene. He has to close the deal. My goal for the evening will be very different."

"Yeah?" she asked over her shoulder as they made their way toward the living room wrapped in each other. "What will your goal be?"

"A whole evening without even a hint of Disney."

If his mom was watching the kids, she'd be subjected to the cartoons, maybe giving them a reprieve.

"Wow," she said, laying her head against his upper arm as they ascended the stairs. "Now I get why the press calls you ambitious."

Brenna and Marjorie were seated on the couch with

the kids on the floor setting up a game on the coffee table.

"Daddy, you be my team," Sky said, lining up the pieces.

"No, Daddy, be my team!" Kye demanded. "Boys and girls."

"How about we each go on our own team?" she said, extricating herself to go sit by Brenna.

It was unlikely they'd finish the game. The twins would lose interest, so it didn't really matter who played with who.

The kids didn't look happy until JD sat on the floor between them. "That's the best plan, you know why?" he said, righting a piece that had fallen. "Because the winner gets a cookie. And I am not sharing my cookie with either of you when I win."

Both kids laughed and jostled him. JD settled the raucous by asking them to explain the game. Didn't matter that he understood it already. Asking them to explain would help them get the rules clear for themselves.

Watching him play mediator and ask questions like he was clueless was funny. JD kept surprising her. Every time she thought she had him figured out, he'd do something that took her breath away.

Even now, while talking to the kids, he took the time to glance up and wink at her. They were a team, and that team was getting stronger every day.

TWENTY-FIVE

HANGING UP THE PHONE, she did her best to remain composed. Others might not see it, sure, but she couldn't hide her discomfort from herself.

Answering a querying call from an assistant assigned to pick up JD's line wasn't unusual. They handled most questions and demands. Just in case of any issues or uncertainty, she tried to be as available as possible.

Something she regretted, given what she'd just heard.

Certain types of appointments were made provisionally by the assistants. While they denied most requests, those in the gray area got emailed to her for approval or rejection.

Once in a while, something urgent or unusual might crop up. In those times, the assistants called through for an immediate answer. Hence the conversation she'd just had.

It didn't matter. At all. She'd done the right thing this time. Made the right decision. They were at work. This was professional, not personal. In that building, it was her place to deal with calls as JD's employee, not the mother of his children.

Still, her insides churned.

Picking up the memos and documents requiring his

review, she put the half dozen phone messages on top, tucking the most recent one into the middle of the stack.

It was time for her to leave, time for her twins, time for fresh air and freedom. One last stop in his office, then she'd be out of there. Holding her breath, she knocked on the door and ventured inside.

JD and Greg were seated at opposite sides of the desk, relaxed, enjoying an informal chat by the looks of things.

Smirking, JD leaned back in his chair, holding a pen by each end in his fingertips. "Did you just knock?" he asked, swinging his chair side to side as she crossed the room. "Did I hear that right, Greg? Did Rylee Hampton just knock on my door?"

Bending over, she put the pile of papers in front of him. While she squared it, his hand slid up the back of her thigh. Oh, no, buddy, she swatted it away. She was not on the menu and wasn't interested in a spot in his schedule.

Greg hissed. "Oh, man, what did you do? You were the Brady Bunch at lunchtime when the sprouts were here."

"Yeah," JD said, curious, probing. "We were. Babe…" He got more matter of fact. "What did I do?"

"Nothing, Overlord," she said, pushing his hand away when he tried to touch her leg again. "The kids have their dental checkups, I have to get going."

"Want me to come?"

She tidied up the other documents scattered around. "No, they're on the dental plan I get through my job. We don't need you."

"Hmm," he said. "You sure I did nothing wrong?"

Greg hid a smile. "This is like the perfect vision of marriage."

"Right?" JD agreed. "I pay the bills. Get put in the doghouse for breathing the wrong way. And I don't get laid."

"Sounds like marriage to me."

The men laughed. Weren't they just hilarious? Ha, ha, ha. Didn't matter they were the only two enjoying themselves.

She snickered out her exaggerated false effort. "You two have to be downstairs for the finance meeting."

"After that I can come and join you," he said. "We'll

take the kids to the burger bar they love… the one with the ice-cream machine… Greg, you want to come? We'll call Nichelle. Last night went okay, from what I saw."

Typical of men that they could get through an entire day without talking about last night's double date. If it could be called that, doubtful. It would've been the first thing she and Brenna talked about if they'd been setting up a friend. JD hadn't even thought to ask.

Sure, it had been a busy day; it hadn't been *that* busy.

"The kids and I are going to stay at Brenna's tonight. Lotta's out of town."

Greg made a sound like he'd witnessed a gut punch.

"When did this happen?" JD asked.

"Brenna called earlier, I said I wasn't sure, but it's on now. We're going to have a sleepover in her living room. The kids love to camp out there. We put two mattresses together and sleep under a canopy. It's been too long since we did it last."

"And I'm not invited?"

"No," she said, setting the paperweight on a stack of papers. As of yet, he hadn't looked at anything she'd put in front of him. "Kye's the only male we need."

"Or I can pick him up? We'll have a guy's night at home. Poker, beer, porn—"

"You have plans tonight. Read your messages," she said, plucking them up to hold them to him, without meeting his eye. "You have a date."

Pushing his chair up from its recline, he frowned. "I have a date?"

Greg pointed at him. "You thought it was cool to set me up. Guess Ry's on a roll and it's your turn."

"Whatever it is, put it off. We didn't eat as a family last night. I want to be with the kids tonight."

"You can't put it off," she said. "You promised your mom you'd go to the dinner party her lawyer is having tomorrow night, and you have the Entrepreneur Association Ball on Thursday."

"Is Mom watching the kids at hers or ours?"

"Neither," she said. "You promised Sky you'd take

her to the ball, so you're taking Kye with you tomorrow. Something your mom's lawyer will probably hate, but he wants to impress you, so he'll let it slide."

He bobbed his head. "My daughter will go to the ball. I remember now."

"Good. You don't have time to go home and change. I'll call Anya and ask her to pick something up from the apartment and drop it here. The royal blue shirt brings out your eyes, but the gray shirt will get you laid… do you have a preference?"

"The blue," he said. "If you're sharing a bed with my sister and the kids, I don't think sex is a good idea, do you, Siren? Unless you want to wait until they're asleep and sneak out somewhere with me…" Propping an elbow on the desk, he stage-whispered to Greg. "From memory, she has a thing for high-class hotels."

"Good thing you can afford it," Greg said, wearing a smirk.

"Bastian owes me."

Shaking the messages at him, she forced him to take them. "You could reserve Buckingham Palace, your cock would still spend the night lonely if it was waiting for me."

Another inhale from Greg.

Slapping his hands on the desk, Greg rose to his feet and pushed away. "You're on your own, man. I'm out."

Moving one memo aside to put another on top, she tapped it as Greg left and closed the door.

"This one's about daycare changes. Read it, it applies to your children," she said and started for the door.

"Babe, don't walk out without—Gabby." She stopped. "What the hell is this?"

About-facing, she saw he was reading the message she'd written.

"She has reserved a table in the restaurant of her hotel, though says the room service is excellent if that's what you'd prefer." A blatant invitation, but whatever, that wasn't her prerogative. "Do you want me to ask Anya to bring condoms too?"

"Babe!" he barked, surging to his feet almost like he

was offended.

"You said she wasn't wild about the idea of kids. If you feel like playing roulette on that—"

"Ry, I'm not going to sleep with her. I don't even want to see her. Why would you arrange a date for me with my ex—"

"Because she wants to discuss the details of your meeting in California next week." That stole some of the outrage from his expression. "Yeah, I loved getting blindsided with that one. Thanks. You're leaving Sunday? You know the kids' birthday party is on Saturday? That's a great birthday present for the kids, JD. Just great. Were you going to tell them or was that going to be left to me? Were we just going to wake up without you on Monday?"

"I… it was going to be a surprise. Greg and I were literally just talking about it. I was going to take you with me, all of you… We can rent a place out there on the beach, take a break from the—"

"That's convenient. You get caught in a lie, and suddenly it's a surprise."

"Ry—"

"Go to dinner with her. Make your plans for next week. Your family won't be home tonight, and there's a gorgeous woman in a private suite with room service just waiting for you."

She began to turn, but he spoke fast. "Wait, Ry, Siren! Babe—"

"You know what I don't get?" Whipping around, she was talking before he got to her. "If you wanted to leave us, you could've just told me. I've dealt with disappointed children before. You think they've never come back from your mom's upset that Daddy never showed?"

"That's not fair! You know it's different now. I would never disappoint—"

"They're used to you at home! They're used to you at bedtime! I told you, I warned you, as long as I didn't doubt your ability—"

"The first day you came into this office we talked about traveling for work," he argued, matching her vehemence. "You know I have to go away sometimes. I told you we could travel together, that's what I intended to—"

"Children need routine, Jamison. You can't just drag them around the world because it suits you!"

"It's their birthday, Rylee! I'm allowed to treat them!"

"You should've talked to me if you wanted to take them with you. Was that it? You wanted to sneak them out the apartment when I was asleep?"

He grabbed her arm. "What the hell are you accusing me of?"

Throwing his hand from her, she retreated to the door. "Take your hands off me!" He backed off a step, holding up his hands in surrender. "Go have fun, JD. We were fine without you for long enough. We don't need you, we never did."

Slamming out of the office, she grabbed her purse and rushed down the stairs. Catching him in a lie cut her deep. He'd only been in their lives full-time for around a month, but she had expectations. That was her mistake. She'd built up a reliance on him, and he'd let her down; something she should never have given him the power to do.

She was hurt and her eyes heated. JD had never made her cry before. She didn't like it and swore right then that it wouldn't happen again.

TWENTY-SIX

"LOOK, you're not going to get anything from me except my complete unadulterated support," Brenna said, watching Kye go back and forth on the swing. "I told you the first night you and the kids stayed with me that my brother was an idiot. I said it last night when you and Sky stayed over again."

Seated on a bench in the park not far from her apartment, the joy on her son's face as he tried to make the swing go on his own gave her hope. He wasn't doing a half bad job. Sky would demand to be pushed, but Kye was all determined effort. A quality magnified since his father moved in. What would happen when said father disappeared from their lives?

At that moment, Sky was at the ball with her father. Her little girl brimmed with excitement all day. Matching her daughter's exuberance wasn't so easy knowing disappointment lurked on the horizon.

"If you don't want Kye and me to stay over—"

"I do, honey." Brenna picked up her hand. "You know I love having you. Lotta will be back tomorrow. I'm not sure how I'll tell her I've been sleeping with another woman the whole time she's been gone but…"

Feeling pathetic, she mustered a laugh, and

appreciated Brenna kissing the inside of her knuckles. "I don't know what to do, Bren. The kids are so psyched for their birthday party in the park this weekend. I don't know how to tell them their dad will be gone twenty-four hours later."

"Make him tell them," Brenna said. "Have you talked to him since… you know… the Gabby date?"

Their fight in the office had taken place two days ago.

"It wasn't the date that upset me, it was the lie," she said for what felt like the fiftieth time. "I've been professional at the office. I haven't been alone with him. I won't be alone with him."

"And you've been sleeping at my place," Brenna said and dragged her across the bench to embrace her. "You know it's your apartment. You can kick him out."

Maybe that was why she'd been staying away rather than asking him to leave. If she told JD to go, she'd be the bad guy in the eyes of the kids, and there was the chance he'd never come back.

"I suppose I'm going to have to make nice before the birthday party. The kids haven't noticed we're not happy with each other because they've been so busy this week. If they have to see us in the same room together or at the same event…"

"Yeah, you two aren't great at hiding how you feel about each other when you're standing side by side."

Her phone made a noise; she pulled her bag closer to get it. "What's that supposed to mean?" She read the text that popped up. "He and Sky are leaving the party."

"It's not even nine."

"This is late for a four-year-old, believe me," she said and stood up, hooking her purse strap over her arm. "Kye! Come on, little prince." When it looked like he was trying to stop without much success, fear gathered on his face. "Just wait, I'm coming, baby."

She and Brenna headed over there.

"You know, you could tell him to stay at the hotel. The event is at a hotel, right? Sky would love getting a big fancy room."

"It wouldn't be fair to do that without Kye," she said,

smiling when she stopped the swing and picked up her boy. "Ready to go?"

"I want Daddy to tuck me in," Kye said.

She made eye contact with Brenna. "I guess we're going home."

***

BOTH SHE AND KYE got ready for bed and were in his room reading when they heard Sky tearing through the apartment. Like a little tornado all of her own.

She'd just put the book aside when Sky ran into Kye's room and did a twirl in her dress.

She'd been the one to put Sky in the dress because JD had meetings at work that meant he only had time to swing by and pick up his date. Yet Sky twirled like she and Kye were seeing her for the first time.

Witnessing her daughter's joy filled her with her own. "Did you have fun, sweetpea?"

"I went to a ball!" Sky said and ran to the bed to climb up with them.

She scrambled all the way to the top and tried to stand up. Settling Sky in her lap, she unbuckled her shoes. Kye was still sitting under her arm, now hypnotized by the intricate twinkling beads on Sky's dress that caught the light from his lamp.

"I know you did, sweetpea."

"Daddy danced with me," Sky said, helping her mom take off her shoes.

JD appeared in the doorway. The moment their eyes met, she distanced herself by loosening Sky's hair. Kye climbed out of bed to run over to his dad, who caught him and picked him up.

"Did he?"

"Uh huh," Sky said. "I dranked shampoo."

"Champagne?" she asked.

While their daughter nodded, she looked to a smiling JD.

"Grape juice," he said. "They put it in a flute for her.

She was the belle of the ball, the most beautiful girl in the room."

With the pins and ribbons put aside, she ran her fingers through Sky's hair.

"Daddy's friend was prettiest. She had pretty sparkles on. Dee-mons."

"Diamonds?" she asked, easing her daughter onto the bed so she could get up.

Kye wouldn't take long to settle, and Sky was hyper. When the excitement wore off, she'd be out like a light.

"Mm huh," Sky said, wriggling to the edge of the bed as her mom removed her pantyhose. "Daddy boughted them for her." That slowed her. Oblivious Sky looked past her mom to her daddy, probably still in the doorway. "I want dee-mons, Daddy. Will you get me dee-moms like Gabby's dee-mons?"

Shock forced her to her feet, anger burning her insides. Only the vision of her innocent daughter wiggling her perfect little toes like Ariel reminded her to grit her teeth and breathe through it.

Slowly counting to ten, she took a long, deep breath before gathering all of Sky's things and taking her daughter's hand. "Come on, sweetpea. Mommy will get you ready for bed."

"Oh, Momma!"

"No, it's bedtime, no complaining."

Sky hopped off the bed and went with her. "Kye is not in bed."

"He wanted Daddy to tuck him in," she said just as they reached the door and she landed a glare on JD. "Put your son to bed, JD."

***

AS SHE'D PREDICTED, Sky dropped like a sack of potatoes when the adrenaline wore off. After changing and brushing her teeth, Sky was dragging her feet. She didn't get through reading two full pages of a story before she drifted off.

When she turned off the light and pulled the door

over, there in the dark hallway was JD, leaning against the wall.

"Are we going to talk or ignore each other for another night?"

She opened her bedroom door and gestured him inside before following and closing the door so as not to disturb the kids.

"You're a brave man initiating conversation with me tonight," she hissed, finding it hard to restrain her anger. "What the hell did you think you were doing introducing your girlfriend to our daughter? I don't care if you guys rekindled your engagement on Tuesday night, you should've spoken to me before doing it."

"Gabby isn't my girlfriend," he snapped and leaped closer.

She raised a hand. "Keep your damn voice down. You should have let me meet her first. We should have had a conversation with the kids. We—"

"Gabby was at the event, just like two hundred other people. Yes, she spoke to Sky, but I didn't introduce them, she introduced herself."

"So you're telling me you can't protect our daughter from your lover? Is that what you're saying? And it's supposed to make me feel better? If I had tried this shit with Baxter—"

"How long are we going to do this?" he asked, his own irritation warming her as he matched her vicious hiss.

"I don't know what you're—"

"I didn't sleep with Gabby. Yes, I went to the hotel to meet her on Tuesday. I met her at the bar. Told her I wasn't interested in anything she had to say and that my family was the only thing that mattered to me. I didn't even know she was going to be at the event tonight."

"That's convenient."

"Not really," he retorted. "Not when I come home to this. Gabby approached us, I walked away. She tried it again, I warned her off. There's only so much you can say in explicit terms in front of an astute four-year-old."

"You've got an excuse for everything. Just like when I found out about California—"

"Oh, come on, Rylee," he said, leaning back and

raising his arms. "You weren't upset about California, you were upset about Gabby calling me!" He let his arms fall and looked square at her. "And you're not upset that Sky met a random person. You're upset that person is someone who once meant something to me."

"Yes! Exactly! I don't think introducing our daughter to your future bride without—"

"How long are we going to do this?" he asked again, seeming less angry.

On the back foot, she didn't expect him to cut off his fury so abruptly.

Adrift, she couldn't adjust. "I don't know what…"

Coming closer, he wrapped his fingers around her wrist to pull her to him, sweeping the hair from her face.

"I want you, Siren," he murmured, gazing down into her. "There, I said it, and the walls didn't come crashing down."

"Stop it, JD," she said. He didn't stop and held her in place when she tried to back off. "This isn't the time for your games or your charm. I'm mad."

"I know," he said, but smiled. "There's nothing to be mad about. I was never leaving you for California. It was a business trip, two weeks max. nothing more. And if you don't want me to go, I won't go… And Gabby's nothing. No one to me. You're the woman who's infected me, my thoughts, my dreams. You've enchanted me, Siren. I want you."

"Stop saying that," she exhaled and dropped her chin; he scooped it back up with a finger. When he dipped lower, she planted her hands on his chest and pushed. "No. You can't, JD. We can't."

"The kids are asleep," he said, stroking her face. "We can."

"No." She shook her head. "We can't… do this… not ever."

He lost some of the drowsy, bewitched desire that had clouded his expression and frowned instead. "I don't understand. I know you're attracted to me."

She kept her pressure on her palms against his chest. "That doesn't matter. We can't be together."

Offence gathered in him again. "Why? Why not?"

"Because we have two children."

"That would seem like the perfect reason to me."

"We have to parent them first. That has to be our primary priority. We can't play at boyfriend and girlfriend in front of them. We've never been together in a relationship to know how it would work out. Being friends for a few weeks is not the same as a long-term, permanent relationship with all the trials that brings."

"Rylee, I—"

"Don't you see? We'd be serious from the moment of the very first kiss. We can't date, see how it goes and just break up like we would with anyone else if it wasn't working out, like we did with Baxter and Gabby. We're parents… and parents who live together at that. I've been terrified of how we'll tell the kids when the time comes for you to move out because they've gotten so used to having you here. How do you think they'll feel if their parents get together, fool around for a few weeks and then break up? Right now, we can work through things as co-parents, because we're both prioritizing the kids. How long do you think we can keep doing that, or working together at Duo, if we let messy, complicated emotions get involved?"

Letting her go, he moved away from her, running a hand through his hair. "You've thought about this," he muttered.

"Yes, I have. Probably more than I wanted to admit to myself."

He turned around to look her in the eye. "I want you."

So damn sure; that certainty was humbling and flattering. That he was making his admission, and allowing her to make hers, put a lot of things about the week suddenly into perspective. His accusations weren't wrong.

"I believe you, JD. I do. I hate myself for believing you, but I do. But we have to look beyond what our hormones want from us."

Sinking down, he sat on the edge of her bed. "What do you mean?"

"I want to get married one day, JD," she said. "You backed out of one engagement already. Maybe marriage isn't something you want."

"Ry, that was—"

"And you said you want the option of having more children in the future… I'm not sure I want more kids. Maybe I do, maybe I don't. I haven't decided on that yet." Seeing his internal struggle drew her closer until she was kneeling on the edge of the bed beside him. "We acted on pure instinct once and, yes, it gave us the most incredible children, who I wouldn't trade for anything, but it altered the entire course of my life." Letting the back of her fingers drift up his five o'clock shadow, she tempted him to see her smile. "You're a good dad, JD, and you've become a good friend. I don't want us to compromise either of those things just because your suite has a bar… you know?"

Taking her hand from his cheek, he pressed it to his mouth. "It's more than that, Siren."

"I know," she whispered, ignoring the tear that tracked down her cheek. "But we are for what we created. We're irrelevant."

Their feelings, whatever they were, had to be ignored in lieu of their duties and responsibility to the kids. She could kiss him and they could fall into bed, but what would tomorrow bring?

They had to put a stop to this before it started. California couldn't be coming at a better time; distance might be their only saving grace. If it was, they needed to put as many miles between them as they could… and fast.

TWENTY-SEVEN

JD WAS MAKING NOTES in a report when his office door opened. He didn't look up, he didn't need to when he recognized his sister's voice.

"I need to borrow your wife," Brenna said.

"For what?" he muttered.

Coming into the office, Brenna took her time closing the door. "That's an interesting turn, you're not going to ask who I'm talking about or deny that I know what I'm talking about?"

"You're talking about Rylee," he said, scrubbing out a whole section. He glanced up when she stopped on the opposite side of the desk. "You think you're the first person to make that kind of comment about our relationship?"

Brenna took a seat; he went back to his report.

"Guess you and she talked last night."

"We did."

The air around Brenna was uneasy, yet eager, like she didn't know how to approach the situation or exactly what to say. She wasn't nervous, his sister never was, she just wanted to maximize results. Brenna was an efficient woman. He tried to concentrate and avoid getting sucked into his sister's obsession.

"I tried calling her this morning. Her phone went to voicemail… I guess she was busy."

"She has better things to do with her time than sit around waiting for your calls. Don't you have a girlfriend of your own to bug?"

"I'd rather bug yours… So… you talked…"

"Mm hmm."

He sensed the expectation. Brenna was waiting for him to say something else, to leap in and answer the question she hadn't posed. He wasn't going to do that. For one thing, his head was still so fucked by what Rylee said last night that he couldn't think about it without getting a sharp pain in his temple.

"Well? Come on!" Brenna screeched.

On a breath and a slow blink, maintaining his calm, he raised his eyes from the paperwork, contrasting his mood to his sister's hysterical mode.

"What?"

She glared at him. "Don't play dumb. Tell me what happened!"

"We talked, you said it yourself."

"What did you say?" She bounced to the edge of her chair. "What did she say? Is she pregnant yet?"

Slapping a page of the report into the done pile, his restraint wavered. "I am not going to gossip with you, Nana. If you want details, talk to Rylee."

She growled. "She's obviously not open to talking, or she would have called me back."

"Then I guess you'll have to live in wonder."

Growling again, she pushed back to slouch in her chair, wearing a sulk that Sky would be proud of.

"You are the most infuriating couple ever!"

"We're not a couple," he muttered, trying to concentrate on his reading. "We won't ever be a couple."

In his peripheral vision, he noticed her spine uncurl slowly until she was sitting upright. "Guess that tells me all I need to know. You fucked it up, didn't you? Shit, Jame, why did you have to lie to her about California?"

"This has nothing to do with California," he said.

"We talked about it and concluded it wouldn't make sense to ruin our ability to tolerate each other for the sake of sex."

She spat out a breath of disgust. "That sounds more like something Rylee would say than you. Did you kiss her?"

"What? No, I didn't kiss her." He would have. He'd wanted to. And Rylee had pushed him away. "She did say it and she's right. We live together now, we get along, the kids love spending time as a family. It's not right of us to screw with their heads by screwing each other; that would take our focus from them. We'd have to deal with all the usual relationship issues rather than just being good parents. This way we can—"

"What? Grow to hate the sight of each other?" she asked. "You think everything will carry on being hunky-dory if you just ignore what you feel for each other? Are you insane? Whoever heard of unresolved sexual tension just evaporating through sheer will? Are you moving out?"

"No. That's the point. Things will continue exactly the way they are."

"With you two showering in the same apartment, sleeping in the same apartment, jerking off in the same apartment."

He screwed up his face. "Bren! Jesus!"

"Hey, I don't like thinking about you touching that part of yourself any more than I like thinking of anyone touching one of those things you have," she said and shivered. "My point is, no matter your mood, or hers, you're going to be living in the same apartment, the same close quarters. So, those nights when you're feeling a little hot, a little twitchy, you have to walk past her bedroom… maybe she's getting dressed…"

Although she was trying to build a picture, it was so insane that she thought it necessary.

The glimmer of a smile he failed to contain quickly grew until he was laughing. "Fuck, Bren, I want her every second of the goddamn day, you think I need to be in the mood or near her bedroom to want to have sex with her?" That shut his sister up fast. "I want her in the office, every minute, even when there are twenty other people in the room and we're dealing with some corporate disaster. Sometimes she comes over to the desk and the smell of her perfume gets me hard. Every time we're in the kitchen at home, she moves in close, helping the kids with something or giving me a hand and her hair falls against my arm. Shit, Bren, it takes every ounce of strength I have not to grab hold of her and kiss the life out of her, even in front of our kids."

For a few seconds, his sister just looked at him, her expression becoming more solemn. "And you think not acting on that will make it go away? Think about the logic of that. I know there's a chance that you will jump in and the relationship won't work out, there's always that chance with a new relationship."

"And then we'll lose what we have now, which is why—"

"You're going to lose it if you do nothing. If you don't try, it's going to eventually get weird. You're going to stop getting close to her so those things you just said don't happen. You want to be near her and horny all the time? It will frustrate you both. You'll be anxious, and angry, and you'll just start avoiding each other. The way I see it, you can try to have a relationship and there's a chance it will work out. If you don't even try, you may as well move out now, and go back to never seeing each other."

He couldn't imagine anything more sickening than never seeing Rylee again. It already pissed him off that he'd missed out on so much of his kids' lives, now he was coming to realize he'd missed out on so much with their mother too.

"The night I met her, I knew she was different," he murmured, picking up his pen to divert focus. "Being with her felt different…"

"But you didn't pursue it."

Because he'd given up, taken the easy way out and gone back to life as he'd always known it without putting up a fight.

"She said it was a one-night thing. Obviously, she didn't feel what I felt, but I don't know… She didn't have a lot of experience. She was twenty-three when we met, for God's sake, she was just starting out."

"So you let her go."

"If it had been supposed to be something, we'd have figured it out by now."

"I disagree," Brenna said. "Neither of you have ever bothered to spend any time getting to know each other until now. Mom and I love Rylee, and she loves us, but that didn't happen in a flash of lightning. We're family. We've spent half a decade getting to know each other, spending time with each other, being there for each other. Rylee knows she can rely on us, and we can rely on her… She's raising the next generation of Dawes and doing a fucking amazing job, I don't know if you noticed."

Pride and appreciation for both the mother of his children and his sister rose within him. "I know she's a good mom… But she doesn't know if she wants more kids."

"And you do?" she asked and exhaled, slouching back in the chair again. "You don't get it. God, I don't know how any woman can have a relationship with a man, you're so upside down."

"Thanks."

"Rylee doesn't want to be a single parent again. She adores her children. Although she'd never say it, raising them has been hard work and she's done it basically alone. I only know from stories she's told after the fact, pregnancy was a slog for her. She had all sorts of issues to work through and she had to track you down and deal with your lawyers too. She hasn't had it easy. So, when you say more kids, all she thinks about is the Everest she's just got through climbing."

His sister was trying to help, but irrational offence surged through him. "It wouldn't be that way. If we were together, she wouldn't have to lift a finger. I'd get her a staff, anything she needed for—"

"You didn't for the last two."

"I didn't know she needed it," he argued.

Brenna waved a hand up and down. "Calm, brother, don't get defensive. I'm trying to explain why she's hesitant." Straightening again, she licked her lips. "Sky makes you watch her Disney movies, right?"

"Yeah," he drawled, not sure where she was going.

"You know what happens right before the narrator says they lived happily ever after? Right at the end, the princess and her prince, they kiss." Eyeing him, she nodded like she was trying to convey something. He didn't get it and shook his head. "Damnit, brother, you have to kiss her!"

"You think that will make everything better?" he asked, recalling what Rylee once said about his kiss.

"I think the movies you watch with Sky represent everything you've been through with Rylee so far. Every kid grows up with fairytale movies. It's only when you're an adult that you appreciate the real story is what we don't see. The real story happens after that kiss at the end."

"Bren—"

"I'm telling you to kiss her, not because I think it will fix everything, I'm telling you to kiss her because that kiss will be your start. It will be the beginning of your love story. Sky's allowed to believe the movie is the toughest trial the hero and heroine will face, she's four. You know better. You need to start your story. Kiss her. Claim her. And deal with the trials together." Damn, he hated when his sister made sense. "You need to kiss her, Jame."

He could feel himself being seduced by the hope his sister offered. Last night he'd tossed and turned trying to come to terms with knowing he'd never have Rylee as his own. All day he'd been on edge and short-tempered, because he didn't like to give up, and that was what Rylee had asked him to do when she'd pulled the brake.

A flash of memory from last night chilled him; he didn't want to hope and be shot down again.

"She doesn't want it, Nana. She told me, we don't want the same things."

It took her a second to gather herself, reminding him of the way Rylee paused before speaking to the kids when they were pushing her buttons. "You're really hung up on this kid thing," she said and sighed. "I think she'd do it. I think she'd have your babies… if you married her, which we both know you would, so don't even pretend to hesitate."

"I don't know, Nana, Rylee mentioned Gabby, and she's right. I didn't marry her, did I? I could have, but I broke it off."

"I didn't know Gabby," Brenna said. "I read about your engagement online." She rolled her eyes in a way meant to chastise him while at the same time communicating that she didn't care enough to dwell on what had been. "You said Rylee was different, that being with her was different… did it feel that way with Gabby?"

Exhaling, he tossed the pen to the desk and pushed back in his chair. "No… No woman's felt like Ry."

Brenna smiled. "You ever think that maybe that's why you haven't settled down? That there was some part of you that wanted to feel the way Rylee made you feel? And because no woman's matched her, no other woman was enough. No woman lives up to the mother of your children and now you've come full circle back to her because she's The One."

Sky would love the story her aunt was weaving.

One thing he couldn't deny was that he'd wanted to pursue a relationship with Rylee when they'd met. He had a vivid memory, that often revisited him in his dreams, of lying in the dark next to Rylee's sleeping form, running his fingertips up and down the center of her naked abdomen, admiring her beautiful body strewn in the hotel sheets they'd made love in. Unable to take his eyes off her, mesmerized, he'd vowed to make her the center of his world.

Pride was to blame for him not following through. She'd basically laughed in his face the morning after when he'd asked about seeing her again. She'd been so young and wanted a casual interlude. To her, he was a one-night stand, a casual fuck; nothing more.

Until that moment, he hadn't admitted to himself that he was embarrassed. He'd lay watching her sleep thinking they were starting something real, and she'd woken up and slapped him down.

In retrospect, he hadn't tried to make her see that he wanted more, he'd just accepted her first no. But he'd been younger too, more conceited, less willing to put himself out there. Experience, age, and maybe parenthood, had made him humbler and more aware of what was important.

The more he reflected, the more he wondered if that night had been a catalyst for him deferring settling down. He'd been rejected, maybe more hurt than he'd realized, and so had buried himself in business.

It was easy to speculate when there was no way of knowing exactly how it would've played out. Even if he'd gotten what he wanted, who was to say his relationship with Rylee would've gone past a few months of fun? The obsession may have dwindled when trying to juggle the reality of a long-distance relationship and they wouldn't have had the twins to hold them together.

Except at some point, Rylee would've found out she was pregnant. Would they have discussed abortion or adoption? Would they have hated each other so much by then that Rylee withheld the truth? He couldn't imagine it of her, but who knew?

Brenna's phone rang, shattering his thoughts, and she leaped up, pulling her phone from her pocket. "Babe? Yeah, I called… where are you?" Nodding, she held up a hand to him, though he hadn't said anything. "No, Jamie says it's okay… I need you to come to the party place with me, finalize things for tomorrow…" She smiled at him. "He says you've to take the whole afternoon off." Shaking his head, he wasn't really saying no, just judging his grinning sister. "Yeah, we'll deal with the party, and then go to the spa… He's nodding his head right now."

He wasn't nodding his head.

Narrowing his eyes, he angled toward her, reaching for the phone. "Let me talk to her."

Brenna edged a little closer. "He wants to talk to you, but I don't think you should talk to him. I think he'll say something inappropriate." A beat or two passed. Brenna laughed and handed over the phone. "She wants you to say something inappropriate."

He knew better than to believe his sister and took the phone without rising to her bait. "Ry?"

"I don't need the entire afternoon."

"Take it," he said, sitting back. "This time five years ago you were less than a day away from giving birth, this is your day too."

"It's taking advantage," she said. The smile in her voice prompted his, though he tried to subdue the instinctual reaction; Brenna scrutinized his every nuance. "Will you pick up the kids?"

"Yes," he said, finding something comforting and appealing about making such ordinary plans.

"And I'll pick up dinner."

Glancing at his sister, he lowered his chin and his volume. "Just us tonight, okay?"

"Okay," Rylee murmured.

Brenna wasn't shy about coughing and traversing one long stride that brought her up against the front of his desk. "You inviting me to dinner, brother? So sorry, I promised my girl candlelight, you know?"

Proving she must've overheard, Rylee laughed down the line. "We'll probably have to invite the kids, you know."

It took him a second to click in with Rylee's teasing. When he did, he relaxed, feeling so much better just to be back in the groove with her. Maybe Brenna was wrong about them getting weird and the necessity of space between them for the sake of sanity. He heard her take the slightest of breaths and his thoughts flew straight to the bedroom.

Damn. Brenna was right. Just Rylee's breathing was enough to turn him on.

"Those little freeloaders are always hanging around," he said. "We should put 'em to work, start charging them rent."

"Kye pays in secret cuddles," she said. "And Sky's probably the best security we could get. She's always at the forefront of any mystery… But we can start setting them chores, they're five now."

"You mean like cleaning the bathroom with a toothbrush kind of thing?"

She laughed again. "How about we talk about it at dinner…? Maybe we could get them a pet."

"What kind of pet? Isn't my sister enough?" he asked and shook his head. "We'll talk about it later, Brenna's waving at me for her phone. I'll grab the kids and meet you at home for dinner. Have fun today."

"Thank you."

"And Ry," he said. "Great job on squeezing them out."

"Five years later and I'm only just starting to recognize my body again," she said. "Speak to you later."

She hung up and he handed the phone to a grinning Brenna. "Jamie and Rylee sitting in a tree—"

"You'll think this is funny 'til I stop paying your rent. I pay more for you than I do in child support," he said, opening the top drawer of his desk to grab his wallet. He slid a credit card from inside and held it toward her. Though she "ooh'd" in excitement and grabbed for it, he didn't immediately let go. "Give this to Rylee." Brenna nodded. "I mean it, Brenna. Give it to her, she swipes the card, you just stand and watch. I don't mind her paying for your shit, but I'm not paying for your lady's candlelight, you know."

He let go and she snatched the card to her body, growling at him as she did. "You're just jealous I'm getting pussy tonight and you're not."

"Get it out your system," he said. "You better show up early tomorrow and remember it's a five year old's birthday party."

"You mean no hot pants and boob tubes?" she asked, walking backwards toward the door.

"I don't give a damn if you come naked, just watch your language."

Opening the door, she snorted. "Mom will be there, only someone with a death wish would swear around her precious babies, and I don't mean us."

Pride warmed him. "My children rule the world."

"Your children? Rylee's kids. We don't give a damn about you."

His laughing sister left, though he wasn't sure she was wrong. That was the way it should be. Adults didn't matter, the kids mattered, just like Rylee tried to tell him last night. But his sister had come into his office and thrown what he thought he knew into the wringer.

The trouble was, now he had to decide, was he going

to do something about it… or not?

to do something about it… or not?

TWENTY-EIGHT

FIVE YEARS OLD. Her babies were five years old. How did that happen? It felt like just yesterday she'd learned of their pending arrival. Now, running around the funfair located in the park just for them, they were fully fledged human beings. It was real. She didn't want it to be. Okay, so she loved to see them so happy, but did they have to keep getting bigger? Crop tops and jalopies got closer every day.

In absolute awe, she couldn't fault any detail of the event. Everything was catered for, every whim satisfied. Every five-year-old's whim anyway. The delight of her babies was enough to skyrocket her own. This was what they wanted and they got it.

A Ferris wheel, a teacup ride, a carousel, on and on, the attractions were in full swing. Various stalls with games like hook-the-duck and a coconut shy kept the adults trying for prizes. The petting zoo, of course, Sky wouldn't surrender the chance to be close to animals. Food trucks were set up for grilling and hotdogs and all kinds of candy. Her children were spoiled. And why shouldn't they be spoiled on their birthday?

All paid for by the sire himself. There hadn't been time to thank him, the day had been manic. The kids got their presents in the morning, followed by a special brunch for close family only. A kind of brunch anyway, one with cake and a chance to blow out their candles.

Afterwards, the fair awaited, along with their daycare friends and extended family. Going from one adult to another, from one group of friends to the next, the twins loved every minute of the attention. Mommy wasn't as exciting, obviously, she'd hardly seen them. They'd get family time at home later, so for now, she'd take a backseat.

JD had said there would be another surprise at the apartment, for just the four of them; she was in the dark along with the twins. Speculating, she wandered to the perimeter of festivities, admiring the vision of happiness created for her children.

That happiness vanished in a heartbeat. A figure broke from the crowd with her in its sights. Was this real? He couldn't be here. Why would he be here? Snapping to, she hurried to meet him.

"Baxter," she gasped. "What the hell…? What are you doing here?"

"I came to get you back," he said, determined, his wide eyes wild. "I can't walk away or live without you."

"You can… you have to," she said, grabbing his wrist to march him away from the party. At the end of the hot dog cart, he yanked his arm from her grip. "Baxter—"

"I love you, Rylee," Baxter declared. "I love you."

Panic surged through her and she grabbed him again. "What has gotten into you? What the hell, Baxter!"

Sinking down onto the grass, he dug in his pocket. "I bought you a ring, Ry. I want to do it. To marry you."

"No, you don't," she said and tossed her head back to growl at the sky before glaring at him. "I will not let you ruin my children's birthday, not for them and not for me. I don't know what is going on here, but we were never in love. You never said you loved me until Jamison came into my life and now you're determined to beat him? Is that what this is?" He gave up rifling in his pocket. "Get up off the ground."

"Rylee—"

"You never met my kids, never wanted to, until their dad moved into town. We didn't talk about being exclusive let alone living together or merging lives. And marriage?" Too astounding for words. "You used to joke with me, tell me you were competitive, but this… I don't know what you expect to happen here. I did nothing to make you believe I wanted us to be forever. We dated, we had fun, and I'm sorry if you're hurt that it's over, but my kids are my priority. They will always be my priority and I'm sorry, I don't believe that you would be a positive influence in their lives."

Staggering back a step, he opened his mouth. "You think I'm not father material? That he's better than me?"

"Baxter, I—"

"You can walk away from four months together? You can give up on us? Just like that?" Hurting him wasn't her goal. She could understand his anger, but there was no way to make it better for him without being dishonest and she couldn't do that. "Are you in love with him?"

"Baxter! This isn't about—"

"Tell me," he snapped, grabbing her arm, tightening his grip to jerk her closer. "We were fine until he showed up. He broke us up. He did this to us… Are you sleeping with him?"

She gasped. "That is not your business," she said, filled with her own anger. "If you don't let go of my arm right now, I'll scream. Believe me, you don't want JD's security to come over here."

"I want an answer; I deserve an answer. I'm not afraid of his monkeys."

Oh, the naïveté. "Don't be afraid of his monkeys, be afraid of him. Threatening me on any given day wouldn't be a smart move, but doing it on our children's birthday? At their party no less? You're lucky I'm giving you this chance to leave." She leaned in to snarl. "Walk away, Baxter. We're through. Walk. Away."

He glared for another minute. No problem, she had plenty of practice staring out men's failed attempts at intimidation.

Tossing her arm away with a force that sent her stumbling backward, Baxter swore and stalked off.

As long as he was walking away, she'd let him go.

Keep going. Yep, right around there. Walk away and never come back. He disappeared through the trees at the other side of the field. It took another minute for her heart rate to slow to normal.

If that was their whole dose of drama to be had today, she'd take it and be happy it stayed away from her babies. Returning to her previous spot, she scanned the fairground, assuring herself that all was okay.

The hot dog cart didn't appeal; the cotton candy stand next to it was a different story. How many years had it been since she'd enjoyed cotton candy? A treat would help get her back to the spirit of the day.

The vendor gave her a stick and a cloud of fluffy pink cotton candy. A smile spread on her face, this was exactly what she needed.

"Thank you," she said. "What do I owe you?"

"Your husband covered all costs," the vendor said. "He's some guy."

"Oh, he is," she said, taking a bite. "Thanks."

Wandering, she ate some more and soaked up the nostalgia. JD had paid for the rides and the games to be there, that much she'd known. It didn't occur to her he'd cover food costs too.

And there he was, heading her way. JD was welcome. Very welcome. JD. Going to meet him, she swept a puff of cotton candy from her stick and offered it to his lips the moment they reached each other.

Opening his mouth, he accepted.

She caught some for herself when he rubbed her arms. "Can we talk?"

Nodding, she ate more of the sweet indulgence. "I love this stuff," she said and didn't object when he laced their fingers together to guide her across the park, past the first row of trees, into a quieter space. "Have some more."

Backing her against a tree in the central row, he let her slip some more of the sugary treat between his lips. This time, her finger touched his tongue and trailed free.

He'd been frowning and on some kind of mission it seemed, but when she sucked her damp finger clean, his head tilted. A feral kind of heat tinged his gaze. That was what she needed. Not another manic man with a grievance, this man with one thing on his mind.

"Does cotton candy turn you on?"

"This turns me on," she said, meaning the party, still looking at him. "I'd never have been able to throw an event like this if it weren't for you, JD. Thank you. Did you see their little faces?"

"I did," he said, rubbing her arms. "And it's your birthday next. You'll have to get to work on your wish list."

"How do you know when my birthday is?" she asked, eating more cotton candy. "My employee file?"

"No, you told me your birthday on the night we met."

Had she?

"Wow," she said, the cotton candy falling to her side. "I can't believe you remember that."

"I remember a lot about that night," he said. "More than I let myself admit for a long time."

"Doesn't matter anyway," she said, picking up her snack for another bite.

"What doesn't?"

Stepping forward, she should really check on her children with their aunt and grandmother. "My wish list," she said. "I can't have what I want this year."

JD had other ideas and caught her shoulders to push her back against the tree. "You can," he said. "That's why I wanted to talk. I've been thinking and I need to tell you, you can have what you want."

Dread bled into her tone in an elongating drawl. "J…"

He smiled and sank both hands into her hair. "It makes sense. It makes so much sense. Brenna said something and I've been thinking about it since. In the interests of fairness, I want you to know that I've come to a decision."

"A decision? What decision?" she asked, then gasped. "Are you leaving us?" It would be her own fault. She'd told him to be honest if he wanted to split, so if he did, it was on her head. "Are you? Because you have to tell me. A business trip to California for a couple of weeks, I can handle, if you're leaving us permanently—"

"No," he said, holding her cheeks, bowing to kiss the end of her nose. "My decision is that I want us to be together. I've decided to find a way to make this work, no matter what."

First Baxter and now JD, something about her kids' birthday fired everyone's aspirations.

"We talked about this, JD. I value you too much to—"

"We're going to work it out and we're going to take our time." JD's calmer nature was a welcome contrast to Baxter's mania. He smiled and rubbed her arms again. One spot took her back in an automatic flinch and his smile fell. "Siren?" Examining her arm, holding her elbow, he raised it a little. "Where did you get the marks?"

She could lie and say they came from a ride, though carousel horses weren't exactly known for being violent.

"I—"

"Jamison!"

Recognizing the urgency in Brenna's voice, she pushed past JD. Brenna never used her brother's name like that. Never.

The moment her friend came into view, she wished for the previous bliss. Something had happened. Something bad. What?

Hurrying toward Brenna, she grabbed her the minute she was within reach. "What?" she demanded. "What is it?"

Brenna tore her eyes away to look over her head at her brother who clutched her shoulders, sandwiching her between the siblings.

Her friend swallowed hard. "We can't find Sky."

For a moment, the planet disappeared. In freefall into nothingness, life became—her body weakened and her knees almost gave. A spear of numbing terror shot through her so fast JD had to hold her up.

"What do you mean?" JD asked. "Where was she? Who was she with?"

With his arm around her, he started moving, pulling her along between him and Brenna, keeping quick pace.

"They wanted burgers and to go on the carousel

again. I went to get the burgers, Mom and Lotta stayed with them when they went on the horses. When I got back, Mom was talking to the people running the ride. Lotta was with Kye who fell on the metal platform. His knee was bleeding, I asked where Sky was and… she was gone."

The word rushed bile to her throat. The lights and music that appealed before now seemed sickening, taunting. It all faded away in the hubbub of panicked people gathering around the brightly painted horses.

The crowds broke apart to gawk at her group. Whatever. Let them. All she could feel was the agony of her red-faced son wailing in the arms of his grandmother. Breaking into a run to get to him, his distress fueled her pace. She had to be there. Now. Fast. Faster. Marjorie didn't hesitate to give him up when she snatched him close, squeezing him to her.

A fresh set of tears streamed from Kye's eyes. She clutched his head close to her mouth and rocked with him.

"I've got you, baby," she whispered against him. "Momma's here. Momma's here."

"I'm sorry, Mommy," Kye howled.

Angling his face to her throat, she drove her fingers into his hair, kissing and soothing him. "You did nothing wrong, my sweet prince, nothing."

All around, nothing registered yet she absorbed everything. Her daughter was the only person she wanted to see, but it wouldn't happen. Something in her just knew. The sheer number of people now aware of what was going on meant the vicinity was guaranteed to be Sky-free.

"I want everything shut down," a stern voice called from behind her: JD. "Search everywhere. The cops are on their way and security is holding everyone here. No car leaves the lot."

Whipping around in his direction, JD had a serious look on his face as he spoke to Greg, Jim, and the security man who was supposed to have kept them safe. That wasn't enough. Nothing was enough.

Eliminating space between them, she came up behind him. "JD," she said, her voice hard despite the tremor of adrenaline in it. His focus was hers. "I want the best." Anger, fear, and desperation drove her, but determination had never been more resolute. She blinked at the security guy for only a second, then matched her eyes to JD's. "Empty your goddamn bank account and get your family the best."

He looked only for another second before turning to Greg. "Call S.I.S.," he said.

"He doesn't—"

"He's a father. Tell him what's going on. He'll be in a chopper and on the ground inside thirty minutes… and he owes me one." The security guy was next in his sights. "Contain these people, brief the cops. You will be paid, but you'll defer to the new team."

Kye sniffled and whimpered, his sobs had lost some of their power. Though he was angled away from her, she picked up JD's hand and guided it to their son's hair. He turned slowly, but she buried her face in their boy, her fingers intertwined between JD's on Kye's head.

"Daddy's here," she whispered to her baby. "Daddy's with us."

"Ry," JD murmured, full of his own pain.

Maybe it was the need in his voice or how it emanated from within him. Whatever it was, she stepped in close, sliding an arm around him, pulling him to her and welcoming his arms when they came around her to hold her close, squeezing Kye between them.

Neither she nor JD could break right now. Sky needed them to be strong. Kye couldn't see their fear. The adults needed these few seconds to reassure each other that they weren't alone, that they were united.

The sirens wailed in, forcing them to break apart, though they only went far enough to find each other's eyes.

If Sky had been injured, she would be somewhere nearby, and would've been seen or heard. Her daughter's healthy lungs would've assured that. What were the other options? That her little girl had wandered off or someone had taken her. Someone who could intend harm.

"I have to talk to the police," JD said, bowing to kiss Kye's head.

With his eyes closed, he pressed for longer than usual, then forced himself to turn away.

A sudden thought made her grab for him. "Baxter was here," she said, with a flourish of hope. "He was mad, maybe…"

JD's jaw ticked and he nodded once. He came back to tunnel his fingers in her hair and yanked her close to kiss her hairline.

"I'll kill the bastard, you know I will," he growled against her and pulled back like he sought approval.

"Only if you find him before I do," she said. If she found the person responsible for hurting their family, she'd relish every second of pain she'd cause them. "If they want money—"

"I'll pay every cent. To hell with negotiation."

"I know," she said. Their staring out wasn't about winning anymore, it was a manifestation of their bond and the strength of their certainty. "Bring back our baby girl, Daddy."

"I promise you, Momma," he said, touching the edge of her jaw. "I promise."

She kissed the heel of his hand just a fraction of a second before he spun around and started toward the cops spreading through the field.

Sky was in trouble. Her knees buckled and she collapsed with her son safe in her arms. She barely felt Brenna and Marjorie close in around her. All she could focus on as she sang into Kye's hair was the column of JD's formidable form in the middle of the fray.

If anyone could bring her baby back to her, it would be him. She'd be there at his side if it wasn't for Kye's need. Their boy would feel his sister's absence, probably more than anyone else; the pair had never been parted, never.

She'd settle Kye for as long as she could, but if Sky wasn't back in her arms soon, she'd start taking the city apart, brick by brick if necessary.

TWENTY-NINE

LESS THAN HALF an hour after Sky went missing—she wouldn't say "losing" her—JD was in front of a bank of cameras declaring war on whoever had done this to them. To their little girl.

She couldn't sit still. In the apartment, she was up, down, pacing, worrying her thumbnail. Her little girl was gone and what was she doing? Nothing.

After that news conference, an hour had gone by in a flash. Another dwindled away and another.

The team working in her kitchen, spread out on the dining table, kept busy, talking to each other, doing things with paper and on computers. Some went out, some came back. Activity buzzed and voices echoed.

How long had it been now?

How long had her little girl been out in the world without her protection?

It wasn't right. She'd failed. Her one job was to keep their little people safe. That was a mother's reason, a mother's purpose. How could this have happened? How could she have been so distracted? So selfish? So complacent?

Kye had stopped crying, but he looked no less distressed sitting under his grandmother's arm. Was what people said true? Could one twin feel another's pain? What her babies must be going through, and all because she'd neglected her duty.

Someone knocked.

On the front door.

Her shoulders went back. Since the troop of investigators had arrived, no one had knocked… Oh, God, was it a good sign or…?

One of the S.I.S. guys went to answer it. JD still spoke to the head guy. They'd been introduced, but his name wasn't in her head.

The S.I.S. guy stepped back and a woman came in. A stranger. Short, blonde, beautiful.

Head S.I.S. guy immediately stopped talking to go around JD, though the latter was close behind.

"Rox?" the head S.I.S. guy said and accepted her hug.

"I felt so much better when I heard you were on this," the blonde said and landed her focus on JD. "The coffers are open and the water's on. We're pumping it out as far and wide as we can. Lilya and I are doing the rounds of anyone with any pull. Jane's Knox's ears at the CollCom block here in Seattle. He's working flat out, him and Caspian, to put your daughter's face in front of as many people as possible. Dyce will send out an alert on all devices as soon as you give us the go ahead. We've opened phone lines, email, live chat, and staffed it out. There's a million reward in the pot, but we're keeping that on the down-low, we don't want the kooks jamming the lines. Gauge is flying into New York, he'll take over CollCom there and is pulling in favors with Whey. Our LA troop don't have a lot of sway there. If you—"

"Wait a second," JD said, raising a hand. "Have we met?"

The blonde smiled. "No, I'm—"

"I know who you are, Ms. Kyst. Me and the rest of the planet. You and your boyfriend are on the fast track to owning the world from how I hear it."

"I hope that's true," Ms. Kyst said. "Because the more people listening, the faster we get your daughter back."

JD took a step toward her, his eyes narrowing. "Why would you—"

"We've been introduced…" The voice of another woman rose before she entered the apartment, a hand on her pregnant belly. "Mr. Dawes."

"Ms. Kearns," he said. "Or is it Mrs. Kintyre now?"

"Not yet, but soon."

The pregnant woman went to her cohort's side. "This is why you dropped out of the Gramercy race. Because you know there's nothing more important than family. You let me sit there and lecture you when… It doesn't matter. What you did was for my family, for my child. Let us do what we can for yours."

"Whey tried to play hardball."

"He's ruthless," the pregnant woman said. "But I'm biased."

"You're right. We came to an understanding."

"And we have some dirt in our back pocket. If need be, we'll own Ricardo Whey."

What did that mean? She didn't care who he owed favors, she'd pay them herself if she could. Anything to get Sky back. These women might have come from nowhere, but if they could help…

She descended the stairs from the living room to go to his side. "JD?"

He gestured at the women in turn. "Roxanna Kyst and Lilya Kearns."

"They know our daughter?"

"We don't know your daughter, ma'am," Lilya said. "We just want to help."

And with a child growing inside her, the woman had perspective on the privilege of parenthood.

"You flew straight here from New York?" the head S.I.S. guy asked Roxanna.

"Jane and I were already in the air. We diverted from LA to Seattle."

Chief Security was either grateful or impressed. "You have an audience, Rox."

"Yes. At your disposal. I have a laptop ready to go."

"It's more grassroots than anything we have access to and it's global."

Oh, God, she hadn't thought about that. Would someone smuggle her child out of the country? They weren't just looking in the city, they had a whole planet to cover, and Sky was so small. She'd never been aware of how many closed doors there were in the world. Now, with her daughter captive behind one, they were all she could think about.

"I'll get on it," Roxanna said. "Stone…" That was the head guy's name, yes, she remembered. "If this is—"

"We've got it handled."

Stone touched Roxanna's jaw for a second.

"Where's Zairn on this?" JD asked.

"On calls, audio and video, pulling people out of beds and meetings. He won't stop. Rourke is going higher, to the top. If you need an address or a statement from the head guy, we'll get it. And if you need black ops…" Roxanna took Lilya's hand. "There's no limit to your resources."

"Why would you do this? There's no negotiation—"

"We understand family too. Maybe you were the cousin no one invited to dinner, but you're a part of our sphere. You became one of us the moment you dropped Gramercy for the sake of Kintyre's unborn child."

Unborn. That was the only time a mother could safeguard her child. Even then it wasn't absolute. While pregnant, she took fewer risks, maybe. Either way, she must've done something right. Her children arrived in the world perfect and innocent. Now their parents' deeds could cost one of them their life.

Still saying things that she couldn't hear beyond the ringing in her ears, JD, Stone, and one woman walked over to the dining table in the background of her awareness.

"How are you doing?"

A woman's voice, a…

Shit, it wasn't in her to be friendly. "I'm sorry, Ms. Kyst, I don't mean to be rude—"

"But you couldn't give a shit about small talk right now," the woman said, putting an arm around her to guide her toward the living room. "And it's Roxie, please."

"Do you have children?"

"Not in 3D," Roxie said, earning herself a frown, she

shook her head. "Never mind, sorry. No, we don't have children."

"You're the *Talk at Sunset* woman. Didn't I read somewhere you're pregnant?"

"Just the media making the news."

They sat together on the stairs. "Before this, it didn't really occur to me that JD might be famous… or have famous connections."

"That we hope will come in useful. Fame is one thing and power is another. How long have you and JD been together?"

"We're not, we haven't been. It's…"

"Complicated?" Roxie took her hand on a smile. "Yeah, I've been there."

"Do you think it's why…? JD said he'd pay any ransom, but we've had no communication from—not that they've told me. We've had our differences, especially recently, but… he loves his children."

"I don't doubt that he does."

"And everything he's going through—and I'm just sitting here—"

Tears welled, so her words silenced.

"Men like to fix things, and he's used to being in charge. Letting him take the lead grants him a mercy. They go crazy, men like him, if they're not in control. This is him, doing what he's doing, in a grab for control."

"But he's not in control. None of us are. Only the person holding my daughter has the power to give her back."

"If we can find her, if there's a witness or someone with a suspicion, you can steal that power back. Right now, it doesn't feel like control, but it's progress. Every person and place Stone and JD eliminate is one less place to look." And there was some comfort in that. Miniscule comfort, but comfort nonetheless. "What's she like?"

Her mind had been wandering again. "Hmm?"

"Your daughter. Her name's Sky, right?"

"Yes," she said, a tight, slight smile broke through. "Which is ironic because she's all about mermaids and the ocean right now. We should've named her something water related.”

“A swimmer, huh?”

“We don’t take her to the pool as often as we should. It would be a great time to get her into…” A swim club or a team… Would they ever get that chance? “Sorry.”

“There’s time,” Roxie said, squeezing her hand. “Your daughter will come back to you.”

JD promised that, but they couldn’t know, no one could for sure. Even if she did…

“We don’t know what they’re doing to her. She’s five years old. Five. She knows nothing about… She’s five.”

“Whatever she endures, you’ll get through it. If your JD is anything like my guy, he’s not the type to give up. If your daughter needs help, you’ll both be there for her, to support her with whatever she needs.”

It didn’t bear thinking about. “When is your friend due?”

“End of January.”

“Does she know what she’s having?”

“A boy. No name yet though. He has a lot of aunts and uncles with strong opinions on that subject.”

“JD’s sister, Brenna, is the same. Loud, vivacious. At least she was until…”

Brenna was in the living room behind them with her mother and had hardly said a word. Guilt was going around. No one could claim to be blameless, yet she didn’t blame anyone. No one but herself.

“I have a streaming channel, it’s run through—it doesn’t matter,” Roxie said, raising their joined hands. “I can tell people whatever you want them to know. They’ll do everything they can to help. No bullshit. Me and mine will do whatever it takes to support your family. And if you’d rather I just disappear—”

“No.” Urgency struck her. “Please. Everything—we need as many people fighting for Sky as we can get. I don’t have connections or money, but I’ll spend the rest of my life repaying—”

“Hey.” Roxie cupped her face. “All I want is to meet your little mermaid.”

And she prayed that would be possible. That her little girl would be back with them… and soon.

THIRTY

STANDING IN KYE'S bedroom doorway, she watched her baby boy sleep. Safe. Calm. She'd taken the security of their life for granted. Would she ever be able to tear herself from that spot or take her eye off him again?

Lost in thought, she hadn't known anyone was approaching until two hands squeezed under her arms to pull her back into a tight embrace against a solid body.

"How is he?" JD asked her, resting his chin on the top of her head.

Settling her arms over his, she stroked his forearms, grateful at least for his attempt at comfort. "Asleep," she whispered. "I didn't think he'd ever close his eyes… but as soon as he did, I wanted him to open them again."

"Come on," he said and tried to draw her away.

Clinging tighter, she fought to pull him back. "No, he needs us near."

"And we'll stay near," he said. "We're going to your room. We'll hear if he moves or shouts and I have security at every door." Still, she was reluctant. He kissed the top of her head. "You need a moment to breathe, sweetheart, that's all. We'll come right back in a minute."

Giving in, she turned against him, wrapping both

arms around his waist while he scooped his around her shoulders.

It had been years since the kids needed to be lifted and laid everywhere. Yet without her daughter, her arms were bereft. She couldn't handle them being empty.

JD steered them into her bedroom and guided her to the bed, sitting them both on the edge. For a minute, he held her, probably taking as much comfort as he was giving.

"I'm scared to ask if there's news," she whispered.

"Nothing new," he murmured, still holding her to him, tucking her hair away from her temple with a fingertip at the same time. "We're going to find her, Ry. I won't stop until we have them both in our arms again."

He meant it and she believed in him, in their family. That didn't stop her missing her baby girl.

"Baxter?"

"They have him in custody; they're questioning him."

Just the idea that someone she knew, who she'd been intimate with, could be involved made her so sick that guilt became overwhelming.

Not knowing was worse than anything. No ransom demand had come. No call from kidnappers. The park site had been searched once, twice, again maybe. She didn't care how long it took, they needed a lead, needed to be doing everything in their power to locate Sky.

"I'd give them anything, Ry. Shit, babe, I hate feeling like this. I'm letting you down, all of you down, and I—"

"Shh," she said, sitting up straight to touch his lips. "You've been my rock, JD."

"There's nothing I wouldn't do for you," he said, taking her hand, caressing her face. "Nothing."

Sitting there, not long ago, she'd wanted to console him, and now she was the one in need of consolation. Rising, she touched his mouth with hers. Urging higher, she parted her lips and eased her tongue forward, begging for a stronger taste.

Sliding her hands onto his shoulders, she climbed over to straddle his lap and rocked herself against him, kissing him harder.

"Oh, you're better than I remember," she murmured. "How can that be?"

Breathing in through her nose, she kissed him again, pouring her need into him. If they could forget. If—

The span of his capable hands gripped her waist. Yes, that sensation was security, solid certainty.

He tipped his head back to break the kiss. "Please don't make me say no to you, Siren."

"Don't," she whispered, seeking his mouth again, though it held back. "Don't say no, baby. I want this." With a hold on his forearm, she skimmed his hand up, trapping it between hers and her breast. "Make love to me, JD."

"Shit," he hissed through gritted teeth. She stole his mouth but the kiss didn't last because he leaned back like before. "Ry, you're vulnerable." He clenched his jaw. "Fuck, babe, I want you so bad. Soon as we have Sky back, ask me again and I'll—" Pushing off his lap, she got to her feet, full of pique. He caught her wrist before she could walk away. "I was trying to tell you in the park, Ry, I want this to last… You don't want to have sex; you just want to feel something other than the gnawing hollow despair eating at your guts. I know it, because I feel that way too."

He wasn't wrong.

She swiped away a tear when it cascaded down her cheek. "We'll never be whole without her."

"Listen to me," he said, grabbing her other hand and pulling her back down to sit with him. "We are going to get her back. Our family will be whole."

More tears fell as a sob escaped her. "I can't breathe, JD. When I think about what they might be doing to her."

Holding her face, he brought her forehead to his. "You'll drive yourself insane thinking like that. Just think about getting her back, about holding her again. Come here."

Climbing onto the bed, he laid them both down. Letting the tears win, she clung to him as he held her tight, stroking and soothing her.

If it hadn't been for JD, she wouldn't have had the resources to mobilize such a full-scale search so quickly. Grateful for him, she couldn't blame him. Still, some part of her wondered… Would this have happened if the world didn't know the identity of Sky's father?

Until her baby came back, she wouldn't make sense of anything. Their lives would never be the same, because as soon as she got Sky back, she'd never risk losing her again.

THIRTY-ONE

"HOW IS SHE DOING?" Brenna asked when he returned from the hallway to the vision of craziness.

In the kitchen and around the dining table, security agents and cops worked hard, some were on phones, some were on laptops. Everyone was busy, yet he wanted to yell at them for not doing enough. Reaching for his sister, he caught her shoulder and pulled her into a hug. Everyone needed to draw a little comfort from each other today.

"She fell asleep," he said, wrapping his arms around her shoulders and swinging her a few inches left to right. "Kye's asleep too, I looked in on him… I just wanted to scoop him up and take him to his momma, you know?"

"None of us want to be alone right now," she said. "Mom's taking it hard."

Keeping Brenna in his arms, he twisted to look toward the living room where his mom was being comforted by Lotta. "It's not her fault."

"No more hers than it is mine," Brenna said. "Jame, I'm so sorry. Rylee trusted me and—"

"Hey," he said, taking her shoulders to guide her back and look down at her. "There's plenty enough blame to go around for everyone. Can we just stand together right now?

For Sky's sake."

He managed a tight smile, so she reciprocated, and he hugged her again, using his sister as a leaning post.

"How are you staying so strong?" Brenna asked as he observed the people working to find his daughter.

"Rylee," he answered without thinking about it.

"Rylee?"

"Her focus is on Kye right now, she needs my eyes on Sky. She's close to breaking and when she does, God help us all."

"You think she'll lose it?"

That was his greatest fear. Though it was obvious losing Sky had shaken her, Rylee was strong. That same strength would get their daughter through whatever she was enduring.

One guy on a laptop gestured another closer. After a quick conversation, they called over another person, saying something about footage.

Clinging tighter to his sister, he couldn't hope. Information was coming in from all angles, and these first hours were crucial. Hope was dangerous, yet he had to think it was possible, they would get their girl back. Every lead had to be followed, but not all would necessarily pan out.

Everyone filming or taking pictures at the party was asked to send their files to a central email account. Technological genius Xavien Rourke, courtesy of Roxanna Kyst, had written a quick program to read the metadata of every file and arrange them into chronological order with a sub-path on geographical location.

Their allies had increased the reach of their request too. Rather than just those at the party, everyone in the city, the country, the planet, with any hint of images or video of the park or party, were donating their material to the same program. Anything might be relevant. To see something out of place or unusual, the same people had to see the same area from as many angles as possible. Compiling the data would take time and time was one thing they didn't have on their side.

Those around the table with laptops analyzed every

frame. While he wanted a set of human eyes on every nanosecond, he was also running every piece of media through facial recognition for Sky and having separate files set up for each party attendee. Those closest to the event could be suspects. It might seem like an invasion of privacy but tracking people at the party could be important. As soon as they had Sky back, he'd burn it all. He just wanted to be ready if they identified a culprit.

Letting Brenna go, he went around her to the table. "What have you got?" he asked, startling the men huddled around the machine.

"Maybe nothing. It's something that we want to—"

"Don't fuck with me, Stone, what is it?"

"Rourke's building a 3D recreation with the media we're getting. Putting it all together to show us from every angle—"

"What is it?"

He'd be wowed by the technology another time. After he got his daughter back.

The others stepped away from Stone as he pushed the shoulder of the man in the chair, making him vacate so the boss could sit in his place.

"Getting that back angle of the ride is impossible, the foliage is too thick and there's a wall before the street, but..."

Going around the table, JD bent to look over Stone's shoulder as he restarted the muted video of the carousel just barely peeking through branches and leaves, hidden in shadow.

It was the usual scene, horses going up and down, round and round, kids smiling and waving.

"There's Kye," Stone said, pointing at a particular horse as the ride rotated. "And Sky. Two behind him on the outer row."

They were his kids, yet with such an obscured view, he wasn't sure he'd have ID'd them on that first round. The ride went around again and Stone pointed to each of the kids. JD's smile curled when Sky tried to wave but grabbed for the horse again the moment she let go. Kye didn't even try to wave, but he bounced like he was actually riding a horse, in his own wonderful world.

"She's more of a swimmer than an equestrian," JD said, spying the determination on his little girl's partially hidden face.

The ride slowed and he steadied his breathing, wary of what he might see. Stone paused the footage and clicked it forward frame by frame. Kye went by the camera which darkened and wavered just before Sky came into view. Fuck, that could be his last chance to see his little girl.

The light returned just as the ride came to a halt. Kye was at the edge of the screen, still bouncing up and down. Doing as told, Kye waited until his aunt came up to help him, the two laughed as Lotta struggled to unfasten the strap around his little waist.

"There," Stone said and froze the image.

What was he supposed to be looking at? People freeing the kids from the ride and the dying fall leaves caused chaos, it was difficult to discern.

"What are you…"

Stone pointed at the screen for a second, then lowered his finger to select and zoom in on a specific area. "That's the front of Sky's horse," he said. The nose of one of the horses was just visible through a tiny crack in the melee of nature and nurture. "Gotta be grateful Roxie's guy is recording in the highest def."

Stone clicked something. The image went through a couple of scrubs, increasing the definition until…

"Fuck," JD breathed out and wiped a hand over his mouth.

"That's a hand, a female one I'd say," Stone said. "Just on the nose of the horse, someone is talking to Sky. They took her off the ride… Why wouldn't she scream bloody murder if a stranger—"

"Because that's not a stranger," JD said, pushing away from the table, fury coursing through him when he stalked toward the door. "Stone, bring a guy and grab a cop to make an arrest."

"Dawes," Stone said and whistled. Two S.I.S. men closed in, blocking JD's access to the front door. "You're emotional, too close to this. Who is it? Tell us, and we'll handle—"

"You've got a son, right?" JD asked, grabbing his jacket from the hooks by the door and snatching one for Sky too. "How old is he?"

"Three," Stone said. "We've got a daughter on the way."

The whole room focused on him, but JD didn't flinch. "And you're married?" Stone nodded. "I've known my daughter two years longer than you've known your son. If someone was holding him, keeping him from your wife, would you leave it to someone else to retrieve him? How would you look her in the eye if you sat on your ass and let strangers rush in on your scared, upset child? Back me up or back down. One father to another."

Stone looked at him for another second then breathed out. "Rocco, you're with us. You've been doing the father thing longer than both of us."

One of the S.I.S. men blocking the door spoke up, "Sure thing, boss."

"Shep," Stone said, coming toward them.

Another S.I.S. man fell in at his side. "And here I thought Little Lady had given you your balls back for this mission," Shep said. "Guess I was wrong if you're falling for speeches like that."

JD stepped aside, letting Rocco open the front door.

The S.I.S. leader shoved Shep out first. "Least my lady doesn't chew mine up and spit 'em out like yours," Stone said, pulling a weapon from his hip to check the clip.

"You won't need that," JD said. After they were in the hallway, he turned to look at Brenna standing at the foot of the table. "Let Rylee sleep, don't wake her. But if she gets up, tell her I'll be back with our girl in less than an hour."

Relief put a grin on Brenna's face. "You mean it? You know where she is?" He nodded. "Oh, Jame!"

JD went into the hallway and closed the door to look at the men he had. "We need a cop to make an arrest."

"We'll radio from the car," Stone said. They all started toward the elevator. "Now you want to fill me in on who we're taking down?"

"A very desperate woman."

THIRTY-TWO

SOMETHING STARTLED HER awake; it took a minute to orient herself. In her own bed in the dark, with Kye tucked against her, she breathed out. The horror of the day hit hard, forcing her upright.

Kye mumbled in protest.

What was the last thing she remembered? Falling asleep in JD's arms after putting Kye in his bed. It was dark. Dark! Sky was out there somewhere and—

"Ow, Daddy, stop it!"

No! It couldn't—was that—

Inhaling fast, she scrambled off the bed on her hands and knees and bolted for the bedroom door. Grabbing the frame, she swung herself into the hallway in the direction of the voice and stopped dead. Sky stood in the lit bathroom, her daddy kneeling behind her, trying to brush her hair.

"Momma, Daddy makes it hurt," Sky said, like nothing had happened.

"Oh, my baby," she said and rushed forward, falling to her knees and snatching her daughter into her arms. "Oh, sweetie, my baby, are you hurt?"

Searching Sky for wounds, she squeezed her limbs and explored her hairline.

"Daddy's hurting my hair," Sky said, pushing her away to turn and take the comb from JD. "Momma's better."

"Guess Mommy's the pro," JD said, dropping to the side to sit on the floor. "Go on, Momma."

"JD, what… how…"

"Comb her hair," JD said, nodding at their daughter.

"I…"

At a loss, she did as suggested, crawling around Sky to run the comb through her hair. The tears didn't register until JD reached over to swipe them from her cheeks.

"It's okay," he murmured. "She's okay."

"What happened?" she asked in a rushed whisper. "I don't understand what—"

JD rose on his knees, cupping Sky's head to pull her to him for a kiss. "Go climb into Mommy's bed," he said, stroking their daughter's hair. "Don't wake Kye up."

Sky kissed each of them and dashed off to do as her father said.

"JD," she gasped the moment Sky darted into her bedroom.

He clutched her hand and kissed her knuckles. "It was Gabby." Her mouth fell open. "I don't even know how to tell you I'm sorry. I can't even… Stone's men found an image of her hand, she was wearing a ring… one I gave her incidentally, which is how I recognized it. She had Sky in her hotel suite… Sky doesn't even realize anything happened. Gabby told her they were just waiting for me to go pick her up. She didn't hurt her. They watched movies and ate room service, completely oblivious to all the… I'm sorry."

"I don't—"

"I told Gabby how important my children are to me, that she would never understand or be a part of my family," he said. Hadn't she had a similar conversation with Baxter? "She's so spoiled and entitled that she can't grasp the gravity of what the hell she did to us."

"JD, I—"

"I'm sorry, Rylee," he said, kissing her hand again. "I'm sorry. I had no idea she was capable of something like this. I… I know it's no consolation, but she wasn't acting in malice. She's clueless about the world. Used to getting her own way. She wanted to prove to me that she could care for my children and, in her warped mind… it doesn't matter. What matters is that she's in a jail cell and our children are safe." Picking up both of her hands, he kissed each one, then let them rest in his lap. "If you want me to leave—"

"This wasn't your fault." Still in shock, she stole her hand out of his to clasp his face. "Would you have exiled me if Baxter was responsible?" He shook his head. "She's a crazy maniac, and I want her punished to the full extent of the law. Don't ask me to cut her any slack, this is our baby, anything could have happened to her. I won't forgive this. You and I will have a problem if you're going to ask me to forgive—"

"I don't forgive her, and I wouldn't ask you to either."

Drawing in a cleansing breath, there was a lot to deal with. They'd have to talk to the kids about crazy people and to the cops about the felonious abductress. But it was late and right then, in her home, she had something they'd feared lost.

Climbing to her feet, she pulled JD up with her. "Get ready for bed then come kiss the kids."

She ran her thumb across his cheek again and left him in the bathroom. The kitchen was a mess, but she didn't care, chores would wait this time.

After checking the front door was locked, she went to her room to quickly change.

Both the kids were in the middle of her bed, beneath the covers. Carefully lifting them, she slid in beside them, kissing each and stroking their beautiful faces.

"How they doing?"

Glancing up, JD leaned against her doorframe.

"It's been a long day," she said. "They're out already."

"We'll have to talk to them. About walking off with people."

She nodded. "I thought the same thing. We can't make it seem like we're mad though, I don't want to scare her."

"I think Kye got a bigger fright than she did," JD said. "We'll make bacon for breakfast, that will mellow him out."

Sliding an arm over both of them, such warmth and

relief couldn't be underrated. "They're so precious, JD. Thank you for bringing her back to me."

"I promised you I would. She belongs in her mother's arms."

Bowing, she brushed Sky's hair from her forehead to kiss her. "And her daddy's too. You saved her, JD. You put our family back together."

"It wouldn't have been fractured if it wasn't for my insane ex," he said. "I am sorry, babe."

"Would you stop apologizing." Kye muttered something in his sleep, so she caressed his face. "There, sweetpea. Mommy and Daddy are here, you're safe."

"Get some sleep," JD said and boosted himself off the doorframe.

"Where are you going?"

"I'm tired, babe," he said. "And we don't want to disturb them."

Raising her arm from beneath the covers, she held a hand toward him. "None of us should be alone tonight," she said. "Get in on the other side of Kye, they need us… We can squish."

His glaring surprise was almost funny, but he didn't hesitate. Entering, he closed the door and came over to slip into her bed behind Kye. After dropping the covers, he kissed each of the kids and settled down, reaching over the top of them to rest a hand on her jaw, stroking his thumb up and down her cheekbone.

"Thank you."

"I wouldn't cast you out tonight." She smiled. "Kye was right, we have to squish."

"No one I'd rather squish with."

"Get some sleep, Daddy," she said, taking his hand from her face, keeping it in hers when she slid her arm back under the covers to rest their twined hands between the kids.

"We're going to keep them safe, Siren. Whatever it takes."

She closed her eyes and pulled them closer together. "We're all safe now. All safe."

After the stress of the day, they could do with some

rest; she had a feeling they'd all sleep sound. They'd come so close to her worst nightmare. JD saved the day by saving their baby.

The trauma would probably hit them hard tomorrow, but all she could feel then was relief. They were together, and right now, she couldn't be more grateful for her children, and for their father too.

***

AFTER THEIR DISCUSSION at breakfast, she spent a long time washing and drying her daughter's hair while JD spoke to the cops. When Sky was dressed, she ran to her brother's bedroom where Kye and JD were playing the cartoon game. She stopped in Kye's doorway.

With no regard for blocking the screen, Sky came to a screeching halt in front of the two males seated on the end of Kye's bed.

"Daddy! Daddy!" Sky shrieked. "Look my butterflies." Turning her head side to side, she showed the slides in her hair that she'd gotten for her birthday yesterday. "They sparkly."

"They are, Little Sproutette. I love them."

Kye blew a raspberry and she laughed, just pleased to be breathing normality. Both kids looked at her like she was crazy.

"Sorry," she said and cleared her throat, doing a bad job of blanking her face. "Kye, don't mock your sister."

Chastising him was the expected course. Once she'd fulfilled that presumption, and routine was maintained, they went back to their lives. Ducking down, Sky went into the loop of her father's arms and faced the screen, blinking at the controller in his hand.

"What's this?" Sky asked and pressed a button on JD's controller. "This one."

Rylee coughed. JD glanced up, to the screen and back at her, she side nodded.

"Here, Sproutette, you play." Still pressing buttons even as he handed the controller off to Sky, he lifted a leg over their daughter's head to join her backing into the hall.

"Daddy!" Kye called.

"Back in a minute, Sprout," he said, putting his hands to her hips as she reversed out of the kids' earshot while keeping them in view. "You okay, Siren? What do you need?"

The slant of his smile betrayed his hope for a repeat of yesterday's request. Another source of guilt. In refusing her advances, he'd saved them and touched something within her.

"What time is your flight?" she asked, stroking his hands on her hips.

His smile quickly vanished to a frown. "My… what?"

"California," she said. "You're leaving today, aren't you?"

Shaking his head, the furrow of his brow deepened. "No. No way. I'm staying with my family."

"JD," she murmured, trying to be gentle. "You should go."

Searching her eyes, he tried to figure her out. "You said you wouldn't exile me. Babe, I'm sorry for Gabby. I swear I had no idea she was even capable—"

"I'm not exiling you," she said, brushing her thumb across his chin. "I want you to come back when you're done with your business. We told the kids that everything was going back to normal and this is what normal is supposed to be. You said your security friend was going to set us up, right?"

"Stone," he said and nodded. "He's putting together three separate teams for you and the kids."

"I don't need a team."

His expression stayed the same. "You're getting a team. I've seen Stone with his wife, I know he understands how much I value keeping you safe."

"We should get him something special," she said. "To thank him for his help and for mobilizing so quickly. You said he had kids?"

"A son. His wife is pregnant with their daughter now."

Pregnancy. Casting her mind back to that time in her life, she hadn't acknowledged the challenge of carrying her babies. She'd thought only of the optimism and love she had for the children growing inside of her.

"I was so naïve when I was pregnant," she said. "I had no idea how helpless they could make me feel and how much I'd want to protect them. I wonder if his wife knows."

"I don't know the whole story, but before she was his wife, his best friend kidnapped her. That's how I know Stone understands… We can get them something, anything you want, but I don't know if it will ever be enough to repay him for ensuring my family's safety."

"Maybe something for the baby, to celebrate their family's future," she said and looped her arms around his neck. "That's the only time we can keep them safe and with us every second, when they're growing inside us."

"Has this put you off having more?"

More? "We neglected them yesterday," she said, dropping her arms and stepping away. "We got caught up in us and our babies suffered. I don't know what's happening between us or what will, but… if we hadn't wanted to be alone, we'd have been with them."

"They were with family," he said. "What happened was no one's fault, no one's but Gabby."

"I know," she said, running her fingers through her hair. "I know that intellectually, but I feel guilty. I feel guilty for wanting to be alone with you, for being selfish and enjoying being in your arms. We talked and agreed we couldn't be together because it would lessen our effectiveness as parents. We were right. Look what happened the minute we got caught up in each other."

"Babe, we were alone for a minute, maybe two. We didn't run off, we were in shouting distance and were found when needed. This did not happen because we were together."

"I'm tired," she whispered. "I'm confused. I… It probably sounds stupid, but I… Am I being seduced by the idea of family? By the security you can offer us?" He just listened. "Not the money, the support you can give me… I want your support."

"You have it."

"So go to California, let me and the kids get back into

our groove. If we still want to be together when you come back, we'll talk about it without all the emotional stress poisoning the air."

Moving to her, he pushed her back against the wall, crowding up close. "I wanted to be with you before we lost Sky. I know I'll want to be with you in two weeks. And that's it, Ry, the trip is only two weeks."

Cupping his face, she tried to smile. "Then you shouldn't mind taking some time to reflect and breathe… I told you, if we do this, it's going to be difficult to avoid being serious from the get-go. I don't want the kids to know until we're sure."

"I'm sure."

So much emotional energy had been expended in the last twenty-four hours. Snap decisions couldn't be trusted. If they stayed in the same home, she feared the intensity of their attraction would compel them to act on impulse. Their track record on ignoring it spoke for itself.

All of them needed comfort and craved solidarity. The risk in that was insulating themselves, isolating themselves, becoming dependent on each other. That could damage the kids and wouldn't be a secure foundation for a future.

This trip to California, the time apart, was just what they needed. Once he came back to them, with a clear head, they could figure out what came next for the family.

THIRTY-THREE

"YOU'RE WHAT?" Brenna asked.

On Monday, sitting at JD's desk, figuring out the paperwork was easier than breaking the news to her friend.

"We're taking some time apart," she said again.

"But I thought things were, you know… progressing. Is this my fault? Rylee, with Sky, I never got a chance to say—"

"We're moving forward," she said, pausing to look her friend in the eye. "JD and I talked to the kids. His security man got us new bodyguards and the kids have trackers in the bracelets on their wrists."

Bracelets could be taken off, but that would require any would-be kidnapper knowing they contained GPS. When the devices were delivered to the apartment the previous day, JD had fastened them onto each of their children's wrists without mention of the tech or their motivation. To pretty much guarantee they'd never take them off, JD promised that as long as they wore them, he'd always be able to come back to them.

Both kids cried when JD said goodbye. It wasn't easy to watch. Witnessing the tearful goodbye proved one crucial concern. The kids were attached to him; more attached than they'd been when just seeing him once in a while at Grama's house. Once upon a time, she'd feared breaking the news of Daddy moving out if he got his own place in the city. Their farewell, even with the promises of video calling every night, broke her heart.

They'd gotten used to having him around. So had she.

He left, and she consoled her babies, eventually getting them to sleep. When JD called from the plane, she'd gone through the apartment to show each of them in slumber at his request. The kids might be attached to their daddy, but it was obvious the same barb of familiarity had stung him.

"I can't believe he just left, that he bailed so soon after their birthday."

"The trip was planned," she said. "It's two weeks. I'll run the office here, and we'll get back to some semblance of normalcy."

"And then?"

Giving up on the distraction of the paperwork, her arms flopped on the desk. "I don't know, Bren. If we give in to what we're feeling and it doesn't work out…"

"Jamie told me you said that," Brenna said. "And I know why it sounds logical. But like I said to him, you can't go on like this, just ignoring what you want from each other… You're not afraid that it won't work out. You're afraid that it will… The kids have given you an excuse not to get close to any man. You can date, keep it casual, and use the kids as a shield. You don't need that shield with Jamie. In fact, the kids are a magnet for the pair of you instead." How would she ever figure this out? "My brother's not that bad, you know. You're patient, I'm sure you could tolerate him better than I did growing up."

Appreciating her friend's attempt at humor, she breathed out a laugh. "Your brother is an incredible man. I know you don't like to think about it, but he gets me hot, Bren. He has always had this ability to turn me on, even from twenty paces. I don't know how he does it."

With a theatrical look of disgust, Brenna's top lip curled in time with her sound of distaste. "If you think fucking him will get it out of your system, just get it over with."

"I think if I fuck him," she said, licking her lips. "If I open myself to him like that, I'll never want to let him go…"

Being with JD all those years ago had been a thrill, a novelty, an adventure. She'd been so swept up by how enamored they were with each other that she didn't stop to acknowledge what they'd found was unique. She couldn't have known it, not back then. Her experience with men was limited by youth.

After being with the same man through most of college, her one-night stand with JD had been a springboard into the world of dating as an adult in the wide world. More accurately, sex as an adult in the wide world. At that time, she'd thought their connection was standard, that it would be possible to replicate the sensation of being with him. Then the twins happened. She'd never had the time, or wanted, to sit down and think about how special that night had been.

"I think that's what he wants," Brenna said, without concealing her grin.

Sucking her lips around her teeth, she sat up straight. "I am not going to dwell on this. I'm still reeling from the weekend and how amazing he was. That's a world away from enduring living with him full-time."

Settling back in her chair, Brenna crossed her legs and linked her fingers around the front of her knee to raise it higher. "Something you've been doing for weeks."

"Yeah, but at least my bedroom has been a safe space. If he irritates me or creeps under my skin, I can go in there and close the door."

Her friend's smile stretched. "Yeah, and you still can do that, except if he's your boyfriend, you can drag him with you and screw out that frustration. Take it out on him."

Now that was a thought. Letting it fill her mind, her head sank toward her shoulder. She and JD would have dynamite sex, of that she had little doubt. Sex… JD… Was that all they had? Sexual attraction?

"But do I want to walk down the aisle to him?"

Brenna had brought the conversation back to exactly what she'd been trying to avoid thinking about.

"Who else would you rather walk down the aisle

toward?" Brenna asked. "Seriously, Ry, can you imagine feeling for another man the way you do for Jamie? Can you imagine any other man being a father figure in the twins' lives?"

That offended her. "I would never ask JD to step aside as their father. He's an incredible father."

"Yeah, but if you married another man, he'd be their stepfather, living with them, acting in a parental position." Brenna wasn't wrong. "You belong with Jamie, Rylee. You and the twins."

Could she trust certainty? Was there such a thing? Impulse couldn't be embraced and she didn't trust herself. She wanted to take some time to think about it, to be sure, before opening herself up to him. And another thing, JD had become her friend. Their development as co-parents was positive, those feelings, that symbiosis could be threatened by romance.

At one point she'd loved spending time with Baxter and looked forward to seeing him, now her ex provoked infuriation and impatience. She couldn't bear ever thinking of JD that way; she wouldn't be able to handle it. All she wanted was peace and security, yet her life had been filled with drama and change since JD decided he wanted to settle down.

Life was changing whether she wanted it to or not. How did she want this rollercoaster to end? Did she want it to return to the start and go back to how things used to be? Did she want to take a new track, one that would throw in a few loops, but might end in a happier place?

The trouble? Her natural urge was to shun risk and JD was exactly that: risk. Yet he spelled security for her babies, and they were her priority. Her twins trusted and adored their father. Could she do the same thing?

THIRTY-FOUR

"KNOCK, KNOCK." The call raised her head to Roxie, clutching the door, hanging into the office. "I heard a whisper you were looking for me."

"Stone is fast."

"Let's hope his wife doesn't say the same. Can I come in?"

She gestured. "Yes, of course. Sorry."

Roxie strolled across the office, absorbing the features. "No Dyce glass?"

"Dyce?"

"I'll make a call." Rox descended into the guest chair opposite with cool elegance. "Not a bad setup."

"We're still settling in." Pulling her chair into the desk until it dug into her torso, she laid her hands on the tabletop. "I can't express how much we thank you. I know JD would— that footage, it came from you."

"From a guy who watches my stream." Roxie's head bobbed. "He monitors birds or squirrels or something. It didn't occur to him to check the historical feed until the appeal."

"Your appeal."

Modest in her smile, Roxie shook her head. "This was

not me. This was JD and Stone, his people, and Rourke wrote the program. Don't worry about him, Roux will thank him for you… maybe. She might punish him instead, who can tell with those two?"

The woman was too kind, humility was unexpected. Roxanna Kyst was more than the cover she projected to the world.

"Can I ask you something personal?"

"My favorite kind of something. Go on."

"Zairn Lomond…"

"I think he's seeing someone, but I can ask."

That quick wit endeared her. "Right," she said with a quiet laugh and picked up a pen to distract her fingers. "It's none of my business, but…"

"No, we don't swing." Shock took her eyes to Roxie's smile. "I'll have to keep guessing if you don't spit it out."

"Do people actually ask you things like that?"

"You'd be amazed how brazen people can be. To most of them, we're not real people. Gives them the impression they're entitled to us."

"And that doesn't upset you?"

"You know what would upset me? If Zairn asked that question. If he asked it seriously, anyway. In our world, our life, there are strong boundaries. We know what's important: each other, our friends, the people we care about. Everything else is bullshit; it's theater. Fun that allows us to prioritize our true reality. What we are doesn't belong to them, and who cares if they think it does? I get to fall asleep in my man's arms any time I want. I can pick up the phone and pour my grief or stress into him without question or judgment. We're one unit. Completely open, completely safe. Your guy has to be your safe space. JD seems decent, like he's in it with you."

"We're not together."

"I heard that about you. What did you want to ask?"

"You made a comment about, a joke, about 3D kids."

Roxie cringed. "Yeah, I'm sorry about that."

"No, it's fine, I… Have you talked about it? With Zairn? Having kids?"

"Yeah. We have embryos on ice, just in case. We'll

get around to it sometime."

"Doesn't it scare you? Until recently, people didn't know JD was the twins' father. As soon as we go public…"

"His ex would've been crazy, public or not. But I get it, you're worried his wealth makes targets of your kids. It does. I won't lie to you."

She swallowed. "How do I minimize that threat? Counter the massive imbalance between what he is and what we are."

Another smile from Roxie. "Don't look now, but I think 'we' is growing to include 'he,' or the other way around. There's no imbalance when he's standing on your side. I don't know Dawes, at all, but I saw it this weekend. The way he looks at you, how he was with Kye. Jamison Dawes knows where his family is. In good times, in bad. What you faced this weekend is probably the worst thing any parent can go through." Short of a negative outcome, but she wouldn't give that thought a platform. "You did it together. Didn't you notice?"

"I wouldn't have got through it without him. He saved our little girl."

"And jeopardized her too."

"No," she said, unwilling to accept that. "It's not his fault Gabby is insane. We can't be held responsible for someone's actions just because we used to sleep with them. Would you blame Zairn for the same?"

"Oh, please, we could write a book about that. A whole series on his exes." She sighed. "I'm crazier than most of them." The blonde pointed a straight finger. "Most." She faltered to a grin and whispered, "but I have it on good authority that he loves my crazy too."

"Sounds like quite the guy."

"Yours is too…" Yeah, was that enough or was she being selfish in justifying her desire? "What do you say to going for a drink tonight? No Crimson clubs in Seattle, but we own a bunch of bars and other clubs. We can tear up the town … I've never been arrested in Washington. Not yet anyway. Commits misdemeanors, will travel. Z will be thrilled."

Whatever that meant. "Uh… Thanks for the offer,

but I have two little ones to go home with.”

“Right. Sure, sure. We can stay indoors; I can have fun anywhere. You got music?”

“Music? Yeah, we have music. Brenna’s coming over tonight.”

“Girls’ night! I want to get to know her better too.”

“Not much fun, keeping things clean for the little ones. They could get up any time and Kye—”

“He can hang with us,” Roxie said. “We’ll give him the inside track on the opposite sex before he hits his teens.” God, what a thought. “You don’t want to hang out, that’s fine. But we’re happy to include the kids. Lilya’s pregnant, so we take it easy for her. We’re almost all guy-less up here, why shouldn’t we celebrate the sisterhood?”

With the women who’d saved her little girl.

“Okay,” she said. “If you’re ready for two inquisitive five-year-olds.”

“Jane will melt, I swear to you. They’ll have a lot more aunts before the night is over.”

“Jane? Collier?”

“She lives to care for people. Don’t be surprised if she cries.”

“Why would she cry?”

“She’s… too pretty. We’ll bring the party if you bring the babies.” Roxie showed both palms. “No liquor, no strippers.”

She laughed. “Are those Zairn’s rules?”

“God, no, he’d never put restrictions on me. And I’d never put them on him. We respect each other enough to know the boundaries. Boundaries, boundaries.” Roxie sucked in a belabored breath. “Listen to me, his words in my mouth. Don’t ever tell him I said that.”

Not much chance of her running into Zairn Lomond any time soon. She could see the appeal of Roxie though, how she won friends and brought a light, joyous air to the room. Not something she’d processed the day they met.

***

"IT'S ABOUT THE MAN, GENIUS!" Roxie declared, seated on the floor between the couch and the coffee table. "Pick the man. Everything else gets worked out… Toria told me that."

"You put up all kinds of barriers for Zairn, but he was there, waiting," Jane said. "When you were ready."

Jane, Roxie, and Lilya brought party food and decorations perfect for the kids. The little ones ate it up and loved dancing around the room with their new friends. Still, unfortunately, time marched on. As much as the twins would love to stay up all night, responsibilities waited for them tomorrow. Brenna nabbed bedtime duty and was currently watching a movie with them in Kye's bed. The music was turned down, and the group had become more reflective, giving her a chance to get to know the women better.

"Z was in Tokyo when I was ready," Roxie said, "or mid-air, whatever time zone. My man, the mind reader." She sighed. "I rag on it, but I love it."

"You love him," Jane said. "The wedding will be spectacular! I can't wait!"

"It better be. Most expensive favor I ever gave."

A favor? What was the favor?

"I'm planning it," Jane said, answering her unasked question. "No budget, no boundaries, just the perfect wedding."

The front door opened and their, temporarily absent, last guest came rushing in: Roux Radley.

"Okay, I'm sorry, I'm back." They all gestured to quiet her and she cringed. "Sorry."

Kicking off her shoes, the woman came to the living room and dropped onto the couch.

"That was quick," Jane said.

"Yeah," Roxie agreed. "How did you get all the way to the apartment and—"

"We did it in the car downstairs."

"He drove over here?"

Like it was no big deal, Roux shrugged and picked up her virgin wine from the end table. "He doesn't do well by himself."

"Rourke loves solitude, he hates people, though not as much as K2. You're his exception, Roux, honey."

"I'm not exactly another person in his view, in our view, it's… complicated."

"Never seen anything simpler."

"You relegated him to the apartment," Lilya said. "Why aren't you staying in the Grand with us?"

A sly, smug smile lit the woman's lips. "We have memories in that apartment… And I like to watch him take out the trash."

"Make him work for it, huh? It's because he's the only guy, isn't it? We're intimidating, I get it. With Z, Knox, and Zach in California, JD too, Rourke can't handle all of us."

"He can't handle Roux when they have an audience," Lilya said. "Just standing next to the two of you feels X-rated."

"Xavien," she said. "Xavien Rourke, that's who you're with?"

"Yep. Begrudgingly. He's rich and hung, that's really what it is. And he buys wine, lots of liquor actually, keeps me lubed so I don't wander off. I don't know how I put up with him."

She laughed. "Your secret's safe."

Brazen, Roux blinked. "Oh no, he knows it. I can't stand him; the feeling is mutual. If it wasn't for the sex, we'd murder each other."

"Or yourselves to prove a point."

Uh, okay. That was a setup probably impossible to figure out. Roux disappeared into her phone, so she moved onto the other women.

She pointed at Lilya. "Zachary Kintyre." And got a nod, so switched to Roxie. "We know you're with Zairn." Everyone nodded along. "You know who I'd be fascinated to learn more about?"

When she landed her attention on Jane, the others followed.

The meek woman blushed. "What?"

"Knox," Lilya said. "She wants to know more about your guy."

"He's uh… amazing. Incredible. I'm so lucky to—"

"You'll never get dirt from Jane." Roxie sighed. "She doesn't know the meaning of the word. Honestly, the kind and gracious thing is completely genuine. And, alas, the only antidote is loving her. Try as you might, you'll never be able to dislike her, it'll never happen."

"Knox is private," Jane whispered.

"Doesn't mean you can't gush," Roux said without looking up from her screen, "if that's, you know, what regular folks do."

Roxie and Lilya laughed. "I would love to hear you gush about Rourke."

"Oh, okay…" Putting her phone aside, Roux sat up on the edge of the couch and cleared her throat. "Xavie baby, is uh…" Her jaw moved, she pondered until she hit on something. "I said he was rich, right?"

"You mentioned it, yeah."

"And his cock—"

"He's hung, yeah, you said that too…"

"Okay, uh…" She snapped her fingers. "He knows how to drive a stick."

They all laughed.

"That could have so many meanings."

"Oh no, I'm a better driver there, and his stick is *always* under my control," Roux said and sipped some more wine. "We know each other's guys, for better or worse, we don't know yours."

In the spotlight, she was quick to shake her head. "No, JD and I aren't… We're not together."

Roxie raised a hand. "Been there…"

"Done that," Lilya finished.

"You have two babies together. Live together. Work together—"

"It's temporary."

"Is it?"

And the silence lingered. Each of the women waited. She looked from one to the next and eventually gave in with a groan.

"I have no idea."

"Do you trust Brenna? We don't have to worry about

her being a double agent—"

"No! God, no, she's more on my side than his." She twisted her glass by the stem. "JD and I were a one-night thing, and then the twins… In the years between then and now, we didn't see much of each other. Any of each other, really. His mom and sister moved here to be close to the twins. I had that buffer, there was no need for JD and me to hang out."

"But now you are hanging out."

"We're something."

"If he's hot and rich and good to your kids, what else do you need? Did the sex suck?"

"Nooo," she said, drawing the syllable out. "Definitely didn't suck. I was just… inexperienced."

"Okay, so…" Lilya said, "you're not inexperienced anymore."

"Nice way to call her a slut," Roux joked.

"I didn't mean it like that. She knows I didn't mean it like—you know I didn't mean it like that."

"Nothing wrong with being a slut," Roxie said. "I'm a slut, just so happens it's only for one guy."

Roux raised her glass in appreciation. "Hear, hear."

Back to the point at hand. "I don't want our relationship to impact what we each have with the kids. And since the weekend…"

"She's right," Lilya said. "Going through that, it's too much emotion to process. If they jumped into a relationship now, they'd always wonder if it was real or a result of the intense circumstances."

"Don't be practical," Jane whimpered. "Follow your heart."

"You didn't."

"I did." Jane squirmed. "I just fell a little behind."

"You were terrified." Roxie and Jane's rapport was more akin to sisters than acquaintances. "And rightly so, I was the same. Slow on the uptake. See with guys like ours, they're risk takers."

"So they took a risk on us?" Lilya asked. "Zach was sure before I was."

"My Casanova was in love with me months before I got a clue, goddamn him." Roxie next addressed Jane. "And Knox had to damn near chase you down, woman."

"He stalked her," Roux said.

"No, that was crazy London Guy."

"Uh, the story I heard included Knox traipsing all around the damn world after her."

"Mostly the country," Jane objected, like that made a difference.

A bold knock on the door got them all looking around, confused. All but Roux.

"That's for me, one sec." The woman got up to dash across the apartment on her tiptoes and opened the front door like it was her place. "You do come to heel." Roux was all smug taunting. "Clever boy. Later we'll try roll over. If you're good, you might get your tummy tickled."

"That's it?" an unimpressed, almost deadpan, male asked from the hallway.

"Yes. What a good Boy Scout you are. What a good boy," Roux said as though talking to a puppy, and reached up, maybe to ruffle his hair. "You're dismissed."

As Roux backed off, a hand appeared to grab her back. "Oh no, you don't get off that easy, Babycakes," the guy said and yanked on Roux. "Good boys get treats."

That's when he came into view, locked in a passionate clinch with the teasing woman who couldn't keep her feet on the floor. Out they went and the door closed.

"They'll be a minute," Lilya said.

"I have neighbors."

Who wouldn't appreciate walking in on, whatever that was, in the hallway.

"He pays them off," Roxie said. "Always does."

"It works for them."

"I know, it's tough to wrap our heads around how the rules change in this stratosphere. We come from a different world," Roxie said like she'd read the script a hundred times. "Well, us minus Lilya."

"I am not billionaire rich."

"You come from money, old money. The traipsing

around the world thing isn't a big deal with means like that."

"I traveled for work."

"See." Roxie gestured with her glass. "Like JD."

Again, all eyes on her. "I told him we can never travel together."

"What did he say?"

"That we could bring the kids."

"Yeah, and you can tutor them on the road, if you get to that stage."

"Is that a life for a child? They need stability, structure. Routine is important."

"Your kids are important, no one can say otherwise."

"She uses them as a shield," Brenna said, bringing their attentions around to the hallway from where she emerged. "She's totally in love with my brother. God knows why."

"Are they asleep?"

Brenna came to join her in the armchair. "Both out like a light. We called Jamie."

"To say goodnight? He's adamant about not missing it."

"I left my phone on video in there."

"Aww," Jane swooned, and the other women softened too. "He loves his babies."

"One thing I don't doubt."

"Not anymore," Brenna said. "You used to wonder when he didn't show up. Now he shows up, what's left not to love?"

And that was the crux of it. She had to stop looking at JD like her children's father and instead as a man. Like the night they met. That man. Could heat like that be sustained? Maybe not. But in these last few weeks with him, their desire had mellowed to something richer and more vibrant. Something deeper? JD wasn't just a lay, wouldn't be if they jumped into a relationship. If they were together, one day, the kids would move out and they'd be on their own. Did she want him to only be a father to their children or the man she'd love until death they did part?

THIRTY-FIVE

"WHY DO YOU not be wedded?" Sky asked at dinner that Sunday night.

She stopped eating to look at her daughter straightening her spaghetti. "What, sweetpea?"

"I want Daddy to live with Sky," Sky said. "Always."

Kye's mouth was full when he chimed in. "Me too. Daddy can live here."

JD had been gone for a week, a whole week, yet he was still prominent in their children's minds, and not only because he called every night. He hadn't gone far from her thoughts either; he'd wormed his way into all their affections. Okay, so the twins had always adored him. Still, she hadn't expected her child to ask such a direct question.

Okay, play it cool.

Subduing her shock, she set down her fork. "Well, guys, Daddy and I never got married."

"Why not?" Sky asked. "If yous do it, he'll live here always."

Marriage was so much more than that. Oh to see the world from the perspective of a five-year-old.

Not one to pass up an opportunity, this was a chance to get their opinions. "Would you like him to live here?"

Kye chased a vegetable around his plate with his fork. He wouldn't know what he was chasing, but seemed to enjoy the pursuit, typical male.

"I love Daddy," her distracted son said.

"I love Daddy more," Sky said. "Daddy is my friend."

"Daddy is friends with both of you. He's Mommy's friend too."

Sky stopped eating, blinked once, and twice, like she was trying to put her thoughts together. Being patient, she waited to see what her daughter came up with. A part of her worried the little one might ask something she couldn't answer. No going back now.

"Why did Daddy leave us?" Sky asked.

She took her daughter's hand. "We told you, Daddy is coming back next week, sweetpea. He didn't leave because he wanted to, he had work things to take care of."

"Daddy is the boss," Kye said, sucking the piece of mushroom from his fork between his lips. "And rich."

"Yes," she said. "He has a lot of money. But we don't love Daddy for his money, we love him because he's our friend. He's good to us. He's a nice person and he is good fun, isn't he? You have fun with Daddy?"

Kye grinned and nodded fast, still chewing the mushroom. "Daddy's the best."

"Do you love Daddy too, Mommy?"

That put her on the spot. Sky kept blinking. Her innocent, expectant eyes never wavered. Kye slowed in his chewing and stopped trying to figure out what he'd put in his mouth to await her response. Neither of them appeared too eager, though she got a sense the importance of her answer wasn't lost on them.

For a week, she'd been thinking about JD and what kind of future they could have. What kind of future did she want with him? As usual, she kept coming back to one thing: she just didn't know what the future held.

She could play it out either way. The relationship fell apart, they ended up hating each other and their family ended up full of friction and anger. The alternative was everything went great, she and JD got married, made it work, and life was everything the fairytales promised every little girl.

"I do love Daddy," she answered. The best course of action was the truth. "He gave me you two and I'll always be thankful for that."

"Will Daddy come back and live with us forever?" Kye asked.

Sky picked up a string of spaghetti with her fingertips and sucked it into her mouth. "Always. I don't want him to go away again."

"Finish your dinner," she said. "When you're done, Mommy will call Daddy and you can talk to him while I tidy up."

"Then you talk to Daddy?" Sky said. "Tell him to come home to us."

"He'll come home, sweetpea. But you can ask him during your bedtime call." As the kids always did. "He knows you want him to come back to us."

"And never go away again," Kye said. "Never. Never."

Fearless. Her kids were sure and not afraid to say it. Both went back to their food like their worlds weren't on such fragile foundations. Truthfully, they ate better when a conversation with their father was the prize at the other end.

JD was a good influence on them, no doubt about that. Would she disrupt that if she gave into her feelings for him? If they got to the stage JD couldn't stand the sight of her, or the sound of her voice, the happy setup couldn't continue.

But they were mature adults, right? Surely they could see past their feelings for the sake of the children if need be. Their babies had just told her what they wanted; did she want the same thing?

***

CHECKING ON THE KIDS was part of her routine. Each night, the little ones took turns to have their father in their rooms with them until they fell asleep.

Her dark phone still sat on Kye's pillow next to his

little slumbering head. She leaned over to get it while admiring his peace.

Beautiful. Perfect. She kissed his head.

"When do I get to watch you sleep?"

JD's gruff voice startled her a little. Usually she just hung up, if he hadn't already.

"Shh," she whispered and rushed into the hallway, holding the phone to her chest. "If you wake him, I'll have to take him into my bed."

"What a life, jealous of my own son."

An exhale of a laugh lingered in her voice. "JD…"

"You've been avoiding me."

"I have not." She went into her room and closed the door. "Okay, I have."

What was the point of lying?

"Because…"

"JD," she sighed again and went to sit on the bed, leaning against the headboard, phone face down next to her. "Because I don't think straight when we're together. When you're… in me."

"That's a whole other conversation. One I'm happy to have when you lose the clothes."

"You know, this is exactly what I'm talking about." Her smile was irrepressible. "I hear your voice and feel you close and… I don't know what the hell's going on anymore."

"I wouldn't know either. The office, the kids, those are the only things we talk about. Is this your decision? Are you pulling away?"

"The office and the kids are safe subjects. The cogs are turning, JD. I'm looking after your empire and the future of it. Lilya stuck around to help with some of the executive stuff at Duo." Which he already knew. "She left on Friday. She's an amazing woman."

"I had dinner with them last night."

"Lilya and Kintyre?"

"And a few others," he said. "This feels like we're talking about work again."

"Work makes sense. There's a formula to it. An end goal."

"And there's no end goal with us?"

"What is it you want to talk about, JD?" Irritation tickled her offense. "You want phone sex and naked pictures and—"

"Whoa, whoa, whoa. I said slow, didn't I? I said we were going to do this right."

"And you're rushing me."

"If I am, I'm sorry. If work and the kids are all you want to talk about, we'll stick to them. Can I at least tell you that I miss you?"

And damn him, but that didn't feel like a line. "I miss you too."

Why was she getting herself so deliberately wound up? Was she looking for an excuse to pull away? Whatever the reason, he'd done nothing wrong. It wouldn't be fair to paint him as the bad guy just to give herself an out.

"That's something."

Such patience and understanding. The man from the bar all those years ago had matured, just as she had.

"It's stupid, I know," she admitted. "I'm freaking out."

She flopped forward onto her face, the phone bounced closer to her ear.

"You're being smart. What you said about serious is right. If we do this, there's no going back." Not without leaving carnage in their wake. "It's tough being so far away."

At home, she had work and the kids to give her stability. JD was the one working away from his family, going home to an empty hotel room every night.

She rolled onto her back. "You're not dating down there, are you?"

"If you want to hop a jet, we can do date night any time you want."

"One good thing about dating the father of my children, finding a babysitter will be as much your responsibility as mine." He didn't respond, now who was freaking? "You remember we have kids, right?" Had they been disconnected? "Short, cute, a boy and a girl, there's two of them. We did paternity. Any of this ringing a bell?"

"Just doing a quick internet search. I'll find some stranger to sit with them while we have adult time."

"Uh huh," she said, not buying any sincerity in him being so glib.

His snicker proved her right. "I want to be responsible for all of you, Ry."

"I don't need a babysitter."

"Sure we'll find another way I can play Daddy for you."

"No daddy fetish here. Didn't we cover that the night we met? Although…"

"Although?" he prompted.

"You were right about it being a turn on."

"Ha! Playing daddy does turn you on."

"Not in a sex dom kind of way. I… love the way you love them." For lack of a better way to put it. "Other people love our kids and find them adorable, but they don't get it, get it. These last few weeks, seeing you interact with them daily. Now you get it like I get it… don't you?"

"Truth?" Always. "I regret ever spending a second away from them."

"Ah!" she teased. "So my heart's just collateral damage in this. You're seducing me to get close to them."

"Is it working? The seducing?"

Boy, he had no idea. "Maybe."

"How about your heart? It in deep enough to get hurt?"

Angling the phone, she focused on the screen, on him in the dark, sitting up, the phone obviously lying at his side.

"Look at me, JD."

He picked up the phone to do as she asked. "Hey, babe."

Smooth, yet genuine. "We almost lost our little girl."

"Siren—"

"Let me finish."

"I'm afraid if we get caught up in each other that the kids will suffer. But I'm also afraid if we don't see this through, we'll always live in wonder. Be each other's 'the one who got away.' Are we going to turn around in ten years or twenty, at

Sky's graduation or Kye's wedding, and still not have the answer to the question?"

"You know my stance. You know what I want."

"I never want to go through what we did with Sky again. Yes, it's made me more aware of how precious they are and how we have to keep them safe. It also skews perspective. We get caught up in the BS drama of life and fail to see what's important."

"The kids have always been important to you."

"I'm not just talking about the kids." She licked her lips and shifted to a more comfortable position. "Sky asked tonight why we weren't married."

He laughed. "That's our girl, straight to the heart of the matter."

"She's never shy."

"What did you say?"

"Just that we never did. They want you to stay here, at home, with us, always."

"That's what I want too."

And she was the only holdout.

"What if it works?" she murmured. "What if we try the relationship thing and it works out?"

He squinted. "I fail to see the problem."

"What have we been doing for the last five years? If we're meant to be together, why the fuck have we wasted all this time?"

"Only remedy to that is not to waste more. You said the night we met we'd have to see how this played out and the movie isn't over yet."

So long as they had kids, the movie wouldn't be over. "And you said that same night you're not the kind of guy to move on or be dissuaded. Are you sure you want this? Have you really thought about what it will mean to take on a relationship and fatherhood on a permanent basis? You can't just do whatever you want anymore, you'll be answerable to me and the kids. You'll have to factor us into your plans, discuss and debate rather than just suit yourself."

"Someone once told me they wanted their own slice of the world. Their own little corner. Somewhere safe and happy. At the time, the notion passed me by. I didn't get it. Now I know where my corner is, my slice, and I want to share it with you and our children."

"And if the twins are it? If I don't want to have more children?"

"We'll talk about that," he said. "Together. I wouldn't walk away from you if that was your decision, I can tell you that." Which was a lot given he'd walked away from Gabby for that reason. "But I would expect you to hear me, to give my perspective a fair hearing."

"We'd be equals, in everything. I won't defer to you."

"I wouldn't expect you to defer; we have met. I want to be the one who props you up, Siren. You've done that for me for five years without either of us realizing it. It's your work with the kids, your willingness to let them build relationships with my family that has ensured my connections with them. I'm sorry you went through so much alone, babe."

"I wasn't alone. My babies got me through every day, and you're as responsible as me for their existence."

Quiet settled over them. Not uncomfortable, just joint appreciation for their positions.

"My norm is deciding and going with my gut. Yours is to be practical. I expected this. Once I thought about it, made my decision, I knew you wouldn't give into me on impulse."

"Again. You knew I wouldn't give into you on impulse again." They shared a smile. "If I was a believer in destiny…"

"You'd say the kids forced us together. I don't want it to be that way, Ry. This is about us. You and me. The kids are fine. Our relationships with them are not in question. It started with us, baby…"

Would it end with them or simply end them? JD. Hers? Could she give herself to him in return?

THIRTY-SIX

TWO WEEKS DIDN'T sound like a lot until one was living it and separated from something valuable. Life was topsy-turvy. No longer was she an inconsequential creative consultant in the marketing department. Somehow she'd graduated to the CEO's desk on the top floor.

The trip that was meant to take only two weeks had spilled into a third. JD promised her and the kids he'd be back by Friday. On Tuesday, time dragged. The whole spell without him had actually. Could she get through another three days without him? Although finding her rhythm in her new professional role, she didn't feel like a natural.

When it came to work anything, JD had been on the end of the phone whenever she needed him. Even in her uncertain moments, he'd shown nothing but confidence in her and wouldn't even think of giving her a reprieve.

As long as she believed in herself, she could do anything. His words. It sounded like some baloney he'd feed the kids, but she accepted it and followed the adage of faking it, not that she really thought she'd ever "make it".

"I'm sorry, gentlemen," she said to the ten men seated around her conference table. "Those factors simply will not affect our timeline."

At the end of that sentence, a familiar figure sauntered into the doorway, his hands sunk in his pockets as he propped himself against the frame. Fuck, her stomach flipped. Her skin shimmered and her heart sped up. JD. God, relief! No, calm, keep cool. What was he doing there three days early? Who cared? He was a welcome surprise.

Their eyes met and she smiled but had to quickly forget his arrival when one of her guests spoke. "But Miss Hampton, we—"

"I'm sorry," she said. "Duo will not expedite their order. If this creates a problem for your company, we'll be more than happy to take our business elsewhere. We would not want to inconvenience you in any way, we value your corporate friendship."

Twisting in his chair, her guest appealed to the man in the doorway fixated on her. "Mr. Dawes, please, can you—"

"Miss Hampton is doing just fine," JD drawled, a smirk touching his lips. "Please, carry on."

"Actually, we're done," she said, picking up the documents from the table and gathering them into their binder. "Thank you for your time, gentlemen. Mieux will show you out."

The men took a second to catch on that they were being flung out. Eventually they blustered and rose, forcing JD to step inside out of their way of the exit. Ignoring their appeals, his focus remained on her.

He waited until they were all gone before speaking. "We wouldn't want to inconvenience you," JD quoted. "We value your corporate friendship. What a nice way to say go fuck yourself, but we might use you again in future."

Getting up to round the table, she hugged the binder to her chest. "They'll call."

He pushed away from the wall. "How do you know?"

"They always do," she said. "And we'll get a discount."

"What makes you so sure?" he asked, coming to a stop in front of her.

No way he didn't know the answer to his own

question, what was the harm in humoring him?

"He wants to bolster this quarter's numbers to appease investors. Without our order, he won't do that. Investors will be edgy, and Pullen has a hair trigger. He'll solicit our order next quarter, I'll hesitate, question his ability to deliver, and he'll panic." Straightening JD's tie over his buttons, she laid her fingers on the fabric for a brief second. "He can't disappoint his investors two quarters in a row and his relationship with your affiliates has shored up support from his investors in the past. If it seems he no longer has the ear of the boss, you, investors will threaten to bolt. I'll hint at a discount, he'll sell it to investors by citing your friendship. And we get a boost in our quarterlies, which will coincide with Duo's major relaunch thus, it will help us attract new clients."

"And you figured all this out…"

"Around the same time I saw how tight he was clutching his briefcase… Don't underestimate the importance of body language," she quoted.

His smile betrayed his own recognition.

"Our daughter just keeps on giving, doesn't she?"

"Have you seen them?"

He shook his head. "I thought I'd surprise them, pick them up, take them home… but I wanted to check in with you first."

She grinned and pulled the binder higher. "Check I hadn't wrecked your company?"

He trailed a fingertip down her jaw. "Did you hear me ask about the company?" he murmured. "All I've thought about is you. You and the kids. I had to see your face, to look at you."

"I thought you weren't coming back until Friday."

"Sorry to see me?"

"Not even a little," she said, curling her fingers around the back of his neck to try drawing him down.

Despite the moment of subdued surprise on his face, he didn't fight her. Except they never got the chance to see where the moment might have gone because Greg and Jim walked in.

"Hello, Rylee!" Jim declared.

Letting go of JD, she backed up, hiding her smirk better than he hid his irritation. "Nice to see you, gents," she said, going over to offer each a kiss on the cheek. "How was your trip?"

"Had its ups and downs," Greg said, rocking back on his heels. "Boss got a little testy at times."

"Would you gentlemen like to join us for dinner tonight?" she asked. "I still have an hour or two here, but I can rustle something up, if you want to come over—"

"No," JD said, becoming the center of attention. "You're uninvited."

Talk about rude. Even the glare he wore was unnecessary.

"JD," she said. "Wow, what happened to your manners? There's plenty of space at our table and the kids like entertaining."

"Daddy has plans for tonight," JD said, taking her shoulders.

She drew her eyes to his. "You're not getting laid, JD."

Greg laughed and Jim sort of choked.

The man at her back just gave her shoulders a squeeze. "I have plans for my family tonight and you two are not a part of them."

"I think Rylee just nixed your plans," Greg said.

Leaving JD's grasp, she opened the binder to sort through the papers as she passed the men to leave the conference room.

At the desk that used to be hers, a little brunette wearing big glasses bounced to her feet. "Can you copy these and send them?" she asked, handing off a couple of sheets to Mieux who nodded and righted her glasses while looking behind her. She glanced back to the trio coming toward them. "Oh, that's Greg, JD, and Jim. They lurk and have the fancy job titles, so you know, we pretend like they're in charge and important."

Carrying on into the office, she zipped her binder and tossed it to the desk before bending over to pull off one heel and then the other.

"Got a round up for us?" Greg asked.

"I kept JD in the loop every day," she said, sitting in the chair and logging into her laptop. "I tell you, I won't be sorry to hand you back the reins, Overlord."

"Sorry to disappoint, but you won't be," JD said, pushing aside something in her in-tray to look at what was beneath. His brows rose and he picked it up. "What's this?" He leafed through it. "Apartment details?"

"It's nothing," she said, boosting up to take it from him.

He just smiled and slipped his hands in his pockets. "For me or you?"

"It's something stupid, a misunderstanding," she said, looking through the pictures in the document. "The apartment upstairs from us is on the market. I called because I wanted to be nosey, and you know, we don't need eight bedrooms, but it wouldn't be an insane idea to have more space. You need a proper office, and I don't want the kids to have computers in their rooms, so a den might be a good idea, and…" When she peeked up at him, he was grinning. "What?"

He feigned confusion, like he was trying to figure something out. "That sounds… wait, does that sound like maybe I am going to get laid?"

Slapping down the schedule, she glared at him. "Not any time you're wearing that smirk," she said. "You don't think we need more space?"

"Depends how many more kids we're going to have. Wouldn't a house make more sense?"

"Too far outside the city. If you're going to be a father to my children, I want you to be a present one… and I like apartment living… and what did you mean about not taking back the reins? I want you to have the reins."

"I have an architect coming tomorrow," he said. "A friend in California inspired me. I was thinking, maybe glass bricks or something, we can split this office down the middle. There's plenty of space in here. We cut a wedge behind the assistant's desk and we can have two doors… though we'll need one between the offices too, for sex in the afternoons."

Folding her forearms on the desk, she leaned across

them. "Going to schedule that, are you?"

Greg cleared his throat. "We're just going to…"

He pointed over his shoulder before he and Jim slipped out.

JD came around the desk and propped himself against it just beside her. "Can you be home in an hour?"

"I have some calls to make," she said. "Emails to deal with."

"If I do the emails, can you be home in an hour?"

She nodded. "Sure, if you need me to be, why?"

"I've got something cooking," he said, touching her face. "The surprise I never got to give the kids on their birthday, I've got someone setting it up now."

"Go to them, JD. They will burst when they see you. They've missed you so much."

"Are they the only ones?"

She smiled and wasn't surprised to see him enjoying her reaction. "Your sister has been on my case since you left. You haven't lost an inch of ground, I'll tell you that."

Bending down, he traced his lips over hers. "I want to gain ground with you, Ry… I want it all." Tipping his head to the side, he focused on the apartment listing on her desk. "I'll buy you a building if it makes a difference."

"I don't care about the money, I never cared about the money," she said, rolling her chair closer to fold her hands on his thigh. "We do need to talk, but the kids… I want them to be your priority."

"I'm going to pick them up and take them home now," he said. "I want Mommy home soon."

"She will be. Brenna and Lotta are taking the twins camping this weekend. Maybe you could spend tomorrow with them? They're leaving on Thursday and won't be back until Sunday."

With a fingertip on her jaw, he stroked her, considering something for a few seconds. "You thought I was coming home on Friday… they'd have been away… we'd have been alone."

She laughed. "It wasn't orchestrated for the benefit of your cock. They got the opportunity through a youth group

Lotta volunteers with. I wasn't sure about it, about letting them go, but I told the security guys to hire some more people and bill you."

"No argument here."

"I know," she murmured and rose from the chair to lean in against him. "That's because you're a good father."

"Turning you on again?"

She nodded slowly, her focus on his lips.

JD grabbed her so fast and tight that she gasped. Her heart rate rose when he gathered her skirt into his fists, slow, his gaze mesmerizing her.

With her skirt at her hips, ass exposed, lines between them warped and faded. "This is sexual harassment."

He snatched her against the desk, boosting her onto it to move between her thighs. "I'm not on the clock," he said. "We're not colleagues, we're parents."

"You're distracting me."

The heat of need and intensity of arousal tempted her to further part her legs when he ran his fingertips up the back of her thighs.

"You've been distracting me since the goddamn minute I got here," he said, leaning over her, raising her knees to his hips. "Ask me again, Siren. Ask me now."

Sliding a hand up the middle of his chest, she licked her lips. "Not yet," she whispered. "Not here. This weekend will be ours, JD… if you want it."

"Oh, I want it," he said. "They're leaving Thursday night?"

"Afternoon."

"I'm coming into the office tomorrow; we'll get through this week's work. Thursday morning will be quality time with the twins… We're both taking Friday off."

Curling her fingers around his tie, she pulled him further down as she reclined, holding herself at a forty-five-degree angle, crunching her abs.

"You think you're getting something from me that we'll need a whole day together? Alone?"

"I think I want to find out."

The phone beside them rang just before his mouth

met hers.

Without changing position, she grabbed the handset. "Rylee Hampton."

"Just checking in, Rylee," Marie said. Daycare had her direct line. "What time will they be picked up today?"

Given she sometimes had more or less work on any given day, the kids' pick up time varied. Sometimes their aunt or grandmother were the ones there to get them.

"Their father's coming to surprise them now," she said, smiling at JD. "Can you help them put on their shoes? Don't tell them who's coming."

"They'll be thrilled," Marie said. "We'll get them ready."

"Thank you," she said and hung up. "They're waiting for you."

"And we'll be waiting for you," he said and dipped forward to steal her mouth.

Oh, he knew how to draw her in. His kiss was too much to resist. Sinking into the seduction, a whimper slipped from her mouth to his. Giving more of herself, her legs rose higher. They should never have started, how would she avoid giving in now she'd had a taste?

She didn't hear the office door open, just the gasp from that direction. "Miss Hampton, I'm sorry."

JD stopped kissing her and straightened up, helping her sit.

Perched on the edge of the desk, she twisted to look over her shoulder. "It's okay, Mieux," she said, patting JD's chest and sliding off the desk to sit in the chair again. "JD is the father of my children."

"I didn't know you were married," Mieux said, tentative in coming across to put files on her desk.

"We're not," JD said, slipping his hands into his pockets. "Yet."

She pulled herself in at the desk and picked up the file to see the list of calls inside. "Oh, now he wants to get married."

"Only because I want to get you pregnant," JD said and bobbed his brows to the blushing Mieux as he sauntered toward the door. "Hurry home, honey, we'll be waiting for you."

THIRTY-SEVEN

IF SHE HADN'T been crazy for JD before arriving home to find her living room transformed into an underwater grotto, she was after. There were rocks on the floor, sand, some kind of plants bedded in like seaweed strewn through the waterfall wall features. Interspersed were built in fish tanks containing all kinds of wondrous aquatic creatures. Special lighting and a sound system brought the illusion to life.

Sky hadn't wanted to leave, so all of them ended up sleeping there in the ocean together. The wonderland was still there when the kids were packing up for their vacation with their aunts.

"Please, please, please," Sky begged. "Mommy, please—"

"Daddy promises the ocean will be here when you get back," JD said.

It would? That didn't seem smart. Okay, so the installation wasn't doing anyone any harm exactly. To nothing except her furniture, which was stuck in storage until they dismantled the scene. But was it realistic for it to be there indefinitely? The kids needed boundaries.

JD had prepped and packed the kids ready for Brenna. She herself had run home just in time to see them off.

"Say goodbye," Brenna said. "Lotta's waiting downstairs."

"Oh, babies, I love you," she said, kissing them both at the door.

"We have to leave," Brenna said. "We'll call you from the road."

Both kids waved and hugged her again. Brenna took their hands and led them out, leaving her staring at a closed door. She had never been so far apart from her babies before. Even when they went to stay with their grandmother, they were right across town. This was a different thing.

No, no, she'd made a terrible mistake. They wouldn't have gone far, she could get them back—

JD's splayed fingertips touched her head. "While you're down there…"

Spinning around, she turned before surging to her feet. "Don't you miss them already? What if something happens or they're hurt?" she asked, glaring. "How can you make jokes?"

"They're both wearing their trackers, and have enough security to raise their own army," he said, winding his arms around her. "Now you're all mine. I'll distract you. What do you want?"

"What do I want?" she asked, suspicion narrowing one of her eyes. "That's your seduction? Excuse me while I swoon."

"I had a plan," he said, one side of his mouth rising. "But you're not shy about giving me direction and I don't want to get it wrong. A misstep would be catastrophic."

Coiling her arms around him, she lured him close. "Not getting laid is catastrophic?"

"You've made it clear the kids can't know what's going on between us. We're on a clock, every minute counts."

"Yes," she whispered. "Every single minute."

Which may be why he'd promised their daughter her grotto would remain. Who had time to tidy up when sex was the alternative?

Rising high on her tiptoes, she kissed him, barely letting their mouths linger before pulling away. Taking his hand, she led him down the hallway to her bedroom. Inside, she closed the door and kicked off her shoes.

"Are we changing?" he asked, probably meaning clothes.

Her answer came in stripping while backing toward the bed. "Do I have to spell it out…? I'm asking again… Make love to me, JD. Take advantage of every minute."

Yanking his tee-shirt over his head, his jeans were on the floor too before he even reached her. Laughter left her when he picked her up to lay her on the bed, falling down over her.

"I want this to last, Rylee."

Sliding her hands up his bare back into his hair, she pulled him down for a kiss. "Then think about baseball," she said. "'Cause if this isn't as good as the first night, this relationship could be the shortest in history."

"A relationship? Is that what we're doing?"

"Let's find out."

Seeking his mouth, she kept control of the kiss while his hands went wandering on her body. He freed her from her underwear and tossed her bra aside, dipping lower to taste her breasts while she whimpered his name.

His insistence fought hers. Was it in him to surrender? No more than it was in her.

"JD," she murmured, scooping his head into both hands, marrying their eyes.

"You putting on the brakes?" Kissing her quick and hard, he inhaled through his teeth. "Who's in charge here?"

Her mouth leaped up to steal her own kiss. "Might take a while to figure that out."

Hence why they had an entire weekend ahead. Their next kiss slowed, like their tongues needed to get reacquainted. Years had passed, paths diverged, but the truth, the need of their magnetism, hadn't waned.

This was what they needed. Everything else faded away. Hands slid from faces, into hair, over sensitive flesh. Satisfying a need in their exploration, nothing but possibility lay ahead.

Moving beneath him, rising, breathing, writhing,

contentment within burned to a searing passion.

"Siren," he whispered on her lips.

Something passed to her, knowledge of his need and how it matched hers. Words, action, potential, a unity built to a drowning aura that consumed them.

Was it possible? All he wanted and the future he proposed? Men were second to her kids. Life with the twins was all she craved.

Or all she had craved until right then. Grabbing for his waist, she tried to push, tried to switch their places. She wanted control, progress, satiated. If he couldn't—

"I got this, Siren," he grumbled into the top of her head and surged up, plunging himself into her.

Relief and joy collided in a yelp of delight. Yes, yes, this was it.

Her body remembered how to move with his. It remembered how best to please herself and impart pleasure. A rush of deep longing raced him to work harder, faster.

"JD!"

Had she told him to think about baseball? God, she couldn't wait, couldn't hold back. Nothing could restrain the rush of endorphins and cascading hormones that tightened and loosened all her muscles at once.

Yes. A man. The man. Sex wasn't just sex with Jamison Dawes.

"Baby," she begged, but he kept going.

Why should he stop? Why would he? Panting, heaving, needing, wanting. Neither were shy about filling a silence, not then, not ever. Rather than words, she communicated in sound, whines of appreciation, whimpers for more. Either he read her mind or tortured women all over with that quick angling of—

Shit. How was he doing that? The thrust and ripple of his pelvis tormented her inside and out. Orgasm ripped through her so hard, her belly clenched until it hurt.

"Shit. Fuck. Siren," he barked and flipped them over, driving into her from underneath like she was a sex toy that existed only to take his seed.

What just happened? Was she still breathing?

"It wasn't… It wasn't like that our first night, was it?"

That intense. That overwhelming. That all-consuming—

"Been downplaying me?" He rolled onto his back next to her. "That's a survival mechanism. The way you've protected yourself from chasing me down to mount me."

"Romantic," she said, straddling him, spreading her hands on his chest.

"You just can't help yourself."

With full entitlement, he wasn't shy about sweeping her hair away from her breasts.

"You know those guys, the ones women say can impregnate them with a look?" Her fingertips roamed his physique. "You're one of those men, Jamison Dawes."

"A man can dream," he said, stroking her stomach. "You feel pregnant?"

"I'm scared to answer that question. Notice you forgot to ask me about birth control. You didn't ask the night we met either. Never learn your lesson, do you, Dawes? I'm having the safe sex talk with Kye when the time comes."

"I'm all about safety," he said. "Depending on the woman."

"Oh, yeah? What does that mean?"

"It doesn't matter."

"I say it does."

"It docsn't," he said.

She plucked a hair on his forearm, growling. Rather than be mad or annoyed, he laughed.

"What woman am I?"

"The only woman."

Suspicion narrowed her eyes, though she didn't object to him taking her hips to force them closer.

"What does that mean?"

"It means it doesn't matter about other women. You're the last woman." That didn't enlighten her. "Whatever your sex rules, baby, I'll comply."

"Oh, so I get to make all the rules?"

"If they get me laid, I'm happy." As she rolled her eyes, amusement left his lips. "You want to talk birth control?

Okay. I didn't bring it up because you know my stance."

"You want babies."

"If it happens, I'll be happy, yeah. I won't lie to you. I'm not actively aiming for it though."

Were they too different? His ease bordered on aloof. He might be okay making it up as they went along, in her view, the time for that had passed. They weren't kids anymore.

"Please take this seriously."

"Okay," he said on an inhale and scrubbed his hands through his hair then across his stubble. "Seriously." Squeezing her hips, he guided her off him and back to her side of the bed. "Don't go anywhere."

"Don't go—" She grabbed his wrist when he tried to get up. "Where are you going? Leaving me in bed after one round is not making this last."

"I don't pack rubbers these days, Siren." He leaned in to kiss her. "I'm a family man now. I'll have to go out for them."

Hooking a hand around the back of his neck, she yanked him down on the bed again. "I'm on the pill, smart guy." She kissed him. He dropped onto his back, his hands in her hair, taking her with him, putting her on top. Planting her hands on his chest, she put a little space between them. "I was on the pill when we conceived the twins too."

He pushed her falling hair back, over and over. "You want me to wear a rubber? I will."

"It's a different pill and it's worked for the last five years."

"My swimmers haven't taken a swing at it yet."

"Is that what this is? What I am? Your baby machine?"

This time she tried to get up, but he pulled her down to lie above her again. "You are my future, Rylee. You need me to get the snip to prove it? 'Cause I will… You're smart, beautiful, passionate, confident. No woman has ever turned me on like you do. This is real to me, if you're unsure—"

"We'll live here. I don't want too much disruption to the kids."

"My beautiful, pragmatic Siren."

"My children will always be the most important thing in my life. Over happiness, relationships, everything. I will always choose them first."

"As will I."

Her stomach lurched again. It was getting impossible to ignore. No matter what she said, this man, JD, had gotten around her defenses.

"Is this real?" she whispered, a little old now for a schoolgirl crush or rushed hormones.

"I love you, Rylee Hampton," he said, caressing her cheek, looking deep into her. "I haven't said it because I promised to take this slow and I don't want to spook you, but I love you. I want to spend the rest of my life with you. Whatever celebrations and challenges that come along in the future, I want you with me and I want to be with you through yours."

And searching his imploring gaze, she couldn't see a hint of doubt. "Sky will be sorry she missed that speech." He laughed, still running his fingers down and across her cheek. "What if they weren't yours? If I was just some woman with kids."

"I love you. You, Rylee."

Maybe that was what kept snagging her. "How can you be so sure of this? Haven't you ever made a life-changing decision you came to regret later?"

"Only one."

"This could be another."

"No." He kissed her. "Because that one regret is you, Siren. I should never have let you walk out of that hotel room without fighting for us."

"We've changed. Both of us."

"Time does that."

There was no going back now.

She laughed; sheer joy rippled through her. "The kids will go berserk."

"We'll get Sky a princess dress for the wedding. And I can buy her diamonds."

"Whoa, a wedding?"

One shoulder shrugged. "Whenever you're ready."

"I thought you didn't want to—"

"I didn't want to marry another woman, any other woman. You, I want to marry."

No cooling his jets or denting his optimism. "If you let Sky pick her outfit, you'll have to let Kye choose his."

"What do you think? Buzz Lightyear or a Turtle?"

Oh, their son would be thrilled.

"Jane's planning Roxie's wedding."

"Yeah, and we're invited."

"We are? Since when?"

"We're part of the family now, apparently. Thank Sky for that one."

"I like Roxie, and her girls."

"They like you too. If Jane does a good job, we can ask her to do ours too."

"No. No way, nothing big and flashy."

"No? What will it look like then?"

And he thought he'd caught her out. Instead of shrinking or backtracking, she grinned, running a fingertip across his shoulder.

"I don't know what it will look like, but I know where it will be."

"Where?"

"The Grand."

He asked, "Which one?" But his expression betrayed he caught on fast. "Santa Clara?" Her touch trailed back. "Bastian will get a kick out of that."

"Bastian?" A whiff of a memory drifted through her mind's eye. "Did I meet him?"

"After the kids' party when—it doesn't matter, you'll meet him again."

"I thought Greg was the closest thing you had to a grown-up friend?"

"Of the variety I see every day. Bastian's more of a… confidante."

"So he knew about the twins too? Was I the only one abiding by the contract?"

"You'll never have to worry about it again. Like I said to Andrews, we'll be signing our names to a completely different contract."

"As soon as I'm ready?"

"As soon as you're ready."

Patient, proud, persevering, JD came with reassuring grace and certainty. In most ways, they were completely different, but they complemented each other. Compromise and communication were the only way a relationship would ever work between them. They were better, stronger, than they had been the night they met, the night the seed of perpetuity was planted.

Her children were her future. And JD? He'd be on that ride with them through every turn. They'd butt heads, sure, but the four of them together, that future didn't look half bad. Now they only had to get on with living it.

THIRTY-EIGHT

"I HAVE NEVER been so grateful to not be a guy," she said, noticing JD's ass first as he bent over the kitchen table to snag something.

He turned. "What?"

Sliding over, she patted his ass. "If I was a guy right now, the world would know it." Her fingers slunk around to his fly. "How do you control these things?"

Grabbing her waist, he swept her around and up onto the table. "Practice," he said, stooping to kiss her neck. "But it's a lot easier when our women let us use it."

Her legs snagged his, winding around him like they'd been most of the weekend. "Any time you want?"

"Any time we want."

The tender kiss became something a lot hotter, a lot more insistent, in super quick time. Hands found their favorite spots to tickle and tease. Grasping and groaning came with fumbling buttons and zippers.

"Guess I don't have to ask how your weekend went."

Brenna's voice broke them apart.

"Shit, Nana, you couldn't have just turned around and walked out, given us some privacy?"

"Much as I'd love you to get back to making more

babies for me to adore—"

The door swung open behind her, and the twins ran inside with Lotta at their back.

"My babies," she said, crouching to catch them both as they threw themselves against her. "Did you have a good time?"

Chattering suggested they'd had fun. Each tried to tell tales.

"We went on a boat, Momma."

"And ate bugs!"

Her gaze ascended to their aunts.

"Chocolate covered crickets."

She cringed.

JD's fingers spread on the top of her head. "Is that legal?"

"It's legal, brother."

"Daddy!" Kye leaped aside to tug on JD's pants leg, father scooped son from the floor. "We was in a tent too." The little one leaned closer, hiding his mouth with a hand. "Wasn't as good as your den."

"Daddy just does things better, son."

Though she swatted for him, she didn't make contact and got a laugh.

"You said they wouldn't be out in the open."

"The campsite was specifically for little ones. It's walled in without access to bodies of water. No animals, no dangers. Plus, we had your super ninjas guarding us every second."

"That's what they're paid for."

"Gimme your backpacks," she said, helping Kye remove his as JD put him down. Brenna handed over the bigger pack when she opened a hand for it. "Both of you come with me."

The kids fell into line behind her, following her into the laundry room.

"Did you have fun, Mommy?"

She smiled. "Yes, sweetpea, I did." She helped one kid and then the other remove their tee-shirts. "I missed both of you, like crazy." Lifting them onto the counter beside the washer, she discarded their little boots. "We have to wash those later. Are you going to help me?"

"Did you get wedded, Momma?" Sky asked.

She hadn't expected the question but wasn't surprised hers had been swerved. "Married, honey. People have a wedding to get married."

"Did you do it?"

Tipping the clothes in the packs into a basket, she sorted them into the washer. "No, sweetpea."

"Why not?"

"Weddings aren't like that. They're not like the movies when it happens overnight. Weddings take a long time to plan."

"Daddy could plan it," Sky said, cupping her hair in a palm to let it slide through, like a pet running from one hand to the other. "We want Daddy to stay forever."

"I know you do, sweetpea, but that's not a reason to get married."

"What is a reason?" Kye asked.

"People get married because they love each other."

Sky's inhale was so elated, it startled her. "Mommy loves Daddy!"

"Baby—"

"Mommy, we love him!"

Cupping one face, then the other, she kissed each of them on the head. "Yes. Because he gave me you. There's nothing in this world I value more than both of you."

"Everyone behaving?" JD sauntered up beside her to plant his hands on the counter on either side of the twins. "Did you miss me?"

Trust him to ask that question. "Can I have their pants, please?"

He got to work balancing each kid to slip off their tiny cargo pants.

"Daddy, we want you to stay here. Not go away like before."

"I am staying," he said. "Don't you worry about that, Sproutette."

"Will you wedded Mommy?"

"Will I what?"

"Madded," Kye said, then frowned. "Mommy—"

"Married," she explained, checking pockets for anything that shouldn't end up in the washer. "You have a wedding to get married."

"You have to wedding Mommy," Sky demanded. "Now, like now."

"Okay." That smirk in his voice tickled the back of her neck. "Vegas?"

"Don't encourage them," she said. Before she could reach up to the high shelf for the detergent, he'd retrieved it for her. "Thank you."

"Mommy says people get wedded if they love each other."

"Yes, that's true."

"Mommy loves you."

"Does she?"

"Yes, she said so. Mommy loves you. Do you love Momma?"

"Okay," she said, getting in there before he could answer. "You two, stop stirring things up." She pointed at each of the kids, then gave JD a shove. "And you stop looking so proud of yourself."

"Come on, Momma," he said, scooping an arm around her to bring her into the circle between him and the kids. "It's an easy question."

"One we won't be answering today."

"I want a baby sister."

"Oh my God," she said, her head falling back as a single burst of laughter came from the man at her back.

"Ha! Sky, sweetheart, you are my hero."

Holding up both hands, she tried to push back, but JD just wrapped his arms around her.

"Did you pay her to say that?"

"That little girl works for me," JD said into the top of her head for all to hear. "We're increasing their allowance."

"They don't get an allowance."

"Not a boy," Sky said, in her own world, as usual. "No more boys."

"Well, see…" she said, bowing closer to her daughter. "That's up to Daddy. He decides whether our baby would be a boy or a girl."

"Daddy, I want a baby sister."

"Thanks, put that one on me."

"Just telling her how it is."

"It's not a conscious choice, Sproutette. But I'll take as many shots as necessary to get you a baby sister."

"You do not mean that," she said, bumping her hips against him. His embrace loosened to slide his hands onto them. "As many shots?"

"Yep." The beaming pride in his tone shook her head. Was this guy for real? "If we get a boy first, second, third—"

"We're out of here, baby Dawes'!" Brenna called from beyond the room.

She put Sky down as JD set Kye on his feet so both of them could run and say goodbye to their aunt. JD turned, but she caught his hand.

"Don't encourage them," she whispered.

He cupped her face. "They want our family together," he said. "They're happy."

"I thought we weren't telling them about us."

"I didn't tell them. Did you?"

Her head fell to the side. "A wedding?"

"You told them you love me."

"That was a different—it wasn't now. I said it in context of—" the sly curl of his lips was far too pleased with himself. "You're making me the bad guy."

"You're not the bad guy, babe," he said, gathering her in his arms. "You're the smartest, most levelheaded of all of us. And Sky knows what she wants, we shouldn't punish her for voicing it." Good point. "Have you decided you'll never marry me?"

"No."

"Have you decided there's no chance of us having more kids?"

"No."

"Then just go with it, babe. Don't break their hearts."

Okay, maybe she was putting more meaning in their requests than they held. "Brenna said they ate. Want to watch a movie?"

"Bathtime first. If we get them in their PJs, it's easier to put them in their beds after if they fall asleep."

"You want me to do that while you do this?"

Not so long ago, the apartment had been hers, responsibility for the kids there had been solely hers too. Yes, she could be a slight control freak, but this didn't feel like him encroaching on her patch. It felt like they were a team, like they were family.

He nodded once and his hand drifted from her cheek. She snagged it again, stealing his attention back. So open, so ready, so raw. There were no misconceptions between them anymore.

Like he read her mind, he came back, scooping a hand under her jaw to stoop and kiss her. They wouldn't stay secret for long if they kept stealing moments like these.

She dipped her head to break the kiss. "We know where that's heading if we don't stop."

"Yep," he said and kissed the top of her head fast. "Don't be long."

Always don't be long. He wanted them together, that much was obvious, in a relationship and physically. It was a cocoon, a safe den they could nestle in, just the four of them. The sooner she could join them, the better.

THIRTY-NINE

WITH HER BACK to the wall by Kye's bedroom door, she waited while JD put their son under the covers and checked his nightlight.

Appearing, he pulled the door closer and smiled when he saw her. Linking their fingers, she led him into his room.

"Why are we in here?"

"Because we shouldn't share a bed," she whispered, sliding her arms around him. "And I want to say goodnight."

"Do you now?"

Her hands slid upward, finding their way under his tee-shirt. "I do."

"I think we should share a bed."

"I know you do," she said, loosening her robe to show her nude body beneath.

His gaze slithered over her. "And I'm going to keep those thoughts to myself," he said, snatching her hips to pick her up and drop her on the dresser. "Until after action."

"Wouldn't want to do yourself out of sex, would you?"

"No." His volume stayed low like hers. "I would not."

He kissed her slow, she leaned away. "We have to be

quiet."

"I'm being quiet." His hands skimmed up her body to the side of her neck, with the slightest pressure, he tipped her head aside and kissed her jaw. "Think you can control yourself?"

"I've never done this… with the kids at home."

"Better get used to it."

Her eyes closed as his lips trailed to her neck, to her breasts, back up to her mouth. Damn, he was good at this. Good at being everything she needed. Not just physically but in her heart, in her soul, in her bed. Even in disagreements, the power shifted back and forth. Neither was more than the other; they balanced each other.

"More," she breathed out the word in unison with his fingers slipping into her.

"Breathe for me, Siren…" Withdrawing and advancing, he teased her clit until her body undulated with the welcome invasion. "You've got it, baby."

"JD…" If he kept on going, she might break her own rule. When his hand drifted away and his knees bent, she grabbed for him. "No, not tonight, I can't." Panting out the words, the effort it took to keep her eyes open was too great. "Oh, this was a bad idea."

"This was a fucking amazing idea," he growled and ignored her plea to crouch and slip his tongue into her.

Tasting her juices, he slowly advanced and stopped only to lick his way up to her clit.

Biting her lip wasn't enough, she'd bloody herself if he didn't show some mercy. "J… Jamie," she gasped his name with the arrival of a climax that squeezed her tight from within.

"Come here." Holding her face, his tongue plunged into her mouth as he forced their kiss harder, faster, more.

"More."

The word was her talisman. There was no more because they'd never be done, more was eternity, the forever they'd spend together.

Delivering his promise, he slammed into her, forcing the air out of her. As her mouth opened, her eyes did too, and there he was, feral, smiling, so happy to weaken her.

No, it wasn't weakness; he gave her strength by exposing her to their truth. Nothing else out there would match this. Resisting was a useless waste of time. And having him there, inside her, was the only time the universe made sense.

Clinging to him, moving to meet his thrusts, her body wanted its pleasure, but that was nothing to its desire to give him his. For all they were, for all he gave her, she couldn't demonstrate how deeply he'd reached inside her.

With a yelp, her nails dug deep into his flesh and he growled against her, emptying himself inside her.

Neither of them moved. His hands were on the wall behind her, her grip on his shoulder and waist, and there they stayed, breathing into the night together.

"I don't know if I can sleep without you next to me," he said. The humor of the quip quickly died when his hands fell and he saw her face. Instant concern seized him. "Did I hurt you? Siren, what's wrong?"

Why was he asking if…? Only when he touched the dampness on her cheek did the gravity of emotion really hit her.

"This…" she breathed. "This is it, isn't it?"

"It?" he asked, his brow lowering. "I don't understand. Are you saying we're—"

"Forever."

"Yes."

"This is it. Our gift. We don't have to look anymore."

Though his eyes still probed hers, his expression relaxed. "I love you, Rylee. I meant what I said. And no, we don't have to look anymore. You're my woman. My only woman. I'll wait as long as you need me to wait. I'm not going anywhere."

Her shoulders dropped. Somehow there was relief in that. Relief in being with him.

The door handle moved, and JD jumped back to straighten himself up. Luckily whoever was on the other side dropped the handle without opening the door. She tied her robe on the little one's second attempt and slid off the dresser just as the door opened and their sleepy daughter peeked in.

"Daddy," Sky yawned. "What's banging?"

He glanced at her, then back at their child. "Well, Sproutette, sometimes when two adults—"

"That's not what she meant," she whispered, slipping past him. "You mean the banging noise? It's stopped now."

JD folded his arms. "Might come back."

"Not tonight it won't," she said, smiling at her child even as she felt his grin burning into her. "You want to go back to bed, sweetpea?"

"Mm," Sky said, nodding.

Rather than retreat, their daughter went past her parents to climb up on her father's bed.

"Looks like you won't be sleeping alone after all."

Sky pulled back the covers to lie right in the middle.

"Daddy has to have a shower and get ready for bed," he said.

Their daughter yawned and turned to bury her face in the pillow.

"Sleep well," she said.

He blocked her route out. "Siren—"

"I'm okay. Look after our girl."

When he raised her hand to his lips, she rested a hand on his abdomen for a second and then departed.

Time for bed. Alone. Was that what any of them wanted?

***

WAS IT WHAT she wanted? Breakfast simmered away, coffee dripped through the machine, and the thought just kept coming back. What did she want? Mores the point, what was she waiting for? It should be a simple decision.

"We'll ask Grama, okay?"

Spinning around, her smile automatically shone at the sight of JD with Kye on his back and Sky clinging to his neck at the front, like a pair of monkeys hanging onto a tree.

"And I thought there would be three separate entities joining me."

"Don't worry, I'm bigger and stronger than these two tearaways," JD said, plucking Sky from him to sit her down.

"We're gonna ask Grama," Sky said, wriggling in her seat.

"We're going to ask Grama what?"

JD poured milk for the kids. "They missed her this weekend. I said we'd invite her over for dinner."

"Okay." Did he read her tone? Still pouring, his questioning gaze ascended to hers. "Or they could eat at Grama's."

He winked and put down the jug. "Or that."

"Baird is supposed to call from Italy at three."

"His time or our time?"

"Our time."

He stopped spreading jelly on toast to frown at her. "What's he doing calling you at midnight?"

"You'd have to ask him."

"I will ask him," he said and finished the spreading to cut the toast in triangles, giving two quarters to each of the kids. "Mommy made your snacks already, but you'll have lunch upstairs with us."

"Is Daddy staying?" Sky asked, bypassing the man at her side to blink at Mommy.

Always at Mommy. "Yes." This obsession was strange. "Why are you suddenly so worried about—"

"Gabby said Daddy lives in her house. He can't live here if he has another house."

Their eyes met.

JD pushed out his chair to take their daughter into his lap. "I told you Gabby isn't well. My house is here, my place is with you and Kye, and with Mommy." Tucking her hair back from her face, he curled a finger under Sky's chin to raise it up. "If anyone ever tries to tell you different, you laugh right in their face, okay? Because, Sproutette, I'm not going anywhere." Reaching over, he caught Kye's hand too. "We're a family. Nothing gets in the way of that."

Nothing except her.

He put Sky back in her chair and like nothing had happened, Sky got to work educating the boys about mermaids.

After breakfast, she cleaned up the kitchen as JD got the kids washed and dressed. She went through her own motions and stepped into the hallway as the three of them traipsed down it.

"We're all ready, Momma, how you doing?"

How was she doing?

And right then, in a snap, it felt urgent.

"Go play Kye's game for a minute," she said to the kids.

"Mommy, we're ready for—"

"Yes, and we're leaving. Mommy needs to talk to Daddy for a second."

"Play nice and you'll get a cookie in the car," JD said.

They turned on their heels to run into Kye's bedroom.

"What is it?" he asked, all concern. "What happened?"

"I…"

Her mouth dried. She'd never been nervous talking to JD, talking to anyone really. Something about the gravity of her clarity got her worrying she wouldn't do it justice.

He stroked her hair above her ear. "If you don't feel good or need the day to—"

"We have to tell them." In surprise, his mouth opened to no words. "You told me—you said that, uh, that you missed out on the pregnancy."

"Yeah."

"And I didn't get it—it didn't occur to me until… I missed out too."

"You missed what?"

Her mouth was still dry, but she kept going anyway. "I never saw you hold them, feed them, change diapers, put them down at night…" She swallowed. "You missed the pregnancy. You missed witnessing me as a mother to them, and I missed watching your devotion to them grow. I want to…" Her heart raced. "I want to see you with them. I want to see you hold their tiny, wriggling little bodies and soothe them to sleep. I want to see you up in the night talking about whatever you talk about when they lie there so innocent and helpless. I want to come home and find you in a mess of toys and chaos, asleep with our little one."

"You missed out," he murmured.

And as her smile formed, a tear slipped from the corner of her eye. "Our twins are the most precious thing in the world." She took his hand. "I know you know that. No one else knows that like you and I know that. It's a journey I thought I would never want to experience again. The thing is… I hadn't realized…"

"Hadn't realized what?"

"That the only person I ever want to share that journey with is you." From the way he searched her, all she got from him was confusion. "It's like you said. I don't want to have children with another man. You're the last man. My last man. I want to have your baby, Jamison Dawes. Only yours. Real, the whole deal, from the very beginning."

"You want to…"

"Baby, babies, whatever you want. I didn't want a family with anyone else because my family is with you. It's with our babies, no matter how many of them we choose to have."

"You want to have my baby."

"Again."

"Again," he murmured. "You want to have my baby?"

After a beat, a grin burst on his face. He grabbed her up in his arms, sweeping her clear off the floor. She laughed and clutched him tight, desperately trying to kiss him. When he turned to meet her mouth, the moment switched in one heated instant and her back hit the wall.

Holding his face, she broke their union. "Not right here in the hallway though."

"Daddy?"

Both kids were there, outside Kye's room, peering at their crazy parents.

"Beautiful sprouts," JD announced and kissed her again before putting her back on her feet. "Mommy and Daddy are going to get wedded."

She laughed again. "Okay, let's not get ahead of ourselves."

Too late. Sky was already shrieking in delight. JD scooped the twins up from the floor and kissed each one.

"Wedded and then you'll get your baby sister."

"No matter how many shots it takes?" she asked.

He glanced back, admired her for a second, then put the kids down. "Go play more game, we'll get you in a minute." As they trotted off, he called after them, "Daddy's taking you out somewhere special today, put on whatever you want!"

"What about work?" she asked. "Your mom—"

"You've just made me the happiest man alive, you think I can sit in a chair and listen to anyone today?"

"You can sit in a chair and listen to me," she said, sauntering over to loosen his tie. "I have some criteria."

"Another contract. This should be interesting. Hit me with it."

"We both have to be involved, fully committed involved. I want both of us to have time off after any births. We raise our children together. I don't have a problem with having an office here, so we can work from home when necessary. But you have to take off as many days as I do, we split caring duty, whatever it takes."

"You want me to be a stay-at-home dad? Play with the kids all day and impregnate you at night? I can get onboard with that."

Oh, he thought he was so funny. Trouble was, he was just the right kind of crazy for her. Yes, just like Zairn and Roxie, she loved his crazy too.

"This is a long term project, not something that can happen overnight. We need to think about space, if we have to move—"

"I've taken care of that."

Huh, uh… "How did you do that?"

"We bought the place upstairs."

"When did we do that?"

"Last week."

"You know I rent this place, right? This apartment

doesn't belong to me."

"No, I thought we'd put it in the kids' names," he said and shrugged. "I bought this one too." Her jaw dropped. "We're meeting with our architect and a couple of contractors this week."

"Why did you—"

"Happy birthday, baby." He leaned closer. "You thought I forgot, didn't you?"

"No, I didn't think you forgot. You don't remember something inconsequential for six years and then forget it when it becomes consequential. My birthday's just… not a big deal."

"Me and the kids are going to make a big deal of it today. I've decided to give you exactly what you want. The only thing on your wish list." When she crooked a brow, he opened his arms. "Me."

"You're my birthday present?"

He nuzzled closer. "Want to unwrap me?"

"Maybe later. Let's get back to, you bought two apartments?"

"For you. For us."

"How did you know I would…? What if I said I didn't want us to be together?"

"That's not the way my mind operates, Siren. If you said that to me, I'd have bigger problems than real estate." He laid both hands on either side of her neck. "You want equal parenting. Want me at home with them at least as much as you are." She nodded. "I want to get married. I really, truly do. Soon."

"JD," she said, pushing his arms.

He strengthened his hold. "I love you, Rylee. I love our kids, our life, and all that lies ahead of us. Sign your name with mine. Let this be forever."

The pleading in his eyes begged her to yield. If it was important to him, and she aspired to it anyway, why should she fight it?

She sighed. "I knew you were trying to pick me up."

His laugh was just so full of joy that she couldn't resist reciprocating. Whatever he wanted, he'd get. Maybe she wouldn't be perfect, but she'd make this man happy in every way she could.

"Of course I'm trying to pick you up." He kissed her quick. "How am I doing so far?"

Looping her arms around his neck, her body sank against his. "Chaos theory, here we come."

Forever and always, their chaos would be their bliss.

Read more from the Roxiverse in
Nothing in Between: Four...

Thank you for reading this tale!
If you can, please take the time to review.

~

Ask your local library for more Scarlett Finn novels!

~

For all things Scarlett Finn
check out:

www.scarlettfinn.com

Next in the

Roxiverse:

SCARLETT FINN